There Are No Rules for This

There Are
No Rules
for This

A Novel

JJ Elliott

SHE WRITES PRESS

Published 2023
Printed in the United States of America
Print ISBN: 978-1-64742-485-5
E-ISBN: 978-1-64742-486-2
Library of Congress Control Number: 2022917186

For information, address:
She Writes Press
1569 Solano Ave #546
Berkeley, CA 94707

Interior Design by Kiran Spees

She Writes Press is a division of SparkPoint Studio, LLC.

To my mom and dad,
my teachers in love and loss.

On who first befriended Feeney Simms, none of us agree. I am sure I met her first, when our daughters were in preschool together. Liddy is positive they met at a yoga class, which is silly because I've never known Feeney to wear pants without a real waistband. Max says her ex-boyfriend and Feeney's husband played softball on the same Rotary team and they met in the bleachers, each toting matching thermos bottles full of chardonnay, which is certainly probable. However it happened, what we all agree upon is that a little over a decade ago, within a few short months, our long-impenetrable trio became a foursome. The decision was both unanimous and never discussed.

Liddy, Max, and I had known each other since high school, and we have the embarrassing photos to prove it. There's me, curvy when no one else was—the body of a woman with the soul of a tomboy. There's Max, loud and funny and raspy and biting, and prone to soul-crushing bouts of depression even then. There's Liddy, Bohemian before it was hip, and by the time it was, she couldn't quite make it cool. Needless to say, we weren't whooping it up every Saturday night as teenagers, something we've spent many, many years making up for.

I often wonder what brought Max, Liddy, and me together all those years ago. Unlike most young female friendships that flourish on mutual interests and common ground, ours seemed rooted in all the things that made us different. Maybe it was the simple fact that none of us slipped easily into those clichéd groups: jocks, preps, nerds, cheerleaders. We were just us, in a world where everyone seemed to be someone else.

Our trifecta wasn't always seamless, however. There were times when we split up and paired off and battled to the point of being sure the damage was irreparable. But it somehow never was. Not even when Liddy slept with Max's boyfriend of four years. Or when Max, in one of her more violent episodes, threatened to kill us both with a Girl Scout penknife. Or when I dated a woman briefly just after college and Liddy accidentally told my old-school dad, who was under the impression that we were roommates.

Feeney was so instantly right in our group that it made us feel like we were all wrong before her arrival, a car that had been limping along with three wheels. She filled in the gaps, softened the edges, made us all a little brighter and better. But that's not to say she was without her quirks. In fact, sometimes it seemed she was all quirk. Like the fact that she set all her clocks in her house to different times. Only she knew at any given hour which clock told the correct time, a fact that was endearing and annoying. Plenty of times I'd say, "Oh for Christ's sake, Feeney, what time is it?" to which she'd just smile and respond, "What's the rush, Ali?" I learned to wear a watch. And while we can't know for certain how she entered our group, none of us will ever forget how she left. A phone call, in the middle of a mid-July night, from her husband. She was gone. She'd done it with pills. None of us saw it coming.

The Time We Drank Tequila in the Afternoon

Eight years before

"I fucking hate it."

"But Max, it must be at least two carats! It's stunning!" Liddy says.

"It's not me. How can I marry someone who buys me a ring—a huge, expensive ring I might add—that I hate? It's a pretty bad way to start a life."

"You said yes," I remind her.

"Ali, he did it on a jumbotron! What was I supposed to say?"

"Certainly not that you fucking hate the ring," Feeney says.

"*Thank* you," Max says.

We're sitting in Max's mishmash of a living room. A kinder person would call it eclectic, but we've been friends long enough for me to say it's a physical manifestation of her chaotic mind. Wall colors swing wildly from hue to hue without reason: French blue in the living room, deep purple in the dining room, tangerine in the kitchen. Art hangs at every level and covers every subject—a pastoral landscape next to a naked man next to bright, abstract splotches that always make me think of a crime scene. In keeping with Max's love of hunkering, however, every chair in the room is as plush and comfy as they come and draped with a soft throw. It's a circle of lifeboats in the chaos. Today is Wine Wednesday, a tradition we've jumped through countless babysitting and work-related hoops in order to maintain. I can count on one hand how many times we've cancelled it. It's our weekly two-hour island amidst the churning seas that are our lives.

At the hub of our wheel is a brilliant, practically perfect two-carat diamond ring. It scatters rainbow light all over the wall and refracts each of us into different emotions. Me: concern. Liddy: joy. Feeney: amusement. Max: it's hard to say. I think at the bottom of her outburst is a growing sense of awe that she has landed such a decent man.

Spence Greene works with my husband, Drew. And because he was one of the only unmarrieds in the office, we adopted him. He always showed up to our dinner parties with thoughtful gifts and usually wrote thank-you notes afterwards. I figured he was either gay or had a sex slave chained up in his garage. No straight man was that perfect. And it wasn't his looks that were keeping him single, that's for damn sure. He was beautiful—somehow both masculine and soft. Like hugging him and having sex with him would be equally satisfying. I often did one, while thinking about the other.

Max was pretty much the only other unmarried person I knew. She was a chronic dater of bad men. Bad in that they cheated on her. Bad in that they were emotionally cruel to her. Bad, one time, in that he hit her, but then she hit him back so hard he had to have eleven stitches above his eye. So when I invited her to one of our dinners, a setup was the last thing on my mind. I honestly just wanted another female opinion of Spence.

Their connection was obvious. They bantered and sparred and flirted like flint against stone. Max confessed her fascination with crop circles, a long-standing source of eye-rolling from Liddy and me. But Spence? He wanted to know more. He drew her out, got her talking, and as I sat there, I watched with amazement as they both unfurled before my eyes.

Feeney lowers her chin and levels her gaze at Max. "Do you love him?"

"Oh Jesus, of course I love him, but I've loved other guys and I haven't married them, have I?"

"Maybe you're just scared about settling down," Liddy theorizes.

"Maybe I'm just not marriage material. I mean, I can be fun to be around and I'm hot in bed and all that, but honestly, you guys know me. Would you want to be shackled to me for all time?"

"We kind of are," I remind her.

"No, not really. You can leave and go home to your own houses and families and not deal with my raging brain. I can hardly handle living with me, how can I expect Spence to do it?"

"Uh huh. And this is about the ring," says Feeney, raising her eyebrow beyond what seems humanly possible. Damn, she's got great eyebrows.

"It is. I fucking hate it." Despite her words, her body language is melting. Max is all strut and bluster until you wriggle a knife beneath her shell.

Liddy leans forward and forces Max to meet her eyes. "You have tried to sabotage this relationship from the beginning, and you have failed miserably. You thought wanting no kids would do it. Didn't faze him. Then you thought he'd run screaming once he knew about your history of psych ward visits. Nope again. Maybe you need to face the fact that this might actually work. And *that's* what you don't know what to do with." She sits back with a mighty flourish.

Max scoffs but stays quiet for a long time. When she speaks, it's in a quiet, atypical voice. "I'm not sure he knows what he's getting himself into."

Feeney hops to her feet and laughs. "Perfect. That makes him like 100 percent of the people who've ever walked down the aisle. I'm not staring at that thing for one more minute without champagne in my system. Please tell me you have some around here."

"I think I need something stronger, " Max says.

Which is how we ended up toasting to Max and Spence's future with tequila and getting drunk at four in the afternoon.

In the end, they eloped. One day, we showed up to Max's for Wine Wednesday and Spence answered the door.

"Are you here to see my wife?" he asked.

We all screamed.

Despite the fact that she never wears her ring, their marriage is still one of the best I've ever seen. Here, I always thought that a good marriage had to start with an ecstatic bride in a huge church, and the best one I know started with an ambivalent bride at City Hall.

Crazy Max. She may turn out to be the sanest one of all.

Healdsburg is centered around a square—a literal town square—which is one of the many things I love about my hometown. Despite being smack in the heart of California's Sonoma wine country, it's never gotten around to being snobby. It tries, but it can't quite hack it. Yes, we have a couple of fancy hotels and restaurants, but it's still the kind of place where everyone knows everyone else and has an opinion about them. And if we don't know you, you're clearly a tourist, a necessary nuisance we'll welcome with open arms if not matching hearts.

Liddy, Max, and I never thought we'd be here all these years later. Liddy was supposed to wind up in New York, having fabulous gallery showings of her critically acclaimed art. Max was supposed to be in San Francisco, kicking criminal ass as a prosecutor. I was the only one without a real game plan, so I took a job out of college as a pharmaceutical rep based out of San Jose. I started out peddling asthma medication, pivoted to prescription-strength antacids, then stumbled into surprising success repping erectile dysfunction drugs. Feeney once made me show her one of my boring, chart-filled ED PowerPoints, and she laughed so hard she peed herself.

But we each came back like dutiful magnets, separately and for very different reasons.

Liddy was back from New York for Christmas when she met and fell for Jack Nash, whose developer father owns a small percentage of Sonoma County. It says a lot for how hard Liddy fell that she hung up her paintbrushes in lieu of becoming a small-town society maven, something she would have considered unthinkable before. Thanks to Jack's father's real estate investments, they're rich. Liddy finds it all embarrassing. I've never known her to spend more than $100 on anything other than art supplies. That said, she plays her part. She's always been good at theater.

Max's prosecutor days took a toll on her. She drank too much, fought too hard, and slept too little. One day she called me from SF General. She had placed herself on psychiatric hold. I picked her up and brought her home to my house, tucking her into our guest bed and keeping a wary eye on her while she slept for the better part of four days. These days, she drives the golf ball picker-upper at the local public course. She loves the thwack of the balls as they hit her caged vehicle, whooping every time, often with obscenities.

As for me, my parents divorced when I was in college. The moment my brother and I were out of the house, the papers were filed. Nobody was surprised nor heartbroken.

My mom moved to Albuquerque. My dad met a woman online and

moved to Palm Springs. My older brother was settled and working in Japan with no intention of ever returning. The house stood empty until I became pregnant for the first time. Suddenly, Healdsburg just made sense. I happily quit my pharmaceutical job the second I saw a positive sign on the pregnancy test. Drew worked his sales job mostly from home and we needed the space, so we packed up the tiny apartment we were renting and moved home. Literally, in my case.

Feeney, however, had a more circuitous trek to our little shop-lined, green-squared town. For a while, her husband Garrett was an investment banker in New York and she was a fashion buyer for Bergdorf's. In her words, they lived a "loud, glamorous, stinky New York life." But then something happened with Garrett's job that forced them out of the city—one of the few stories she never shared at Wine Wednesday. By that time, Feeney was pregnant for the second time, and according to her, she became adamant about California. She didn't crave peanut butter or hamburgers. She craved a minimum of nine months of sun and access to a hospitable coastline. The first time they visited Healdsburg for the weekend, with two-year old Caroline at her side and four-month-old Hannah nestled against her in a cherry pink sling, Feeney sat down on the grass in the middle of the town square and announced she wasn't leaving. She wasn't kidding.

In the summers, the four of us and our children usually spend at least one night a week in that same square of grass, snug in the town's heart, soaking in the cool evenings we get after our blazing hot afternoons. On one corner sits the place we like to pick up sandwiches, though they got so expensive Feeney started calling them "pearlwiches." On another is the tasting room of one of our favorite local wineries. My friends, our kids, this town. Sometimes it feels like an embarrassment of riches.

It's one of those hazy, dreamlike summer evenings, the four of us draped across a park bench, drowsily sated, the paper wrappers and napkins from our sandwich dinners strewn about. We have just reached a rare lull in our conversation when Feeney lobs one of her grenade-attack questions at us. They no longer surprise us.

"One word to describe your sex life. Go."

"Huh?" Liddy says.

"Give me a word to describe your sex life," Feeney repeats.

"I heard you. That was my word."

We laugh and I glance over at her to judge her mood, but she's watching the kids as they splash in the fountain.

I go next. "8.95."

"What does that mean?" asks Liddy.

"We've got the whole thing down to a solid routine. Like gymnastics. I think 8.95 is what even the mean Russian judge would give it, which is pretty darn good."

Max chuckles. "I'd hate to see the dismount."

I check her with my shoulder. "What about our resident sexpert? What's your word, Max?"

"Hmm. I'm going to go with *admirable*."

"You know what they say—booty is in the eye of the beholder," Feeney says, and we all snort laugh.

"And what about you?" Max peers at Feeney and raises an eyebrow.

Feeney shakes her head, the setting sun making her blonde hair look as if it's shot through with metallic thread. "I just ask the questions around here."

"Unfair! You have to give us a word," Max pouts.

"Fine . . . *check*. Sometimes it feels like we're just checking a box. Like we do it because that's what married people do."

Liddy tilts her head and says under her breath, "Not all married people."

I catch Feeney's eye. "Maybe it's time for a date night."

"Maybe. But I'd rather be here. I'm pretty sure without you guys I would have gone crazy years ago."

"Yeah? Well, I'm crazy even *with* you all as friends," Max says.

We smile and raise our glasses and feel smug about our extremely good taste in friend selection. Or at least that's how I thought we felt.

Looking back at this moment, just one in a sea of them, I now wonder if this was Feeney being brutally honest. Maybe her version of going crazy wasn't the one I had always pictured for myself: eating Twinkies all day and not brushing my hair. Maybe she truly feared for her sanity, and she felt that somehow our friendship was her tether. When I think of that, I get a mental image of Feeney at the edge of a cliff, stumbling and reaching for help. Meanwhile the three of us are looking the other way, drinks in hand, admiring the sunset.

I wake up in a panic when my doorbell rings at 3:47 in the morning. Of course, Drew doesn't move. A marching band could honk and drum its way through our bedroom, and he wouldn't flinch. I throw the covers off and run to the door with my heart pounding out of my chest.

When I get to the door, I peer through the peephole to see Liddy and Max standing there in their pajamas. To my newly conscious brain, it seems so comical that I'm laughing as I swing open the door.

"Oh my God, you should see yourselves!" I hang onto the doorway with white fingers to catch my breath. "Oh my God, you scared me." I am just about to ask them what the hell they are doing here in the middle of the night when I feel someone's hands on my shoulders, as if to keep me upright. From very far away I hear Max talking.

"Ali, Feeney's gone. She killed herself."

"What?" I peer up at Max. She's speaking some strange language that doesn't make sense. I become unnaturally still. "Feeney . . ."

"Feeney killed herself, Ali." Liddy's voice is full of tears.

I can't breathe. I'm trying to think. There's that feeling you get when you first wake up, where you momentarily live in two different worlds. You can't decide if what you're thinking is real or imagined. I glance to my right and see a fat snail tracking up the porch wall. Just yesterday, I wrote *snail bait* on my shopping list. Just yesterday, I didn't call her back.

"Ali," Liddy reaches for my hand, and I snatch it away as if she burned me.

"No!" This cannot be real. This is a sick joke, an April Fools', what month are we even in right now?

Max tightens her grip on my shoulders. "Ali, Feeney is dead. Feeney died. She killed herself." It must be true because Max is crying while she's talking and she never cries. Seeing the wet streaks on her face makes it even less real.

I look between their faces, back and forth. They are pale and shaking and the reality of what they are telling me explodes in my brain, buckling my knees. I sit in my doorway, shaking and trying to process news that is unprocessable. They sink to the ground next to me. We sit there in silence gripping each other's hands, paralyzed by a horrible truth.

"Feeney's dead?" I whisper this question, I can't give it the honor of my voice. It's the question you have to ask, even when you know the answer in your bones. *Santa's not real? Dad's not going to live at home anymore?*

"Yes," Max says, nodding. "Feeney's dead." Then she closes her eyes and claps a hand over her mouth like she might be sick.

I lean forward until my forehead touches my knees, the only

sound around us the gentle chirping of crickets. The sweet innocence of their music is jarring. What did we look like, sitting there pooled under my porch light processing the loss of our mutual best friend? Three heads, blonde, brown, and red, filled with nothing but questions that will likely never be answered.

I finally lift my head and ask the thing I don't want to ask but need to know. "How?"

Liddy flinches and starts, "She . . ." Then she shakes her head and can't finish.

Max takes over, talking without meeting my eyes. "She took pills. She was at Drake's Beach. A policeman found her in her car. Garrett called Liddy and she called me, and we decided to come over here." She is as monotone and emotionless as an anchorwoman.

"Oh my God." The words are a physical blow. My mind is flashing with scenes. Feeney and I laughing at an inane inside joke. Feeney kissing the tops of her daughters' heads. Feeney swallowing pills. Feeney dead in a car.

I stand up so fast I see spots. I have to get off this porch. I turn and head inside, not caring whether or not they follow. They do.

I pull out a chair and sit at my kitchen counter. Max and Liddy join me. It's the same worn wooden counter where the four of us have laughed, cried, drank, bitched, yelled, and drank some more, in the same farm chairs where we've discussed pregnancies, marriage crises, kid consternation, and celebrity gossip. It's impossible that Feeney will never sit here among us again.

"How did this happen?" I ask. Then I do it again, as a statement this time, hitting my hand against the counter to the rhythm of my voice. "How. Did. *This*. Happen." I search the faces of my friends, which look older than I have ever seen them.

Liddy holds her stomach and cries silent tears. Max's expression is unreadable. She looks like she's trying to figure something out, deep circles under her green eyes. "It makes no sense," she affirms. "None."

I prop my elbows on the cool countertop and drop my head into my hands, pressing my palms into my eye sockets. "I feel like I'm going to puke."

Liddy pulls a glass out of the cupboard and fills it with water from the sink. We know each other's kitchens like our own. She places it in front of me, but I can't muster the energy to even reach for it.

"Did either of you talk to her yesterday?" I ask.

They both shake their heads, and I see the same guilt and pain on their face that's coursing through my body.

A clock chimes from the living room, five bells echoing through the emptiness of the hallway.

Max clears her throat and shakes her short hair, as if to make it all go away. "I should go. Spence is probably worried about me. I barely told him what was going on then I ran out the door. Lids, I'll drop you." I hear them both slide off their chairs. Someone rubs my back. A few seconds later I hear the sound of Max's car driving away. I can't and don't move.

I'm still sitting like that when Drew gets up. I hear him walk into the kitchen and stop. A few seconds later, he wraps his arms around me from behind. I flinch like I've been stung.

"What's going on, Ali?" There's love in his voice, but I also hear fear.

I open my eyes but not my mouth. If I say it, it's real. I want to freeze that moment so I never have to render the truth with my own voice.

Slowly, I sit up. I look at my hands in my lap. They are stupid.

"Feeney killed herself."

These are the worst three words I've ever had to say.

"What? No!"

"Yes."

"How do you know? Are you sure?"

"I'm sure. Max and Liddy came here at four in the morning to tell me. You didn't wake up."

I know he's reeling, but the last thing in the world I want to do is help him process this information when I haven't done so myself.

I stand up for the first time in hours feeling cold and alone. I walk away as he makes a too-late effort to comfort me. But we're already on separate planes by then. He, among the living and the whole, and me among the dead and broken.

The Time She Knew What to Do

Six years before

After having a normal pregnancy spiked with the typical barfy mornings and fat ankles, Liddy gives birth to a beautiful baby boy with slightly angled eyes and a flat nose. Nothing that would make anyone besides a doctor look twice.

Liddy's husband Jack texts the three of us mere minutes after he is born—*It's a boy! His name is Luke! Come meet him!*

A few hours later, Max, Feeney, and I arrive at the hospital with the requisite flowers, cookies and wine, only to find Liddy hysterical and alone in her hospital room.

We look at each other and at our less-than-four-hours-postpartum friend and are at a loss. Liddy is crying so hard she can't form words.

There are some feeble attempts. I start a sentence with "Oh, Liddy, what . . ." and then just trail off. How exactly should I end that sentence? *Is wrong? Happened to your baby?*

Max, never short on words, keeps opening her mouth like she's going to speak and then snapping it shut again.

Feeney, however, climbs into bed with Liddy and pulls her head over to her chest, stroking her hair whispering over and over, "We're here. Everything's going to be okay."

Eventually, Liddy stops sobbing and just lays on Feeney's chest. It's eerily reminiscent of my own newborns lying upon my chest after the initial shock and chaos of entering the world. Max and I simply stood around like the labor nurses who become instantly irrelevant in the moments after a baby is born.

A whisper.

"Luke has Down syndrome."

Max and I trip over each other's words in a clumsy attempt to console her.

Me: "Liddy, that's not the end of the world." *(Cringe.)*

Max: "My mom's cousin has Down syndrome and is awesome." *(Oof.)*

But Feeney just continues her mantra. "We're here. Everything's going to be okay. We're here. Everything's going to be okay."

It wasn't until later that I realized that, if we were being honest, that's all any of us should have been saying. What did we know about raising a child with Down syndrome? Those of us who only ever had to decide, with much discussion and hand-wringing, which vaccinations our children would receive and at what time? When to introduce solids? Whether an hour of screen a day would fry our children's tiny developing brains while giving us time to shower and send a few emails, and, even if it did, whether or not we cared?

Instead, with the exception of Feeney, we rushed to normal, when it was anything but. I think that when you've known someone a really long time, it's especially excruciating to see them in pain. You're not just hurting for them right here and now, you're hurting for the six-teen-year-old girl that used to imagine naming her two imaginary children with matching *L* names. You're hurting for the nineteen-year-old girl whose mother told her she'd never make anything of herself because she wanted to leave university to go to art school. You're hurting for the woman who had one healthy child followed by three brutal miscarriages before finally carrying this child to term.

You're hurting for the lost dreams of everyone, of which there are too many to name.

But Feeney met Liddy right where she was and didn't try to fix the pain. She received it, held it, and responded in the only way that was honest—by reminding Liddy of our permanence in her life.

We thought it would always be this way.

I'm lying on top of my bed staring at the ceiling. My thoughts are terrible and circular. *Feeney's dead. She killed herself. I'll never see her again.* The loop never stops and never makes sense. I need to get the kids up for summer soccer camp, but I can't bring myself to do it. I don't want them to wake up to this day.

I force myself to sit up. My phone is on the nightstand, but the only person I want to call is her. It makes no sense. Feeney is dead, and I want to talk to her about it. I dial her number and listen to it ring. Where is it ringing? What happens to someone's phone when they die?

Then, her voice. "Be honest. You were hoping to get my voicemail. Lucky you."

The normality of her tone is almost more painful than the knowledge that she's gone. The Feeney who recorded that message can't possibly be the same one who died. The world doesn't work that way. My world doesn't work that way.

The tone shrills in my ear and I hang up, only to dial again. I do this five, six times in a row. With each listen, I press the phone harder to my ear, trying to catch some hint, some vocal cue, that makes sense of how we got here. Then I remember, with a dizzying swoop in my stomach, that I got a missed call from her yesterday and didn't call her back. I got busy and distracted and told myself I'd call her back tomorrow, which is now today, and today she is gone. I drop my phone and run to the bathroom, barely getting there before emptying my stomach. There, kneeling on the cold tile in front of my toilet, is when the tears come. I cry with my head against the porcelain until there's nothing left inside.

After what could have been ten minutes or an hour, I pick myself up and stare at myself in the mirror. I've never seen this Ali before, the one who has lost her best friend. I splash my face with cold water until it hurts. If I don't go forward with this day, I'm afraid I'll never leave my room again.

I knock softly on Lachlan's door. He is thirteen, vacillating moment to moment between little boy and burgeoning man. There are grass stains on his knees and the beginnings of whiskers on his cheeks. He still loves snuggles, but I can't kiss him in front of his friends. The musty boy smell that normally makes me roll my eyes is, today, my favorite scent on earth. It means sweat, dirt, grime, socks. It means life.

I sit on his bed and stare at his sleeping profile. I've never lost anyone before. I have four living grandparents. Our family dog, Boomer, died when I was eleven. I had been at summer camp, I came home to find his frayed collar on the mantel next to a photo of him jumping into a lake. I'm pretty sure I cried. When the kids' betta fish died a couple of years ago, we flushed it down the toilet while singing taps. Drew played the kazoo. It was surprisingly emotional.

Now, everything seems precarious. I feel like I was happily climbing up a ladder when suddenly all the rungs disappeared. I'm hanging onto the rails with no way to go up or down.

Lachlan snores lightly, the same snore he's had since he was a baby. I ruffle his hair.

"Morning, Loch Ness."

He groans and rolls over, leaving just a sprig of his hair visible. Impossibly, I smile.

"We're leaving for camp in half an hour. I need you up and dressed in ten minutes. Grunt once if you've got the message."

"Unh."

I walk down the hall to Devon's room to repeat the ritual, feeling out of body yet grateful for the muscle memory that's allowing me to move through this day.

Max never wanted children. We all knew this from the start. She and Spence have a tortoise named Dave and she's the world's best auntie to all of our children.

Lachlan is the eldest of our kids. My Devon and Feeney's daughter Caroline, both eleven, couldn't be more different girls. Caroline is mature and polite and seems totally unflappable. My Devon is pretty much all flap. Despite their differences they have a solid friendship, though it's based not as much upon mutual desire as much as sheer time spent together. Hannah, Feeney's youngest, is extremely shy and anxiety prone. Feeney was often reading books and articles about introverts, as if the very idea of it was a foreign concept to her, a nut she was determined to crack.

Liddy's daughter Lily is nine and wise beyond her years, probably exacerbated by five-year-old Luke's Down syndrome. We all love Luke to distraction. He is pure, unadulterated love incarnate. That said, he's also a lot of work. And he has periodic health scares that are nothing short of harrowing.

I often feel like our kids are our engines, moving us forward into a world of unknowns. Their little bodies are constantly humming with the energy of life, the wonder of innocence, and the spirit to take it all on. We're holding on to their coattails, not the other way around.

We liked it this way. The four of us were always able to exist in a bubble outside of the school, work, and community relationships that constantly seem to drain us of our life force. When we were together, we built each other back up, fed each other's souls and fortified each other to go back out into our own real worlds. We were each other's personal pit crews.

But the bubble has been ripped open. The world is garish and loud without the armor of our foursome. Everything seems dangerous, terrifying, loaded.

Maybe it will help to focus on the mundane. There's dried toothpaste on the sink; I need to scrape it off. My birth control pills need to be picked up at the pharmacy. The dog has a bald spot—I should talk to the vet about that. My new rug is shedding, and there are dust bunnies hunkering in the corners of my living room. Feeney always called them fuzz rabbits.

Nope, not even the mundane is safe.

After drop off, I arrive back at the house and see that Drew's car is still parked in front of our house. He's usually off by now, working out or making sales calls. My heart sinks. I have no idea what I need right now, but I'm positive he can't give it to me. If he hugs me, I'll fall apart. If I talk, I don't know what will come out.

I open the door, and he's standing right there in the entry. There is naked emotion all over his face. He starts toward me and I freeze, my hands flying up, splayed out as if warding off an attack. "No. No, I can't." I drop my purse and weave past him, running up the stairs to our bedroom and shutting the world behind me.

As I'm leaning against the door, heart slamming, skin seething, a thought pops into my head, uninvited yet inescapable: *I wish it had been Drew who died.* I have to sit down for a few minutes to let the shockwaves pass.

The four of us were supposed to grow old together. I know that's what you're supposed to think about your spouse, but for me, it was my friends. When I imagined my golden years, it was always the four of us, a little stooped, a little shriveled, but together as always. My friends were my dock, each holding up an essential piece of what was keeping us all above water.

If Drew died, I'd be a widow. If one of my parents died, I could expend understandable grief and people would write me nice cards. But there's no name for what I am. I've lost a best friend, a sibling I loved more than the one I'm related to, a soulmate I didn't realize how much I needed.

I've lost more than I ever knew I had. There's no word for that.

I want to crawl into bed and never leave. But the minute I lie down and close my eyes, Feeney's face fills my mind. I flip onto my side and am confronted with a framed photo of Feeney, Max, and Liddy, one I'd taken recently and especially liked.

I have to get the hell out of this house.

I leave a note for Drew that I'll call him later and slip out the front door, climbing into my dirty, ancient Jeep Cherokee with no intended destination. I start the car and sit in it while it idles. What am I doing? What am I going to do? What am I going to do without her?

Feeney in my life was like breathing—understood and necessary. Now she's gone, and somehow I'm still here. My hands are right there on the steering wheel, freckled with sun and starting to get wrinkly. There are my knees, scarred from years of sliding into bases, peeking out from beneath my cutoff shorts. I'm so very here. Where the hell is she?

The "every other" times mock me. Every other time I sat in this same spot, ready to muscle the car into reverse to head off on some adventure with her. Every other time I put her on speaker to talk about our kids, our husbands, or nothing at all. Every other time I had courage to head out into life knowing she was in my corner.

Eventually I pull out of the driveway. I sense rather than know that I am driving to Max's house. I don't have any feelings about this one way or another, but it's what I'm doing. Some part of my brain has taken over, flipped into autopilot.

Liddy's car is already here. I feel the unwanted churn of jealousy. *Why didn't they call me? And why didn't Garrett call me first?* I park and exhale, willing myself to focus on what matters: Feeney.

I let myself in like always. Max is sitting in her favorite chair, her hands gripping a mug like it's her handhold on life. The highways and intersections of veins on her hands stand out like a topographic map. She lifts her eyes to me. We don't speak. I sit down in the chair opposite her, listening to the sounds of Liddy bumping around in the kitchen.

"I didn't know what else to do or where else to go."

"Yeah, me too," Max says.

"I keep thinking I'm going to wake up and this will all have been a shitty dream."

"Yeah, me too." Max looks up at me, her eyes fierce with swirling emotions. "I can't help but think it should have been me, Ali."

I almost say, *"Yeah, me too,"* but I manage to keep it in.

Liddy comes into the room and startles when she sees me. "I didn't hear you come in. Do you want some tea?"

"No, Liddy, I don't want any tea, I want my life to make sense again." I close my eyes and squeeze the bridge of my nose until I see stars. "Tell me again about last night."

Liddy sits down next to me and goes through it again, her voice patient but robotic. It's as if I pulled a string on her back and out came the awful details of the last twenty-four hours. But I needed to hear it again, the same way I need to push on a bruise to see if it still hurts days later. When she's done she pauses, then clears her throat and turns her body toward me.

"Max and I were just talking. We need to go over to Feeney's to see what Garrett needs and be there for Caroline and Hannah."

My stomach heaves and panic rises in my chest. "No."

Liddy's eyes snap to my face and widen. "No?"

"I don't think I can see Garrett." I say. I run my hands down my face. My anxiety is full blown, roaring in my ears, prickling my scalp.

"Why not? He needs us, Ali." There is no shortage of confusion in Liddy's voice.

"I just . . . oh, God." I feel like I can't catch my breath. "I keep thinking this is my fault. I mean, I was her best friend! Shouldn't I have known how she was?"

Max meets Liddy's eyes before settling on me. "Ali, we were all her best friends. None of us knew this could happen. This is not on you, just like it's not on us or Garrett."

I wave off this logic. "You guys were never as close to her as I was. If anyone should have seen this coming, it is me."

Liddy stands up fast. "Are you pulling rank? Right now?"

Max nods. "Yeah, this is some pure bullshit, Ali."

I fling myself back on the couch, frustrated and pissed and bereft. "I'm trying to explain why I can't face Garrett! I'm trying to tell you how I feel! Jesus, would you stop jumping down my throat?"

"No, Ali, you are establishing some sort of posthumous pecking order that never existed, and I can't for the life of me understand why," Liddy crosses her arms and tips her head to the side, amber curls sliding down her shoulder.

I sigh, anger slowly receding to pain. "She just, shared things with me. We were like sisters! I feel like I must not have asked the right questions or wasn't paying enough attention."

"Well, I have news for you, Ali," Max says. "Feeney shared stuff with me too. Lots of stuff. Even dark stuff."

"Yeah, me too," Liddy adds.

I sputter. "Then why didn't *you* know? Why didn't Garrett know? How could so many of us who loved her have missed this? How the fuck does this even happen?" I feel myself careening toward desperation again. I'm mad and sad and jealous. I truly thought I was special to Feeney. Maybe she was just one of those people who made everyone feel special. It feels like another, deeper, more personal loss.

"There are way more questions than answers right now," Liddy says. "But either way, we need to go over to Feeney's to see how we can help Garrett and the girls. We are their family, and sitting here wondering who knew Feeney better or loved her more is doing nobody any good."

God, there's nothing worse than being pegged. Especially when you're already as low in the hole as it goes. I can't figure out who I'm angriest at—myself, my friends, Feeney, Garrett, Drew. All the people I love, and not one of them can make me feel the slightest bit better. "I hate you both right now."

Max stands up and grabs her purse. "Fine. Hate us while we go check on Feeney's family."

I dig my nails into my scalp to center myself and do the breathing exercises I learned years ago in yoga class and never use. Little by little, my body starts to regulate. My skin stops being electric, my hands relax just enough to stop shaking.

Liddy holds her hand out to me, a peace offering and a lifeline. "Come."

Resigned, I hold out my hand and allow myself to be led to the door.

I am sick to my stomach as we pull up in front of Feeney's house. It stands there with improbable normality, a grey bungalow with white trim and a wrap-around porch. The Dutch door she and I spent weeks debating color choices for stands partially open. It's Benjamin Moore Sunburst Yellow.

We trudge up Feeney's aged brick walkway. How many times have we made this exact trip? How many times has Feeney swung this door open for us, arms and smile wide?

It occurs to me in a strange, disembodied thought that this is no longer Feeney's house. I bat away the thought and swallow my rising terror.

"Hello? Garrett?" Liddy pushes the door open, and we step into the entryway, which already feels wrong and hollow. The sounds and smells are familiar, but it's as if some stagehand has dimmed the lights. I feel like my skin is stretched too tight across my face.

We turn the corner into Feeney's kitchen and stop short. There are other people here, random humans in our best friend's house. A couple of men I don't recognize introduce themselves; apparently, they work with Garrett and came to be with him when he called to say why he wouldn't be in. The next door neighbor, Patty Sweet, is busying herself with a dishtowel. Ever since an incident involving her car and Patty's mailbox, Feeney has called her Patty Not-So. Everything seems like it's happening a few beats too slowly. We're told by someone that Caroline and Hannah know and have been picked up by the mothers of school friends to keep them occupied while "arrangements" are made. We're told by someone that Garrett is in his office calling family members. We're told by everyone that nobody needs help, thank you very much.

For the next hour we are the silent audience of a bizarre play. Patty Not-So appoints herself master of ceremonies. She has a pink apron tied over her ample bosom. Is that Feeney's? Did Feeney even own an apron? Did Patty Not-So put it on before she arrived? *There's been a suicide next door, time to don my pink apron.*

Over and over we hear the doorbell ring, see Patty Not-So swing open Feeney's Dutch door, and overhear a barrage of condolences. Patty Not-So accepts food and hugs from strangers while we sit in paralyzed shock in our best friend's living room. Every so often someone we recognize will look over Patty Not-So's shoulder at us with a searching expression. Perhaps they think we have answers. We do not.

It takes us a while to realize we are doing nothing and helping no one. Feeney always made us feel like the center of her universe when we were in her home, now we are superfluous. It's for the best that nobody needs us to do anything because we are capable of jack shit. We tell the strange men to tell Garrett that we'll be back and we get the hell out of there.

Back at Max's, some of the blood starts returning to our emotional limbs. Shock begins to give way, and anger rushes in to fill the space. Our shared contempt for the people filling Feeney's house smooths over the ice between us, at least for the moment.

"If I hear the word *condolences* one more time I will spit," Max says under her breath. "'Thanks for your *condolences*. Your *condolences* mean so much. Who uses that word in real life? It's a word that's only supposed to be printed on Hallmark cards. And don't even get me started about Patty Not-So."

Even Liddy is annoyed. "She was way too comfortable in there. Why was she wearing an apron? And did you catch a glimpse of Garrett in the back office? He had on a *braided leather belt*! Shouldn't a newly widowed husband be wandering around the house in a bathrobe with a five-o'clock shadow?"

"You mean like how I look right now?" I ask. I am wearing black yoga pants that are now covered in fur from Feeney's two cats, Roddy and Andi McDowell. I have on a decades-old, holey UC Davis sweatshirt, and my hair's in a messy ponytail. I can't imagine I'll ever give a shit about how I look again.

"Do you think Garrett will talk to us about it?" Liddy asks.

I pull at the unraveling hem of my sweatshirt. "I don't even know what to say to him. Do we ask him why he thinks Feeney did this?"

Max looks at me hard, and I can tell she's revved up. "Trying to make sense of suicide is a losing proposition. Feeney obviously didn't want anyone to know how she felt."

"But why not?" I feel like a petulant toddler that's trying to make sense of the world. It's grief and anger and a hefty dose of guilt.

Max just shakes her head and closes her eyes. She takes a breath like she's going to say something and then swallows it.

Liddy fills the void. "I remember years ago at our attempt at a book club, we read *A Moveable Feast,* and it got us talking about Hemingway's suicide. Do you guys remember? We were wondering how someone so seemingly full of life and pleasure could want to die. I'll never forget what Feeney said: 'I've always thought that people who kill themselves don't really want to die. They just want to get off the ride.' I remember it because I thought it sounded so poetic, but now . . ." Tears fill her eyes, she shakes her head.

I feel a burst of angry protectiveness. "Let's promise each other we'll never say the word *condolences*. Or bring casseroles to newly widowed men."

"Let's also promise not to stand up at Feeney's funeral and give some stupid speech about what a good person she was. Let's talk about her as she really was, which is a hell of a lot better and more interesting than 'good,'" says Max.

"If I had wine, I'd toast you, Max," Liddy says.

"Seriously, why don't we have wine?" Max says, picking herself up. "Let's fix that."

A bottle and a half later, we've started telling Feeney stories. For a few fleeting moments, she's with us again.

"There was that time we were at that luncheon for the library and she got seated next to nasty Megan Calder—I remember wondering how she was going to handle it when I overheard her telling Megan that she was *so* terribly sorry but she had an ear infection in her right ear and wouldn't be able to hear a word she said. Then she turned to the woman on her left and proceeded to chat for the rest of the lunch," Liddy hoots. "God I'd love to tell that story at the funeral, but you know Megan will be there pretending to be sad."

"That's exactly why you should tell it," I say. "Feeney would love nothing better than to piss off Megan Calder from the grave." I stop cold. There was so much wrong with saying "Feeney" and "grave" in the same sentence. I look up and the anguish must be etched in my face.

Liddy nudges my knee. "You're up, Ali. Give us a Feeney story."

I swallow my rising dread. "A couple years ago on my birthday, the doorbell rang. I went to open it and there was nobody there. I was about to close the door when I looked down, and there on my doorstep was a gargantuan squash shaped exactly like a penis. I mean exactly, balls and all."

I pick up my phone and scroll through hundreds of pictures until I find it. I pass it to Max, who takes one look and starts laughing so hard she's staring at the ceiling and stamping her feet. I feel a rush of relief that Feeney has, yet again, smoothed out our emotional dings.

Liddy peeks over and then covers her eyes. "Oh my Lord, it's orange! Put it away!"

"It had a big red bow around it and no card, but of course I knew it was Feeney. I mean, who else would find something like that? A cock squash? On my birthday?"

"Did I ever tell you guys about the time she called me from the dressing room at Macy's because she was stuck in a dress?" Max asks. "She was trapped with her hands straight up in the air. She had been there for half an hour and every time she moved she got more and more stuck. I still don't know how she got her phone and dialed it. I'm pretty sure I peed my pants trying to get her out. She kept trying to slap me with her up-in-the-air hands for laughing at her." Max does a Stuck Feeney impression, her arms by her ears, hands flapping wildly as she careens in circles.

Then she stops and goes still. Her face drops and she sinks back into the couch.

"Why the hell didn't any of us see this coming?" Max asks, to all of us and no one.

As quickly as a match sputtering out in the rain, she's gone. It feels a few degrees colder in the room. I shudder and we all hunker a little closer together for warmth.

The Time She Changed the Subject

Five years before

Feeney and I are on a walk in a nature reserve near town. We are striding along, talking about nothing of much importance, when she lobs a big one at me. "How did you know you wanted to marry Drew?"

I'm caught off guard. "Well . . ." I stall for a moment while I try to conjure up the person I was when Drew and I were first together. "First of all, he asked."

Feeney pushes me with her shoulder. "Seriously," she says.

"I know. Okay. So, you know we met at a party. But I probably haven't told you the longer story."

She rubs her hands together. "That's exactly what I want, the longer story."

"When we first started talking, I remember thinking to myself, 'What a nice man. He will make someone really happy.' But I never thought of that person as me."

"Why not?"

"I don't know, he was almost too nice and good. Like I didn't deserve it. Or that maybe nice was boring."

"Drew is so not boring, and you deserve nice."

"I agree! But it took me some time to figure that out. The night we met, we were chatting and I was drinking a glass of red wine. I thought I was so sophisticated. We were talking about an interview we had both heard on NPR. I remember thinking for the first time that I was an official, bona fide adult. But then I noticed he was trying really hard not to smile."

"Because you were so cute?"

"Oh God, no. He stopped me mid-sentence and said, 'I really want to continue this conversation, but I think it's my duty to tell you that you are sporting one hell of a red wine mustache right now.' I excused myself and ran to the bathroom, and, Feeney, it was like porn star thick."

Feeney starts clapping with glee. "This is making me so happy."

"I cleaned myself up and walked back into the party with my head high, hoping to restore my dignity, but the first person I saw was Drew. He smiled and it just shot through me. I started laughing, and he came over and touched my upper lip. He said, 'I kind of miss it.' Then he kissed me."

"What? Just right there in the middle of the party?"

"Yep. I think we were both equally surprised."

"That is really fucking romantic."

"Funny, at the time it didn't feel romantic; it felt kind of buzzy and horny. But yeah, in retrospect it's pretty romantic."

"I'm getting a whole new appreciation for Drew right now."

"Well, don't get too appreciative. He didn't ask for my number. I'm not sure he even knew my name. He left with a bunch of friends, and I thought I'd never see him again."

"Yet clearly you did."

"He woke up the next morning and started making phone calls to figure out who I was and how to reach me. Someone gave him my name and Max's number."

"Oh my God!" Feeney is practically jumping up and down with excitement.

"So he calls Max and says he met me at a party and would love my number. Of course Max was like a cat playing with its prey. She asked him all kinds of totally inappropriate questions including whether or not he was circumcised."

Feeney whips her head at me.

"He is," I say.

She tosses her head back and laughs.

"Finally she gives him my number, and he calls me. The first thing he says when I pick up is, 'Your friend Max is like Terry Gross and Ellen DeGeneres had a baby with ADD.' I think that's when I started to fall in love."

Feeney is cracking up and shaking her head. "That is Max in a nutshell."

"I know. And that's Drew. He can spend ten minutes with someone and totally size them up. Knowing that, and knowing I was who he wanted to be with, it was intoxicating. Before I knew it, I had a ring on my finger and was picking out china. In retrospect it feels like a whirlwind."

"Is that a good thing?" Feeney asks.

I tip my head to one side and consider her question. "For me, yes. I'm such an overthinker that it can paralyze me. It was a relief to get swept up in Drew's confidence. I don't know if I would have made it down the aisle with anyone else."

Feeney stops me with her hand and points to a deer that's grazing mere feet from where we are standing. She grips my shoulder so hard it hurts. The deer raises her head and looks directly at us for several long moments, then flicks her tail and darts away.

"I hit a deer once when I was in high school," Feeney whispers. "I got out of the car and stayed with her. I held her head in my lap."

"Oh my God, Feeney, that's terrible."

"She was suffering, Ali. Finally I just held her nose and mouth shut until she died. There was so much blood."

I reach out and take hold of her arm. I'm not sure if it's to brace her or myself. I have no idea what to say.

She shakes her head and waves her hand as if to push away the memory. "Sorry. It's just, sometimes things that were so long ago can suddenly feel so close, you know? Like no time has passed at all."

I nod, but I had just been thinking the opposite. Meeting Drew feels like a lifetime ago, and it's nearly impossible to return to that moment with much feeling other than nostalgia. But I can tell that Feeney is right back there with that deer.

We continue our walk. The mood has mellowed considerably. I can't get the image of Feeney with the bleeding, dying deer out of my head. Shaken, I steer our conversation back to what I believe is safe ground.

"What about you?" I ask. "How did you know Garrett was the one?"

"Well, he asked," she says, brushing her hair out of her eyes and looking at me with a smile.

"No fair."

"Sorry. To be totally honest, I've never believed in the one. At least not for me."

I peek at her out of the corner of my eye. She's no longer smiling. She's dead serious.

"What do you mean?"

She looks at me and her eyes are now jumpy and fierce. "How are we supposed to know at age twenty-six or twenty-seven or whatever what we will need in our lives forever? It always seemed ludicrous to me. My parents were married for almost forty years before my dad died, and I don't even think they even liked each other. That will never be me. I'm just going one day at a time. Today, I want to stay married. Tomorrow, we'll see."

I'm floored. I've never heard her talk like this, like her marriage was potentially disposable.

"Does Garrett know you feel this way?" I ask. A few minutes ago we were skipping through a meadow, now we're tiptoeing through a minefield.

"Yes. I never wanted to feel trapped like my mother. I told Garrett before we got married that I could promise him fun, but I couldn't promise him forever. He decided to take his chances."

"You guys have always seemed pretty damn happy to me," I venture.

She laughs. "Yeah, that's something I'm good at. Seeming pretty damn happy."

For the second time today, I feel a swell of anxiety. This is a woman whose carpool schedule, menstrual cycle, and sex frequency I know like the back of my hand, but this feels like a place we've never visited.

"So . . . you're not happy with him?"

"I am, mostly. But I miss who I was before we were together, Ali. I felt like I stood on my own two feet and made my way in the world. Now it's all muddled. I don't know who I am anymore."

"Well, I do. You're Feeney, and you're amazing. Full stop."

She looks at me sideways and smiles. "This is why I love you, Ali. When it comes to me, you only see black and white. Not all the gray stuff in the middle."

"Well, are you so different from who you were before?"

She considers this for a moment. "Yeah, actually I am. Back then, I had a job that gave me a sense of confidence I'd never had before. And God, I loved New York. I loved being just another face in that crowd scene from every cheesy movie ever filmed there. I was somebody and nobody. It was my happy place."

"What's your happy place now?"

"Well, I'm in one here with you. And of course when I'm with Caroline and Hannah. But they are few and far between these days. I thought moving here would bring me that feeling of belonging again. And sometimes it does, but then sometimes I feel completely alone and lost to the world."

I put an arm around her shoulders and squeeze. "I'm always here if you need directions."

She shakes her head hard. "Ugh, so depressing. Let's play, 'What's the deal' instead. I'll go first. What's the deal with people who don't pluck or trim their nose hair?"

I laugh. This is one of our favorite pastimes. "What's the deal with arm fat?" I follow up by demonstrating mine's ability to swing of its own volition. "It's like I hit forty and my arms just stopped trying."

"What's the deal with those sneakers with the weird separate toes?

"What's the deal with men having nipples?" I say.

"You mean mipples?" she asks.

Which makes me laugh, which makes her laugh, and then we both have to pee, so our walk is over.

I still can't bring myself to reach out directly to Garrett. But the next time Liddy calls to check in on him, because she is a better human than I am, he asks if we can come over to talk about the funeral while the girls are out with friends. Liddy picks Max and me up, and we arrive at Feeney's yellow door in silence and dread. He opens it and his absurdly handsome face is unreadable. His hair is well-coiffed as always and his shirt looks like it's been pressed, but there's a fatigue about him I've never seen before. His gray-blue eyes are rimmed with pink, his broad shoulders slack with burden.

Liddy opens up her arms and a look of such pain crosses his face that I almost have to look away. We all take turns hugging him, when it's my turn I'm surprised to feel him shaking.

"How are Caroline and Hannah?" I ask when he pulls away.

He takes a deep breath and opens his hands like he's about to explain something to us, but then he just deflates. "I don't know," he says. "I told them what happened and we all cried, but then suddenly there were people everywhere and they got picked up by a mom who has daughters their ages and we've barely talked." He looks panic-stricken. "I've been googling what to tell children about death but there's so much information that it's overwhelming."

Liddy puts a hand on his shoulder. "Garrett, what do you need? Do you want us to talk to them?"

"No, no. I can do it. I'm just . . . I don't know. I'm reeling."

Max, Liddy, and I catch eyes. It's a relief to focus on someone else's grief besides of our own.

"Let's go sit down," Liddy says, herding us all into Feeney's kitchen. She makes tea while we all take seats around Feeney's white kitchen table. All the chairs are different; she found them all at separate flea markets. The one Garrett sits in is the one we always called "the throne" because of its claw feet.

"The thing I need most is help with this funeral," Garrett says. "You know about Feeney's mother, right?"

Max groans while Liddy and I nod. None of us have met her but we've heard enough to get it. "I descended from royalty," Feeney used to say. "Royal bitches and assholes."

Garrett rakes a hand through his hair. "Barbara calls me at least two times a day to talk about the service. I can't take it. She hasn't asked once about Caroline or Hannah, or me for that matter; she just wants to talk flowers and hymns. It's making me crazy." His knee is hammering a mile a minute underneath the table.

"Has she asked anything about . . . what happened?" As I say it, I'm struck by the surreality of this conversation. I'm asking Garrett if Feeney's mom has asked about how Feeney died, which I myself haven't asked.

"This is between us," he says, looking past us into the hall. I follow his gaze and am met with an assault of framed family photos. I look away. "But the fact that this was . . . by choice . . . is not being discussed. It's as if she were in a car accident or something. I honestly think they're hoping people back East won't find out." His voice breaks.

"That is fucked up," Max says, which is true, but it seems the same could be said about this very conversation.

"Have her sisters asked or said anything?" Liddy asks, plunking mugs of tea down in front of us.

"Yes," Garrett looks up at us with wide eyes. "They wondered what the weather was like so they'd know what to pack."

For a couple of seconds the kitchen is perfectly still, then Max slams both her hands on the table and puts her head down. We all look at her with a mix of anxiety and confusion. When she lifts her head, however, we see that she is laughing so hard that she's making no noise. "Stop!" she manages to get out, but it's little more than a squeak.

Garrett looks like he doesn't know what to do, but Max's inappropriateness makes me start to laugh, too. Liddy is trying with all her mature might to keep herself together but I see her fighting a smile.

A brief smile crosses over Garrett's face, and his body language relaxes. "Yeah, I thought that was weird too." He takes a sip of his tea, and he looks years younger than he did when he opened the door.

Max pulls herself together and kicks into planning mode to compensate for her outburst. "Okay, sorry. So what does Feeney's mom want?" She wipes her eyes and clasps her hands together like a schoolmarm. In any other situation, I would make fun of her for it.

"She wants a very traditional church funeral. Communion, hymns, verses, the works."

Liddy and I look at each other warily. Feeney always called Communion "hair of the dog" and referred to herself as a Buddhist Christian. "Both Jesus and Buddha were cool," she'd say. "Why do I have to choose?"

"We've got this, Garrett. We'll figure out what a traditional church funeral is and deliver it. Okay?" Liddy puts her hand on his knee and it stops its frantic thrumming. "We are officially on project Traditional Funeral."

"And give us Barbara's number. We'll be the Barbara buffer," Max says.

"Thank you," he says, choked. "I am lost here."

"We all are," I say, rubbing his back like I do with my kids. I feel a stab of raw pain for him. "But we'll be each other's landmarks."

Half an hour later, the three of us are sitting at the spotless marble island in Liddy's vast gray kitchen. Everything is top of the line—Viking range, Sub-Zero fridge, Carrara marble—all things Liddy could give a rip about, but her husband the developer has certain standards to uphold. It's spacious and beautiful yet starkly devoid of Liddy's personality. The only hints of her creative nature lie in the various misshapen clay animals and vases on the windowsill, handmade presents from her kids.

Liddy is holding court with her iPhone, a pen, and a pad of yellow lined paper, as if this were an extremely depressing board meeting. "Are you ready?"

"Let's get this over with," I say.

Liddy stabs some numbers into her phone and hits the speaker button. After a few rings, a thin, nasal voice answers. "Fox residence, Barbara speaking."

We all freeze and look at each other. It's Feeney's mom. Max kicks my foot, and I clear my throat.

"Hi, Barbara, this is Ali Stirling, Feeney's friend? I'm here with Max Greene and Liddy Nash. We are so, so sorry about your loss. We loved Feeney so much." My voice starts to wobble so I stop talking and press my knuckle against my mouth.

"Oh hello, dears. Thank you. Very kind."

It's quiet on both ends for several seconds. The three of us are looking at the phone like it has answers.

Liddy breaks the silence. "Hi, Barbara, it's Liddy. Garrett asked us to help plan the service and told us you have some thoughts? We'd love to hear them. We'll do whatever we can to make it what you and your family wants."

"Oh, yes. Hold on. Let me get my glasses and my organizer."

Max's eyebrows hit high altitude as she looks at us and mouths, *"Organizer?"*

Liddy shrugs and gets her pen poised as we hear Barbara picking back up the phone.

"Hello? Are you there?"

"We're here," I say.

"Oh good. Let's see. I want to start by singing *How Great Thou Art*, followed by *I Stand Amazed in the Presence*. Then I'd like the priest to read Isaiah 25. The whole chapter. It's not long."

I watch, oddly detached, as Liddy struggles with how to spell

Isaiah. Barbara sounds like she's ordering dinner, not planning her youngest daughter's funeral.

"Um, the church the service is being held in is Episcopal," Liddy says. "It's a reverend, not a priest. Reverend Peter, actually."

"Whatever," Barbara replies.

Liddy's and my eyebrows shoot up to match Max's.

"Then we'll sing *Be Thou My Vision*, followed by eulogies by Eleanor and Vivian. Then the priest or . . . whatever . . . will read Daniel 12:1–3. We'll end with *Amazing Grace*. Did you get all of that?"

Liddy is writing furiously and nodding.

"Yes, got it," I say. "Thank you Barbara. Also, we'd love to say a few things . . ." The words are barely out of my mouth before she cuts in.

"No. Nothing from outside the family. I'm sure you understand."

Max rears back and her face makes it clear that A) she does not understand and B) she's about to tell Barbara all about it. Liddy places her hand on Max's arm and squeezes hard, shaking her head. Max stands down, but I can see the energy pulsing just beneath the surface, frenetic and palpable.

"Sooooo . . . about flowers . . ." I say. I'm starting to not feel my extremities. I can't wrap my head around this conversation, this day, this week.

"Since you all know the church, I'll put you in charge of flowers. And by no means let Garrett have a say! You know men and flowers," Barbara says in a conspiratorial tone.

We all sit back and stare at each other in disbelief. Thank God we have each other to verify that this batshit crazy conversation actually occurred.

Then Barbara says, in an afterthought, "I suppose if you ladies would like to choose the song to play during the slideshow we're putting together, that would be fine. We are all in disagreement over here; another opinion might be helpful. Something appropriate that Josephine would have liked."

Holy shit, I forgot her name was Josephine. There's going to be a slideshow?

Liddy kicks in before Max and I. "Thank you Barbara, yes, we would like that. We'll take care of flowers and a slideshow song and make sure everything is just as you want it." Her voice is calm but I look down and see that she's drawing a circle, hard, over and over again onto her notepad with shaking, white fingers.

"Okay. Goodbye." Click.

I reach over as if in a dream and press the speaker button. The red light goes off and we are sitting in Liddy's kitchen alone. Liddy and I are still staring at the silent phone when Max pushes her stool back with a jarring screech.

She starts pacing and shaking her hands out like she's just hit someone. She turns to look at us. "Did that just happen?"

Liddy brings her hands to prayer position in front of her lips. "That was really weird."

We'd heard so many stories about Feeney's family—the stiff, uptight mother; the cold, remote father; the flighty, superficial older sisters. It's bizarre to have your preconceived notions so resolutely confirmed. I feel like I did the first time I went to Disneyland as a child, seeing the fairy-tale castle in real life—it was exactly as I had imagined.

"Maybe she's in shock?" I ask.

"Ali, *we're* in shock. Garrett's in shock. None of us are talking like fucking robots. That was just . . ." Max shivers instead of finishing her sentence. She starts pacing again.

"I can't believe it," Liddy whispers. She looks up at us with wide, tear-glassed eyes. "We can't say anything at Feeney's funeral. *Nothing from outside the family.* It's not just weird, it's cruel." She blinks and the tears escape and meander down her cheeks.

"We still get to do the flowers and the slideshow song," I say, trying to salvage some part of this day.

"Goody for us! We get to do the fucking flowers and slideshow song at our friend's funeral! Yee-fucking-haw!" Max is getting manic and extremely loud.

Liddy stands up and places her hands on Max's shoulders. Max is skittering with electricity. "Look at me, Max. Look at me."

Max looks up into Liddy's eyes, but the rest of her body is poised to bolt.

Liddy speaks slowly, staring directly into Max's eyes. She nods her head with every sentence. "This is about Feeney. Forget about Barbara."

Max closes her eyes and takes a deep breath, then her eyes snap open again. "I need a few minutes. I'll be okay, just give me a few minutes." She brushes past us into the hallway, goes into the guest bathroom, and shuts the door. I hear the water running.

Liddy and I look at each other. Disarming Max is something we've been doing since we were fourteen. Sometimes I think both of us would be excellent in a hostage negotiation.

I get up and pour us all tall glasses of water. Max comes back from the bathroom still shaky, but a few levels calmer. Liddy picks up her pen and sets her shoulders. "Okay, what should we do for flowers? Feeney loved peonies and dahlias. The brighter the better."

"Remember how horrible she thought those dyed carnations were that you'd see in the supermarket?" I say. "There was that St. Patrick's Day when she bought all the green carnations at the grocery store and put them all around her house because she said it depressed her to think of anyone buying them for real. What Feeney would like most is if we had dyed carnations in gaudy colors all over the church."

It's precisely what Feeney would want, and we all know it. But we also know that it's inappropriate, given Barbara's mandates. What Feeney Would Have Wanted has taken a definite back seat.

"So, we'll do peonies and dahlias but we'll keep the colors muted," Liddy says, back to scribbling on her annoying notepad. I am starting to feel like I am having an out of body experience. "Now what about the slideshow song?"

Max clears her throat. "She loved that Marc Cohn song, *Walking in Memphis.*"

"Had Feeney ever even been to Memphis?" Liddy asks.

"I have no idea, but she did have those amazing blue suede she-booties . . ." I say distractedly.

"Jesus, Ali, we can't pick a song for Feeney's funeral based on a pair of shoes she had!" Max looks at me like I'm crazy.

It happens in an instant, fury taking over my body like a roaring wave. "Why the hell can't we? Why the hell can't we do whatever the fuck we want? That's what she did, isn't it? If she hadn't done this, we wouldn't be sitting here wondering if she'd ever been to Memphis in her fucking blue suede shoes! You guys pick the song, I'm done."

I pick up my purse and run out the front door to my car, jamming my keys into its door. My heart is racing, my face is hot, and I'm breathing in weird little gulps. I throw myself into the driver's seat, crank the car on, and, I shit you not, *Walking in Memphis* starts blasting out of the radio. I slowly crumple, head and hands on the steering wheel, heart squeezing into a tiny mass of pain. I have never cried like this before, like there are not even tears in the universe to wash away how I feel. I don't know how long I'm there, but eventually I hear the passenger door opening. I can tell without looking that it's Liddy, her calm presence seeping into the stale air of the car. I fall onto her lap, sobbing. There's snot; there's mascara; there's anger that's fueled by grief that's fueled by desperation, powerlessness, and loss.

Liddy strokes my hair gently, pausing every so often to wipe away her own quiet tears. Little by little I start breathing normally again. I'm spent, lying limp in Liddy's lap.

After a few minutes, Liddy says in a quiet, gentle voice, "Max and I decided we should all wear Feeney's clothes to the funeral. She'd like that. Plus her clothes are way better than any of ours."

Without moving off her lap I say, "I call the blue suede shebooties."

The Time She Wore White to Wine Wednesday

Seven years before

Max, Liddy and I are already half a glass in when there's a knock on the door. Feeney is always last, perpetually late. She blames it on being from the east coast. "Your six is my nine," she says. "So thirty minutes late to you is two and a half hours early to me."

"It's open!" Max yells.

More knocking.

"IT'S OPEN!"

Three loud dings of the doorbell, one after the other.

Max grumbles under her breath as she stands up to head for the door. She peers through the peephole. Then, loudly, "What the . . .?"

She swings the door open wide and there stands Feeney, all five foot nine of her, in head-to-toe lace and silk. She's in her wedding dress, an ethereal A-line gown with three-quarter sleeves and a full train. I can tell just by looking at it that it's something expensive. Flowing from her head is a spectacular cathedral-length veil, edged in the same lace as her dress. She's stunning.

Without saying a thing she floats in and hands each of us an off-white slab of thick, letterpressed paper, full of words in a font so loopy it's difficult to read. The one thing that I can read, however, is the part that's in her own handwriting. Feeney has crossed out the letterpressed date and penned in today's date.

"Welcome to the reincarnation of my wedding!" she says. "But I'm leaving out all the boring bits, of which there were plenty."

We are giggling and holding our invitations, one of which probably cost as much as the entire lot from my own wedding, beholding our gorgeous friend standing in the middle of Max's living room in her wedding garb.

"To what do we owe this honor?" Liddy asks.

"You guys said you wanted to watch my wedding video," Feeney responds, "which sounded like the worst Wine Wednesday ever. So you'll have to do with this instead. Lucky for you I didn't bring my god-awful sisters to hold the train."

"You look amazing," I say, and it's true. She's a bridal magazine in 3D.

"You're kind," she says. "But the best part is what's underneath."

"That's my girl," Max says, as she fills Feeney's glass and hands it to her.

Feeney takes a huge swig and then places her glass on the fireplace mantel. She spins around slowly to give us the full picture, and when she faces us again she has a cheeky glint in her eye.

"Here's my first secret." She reaches into the bodice of her ethereal gown and shifts her arms a bit. We hear the unmistakable sound of something slowly unsticking itself from something else. Her hand emerges, holding a full-size maxi-pad.

"It was so damn hot that day, and I knew I'd pit out with sweat stains in an instant. I was in a complete panic about it until *ding!* Lightbulb moment. Pads in the pits!"

As we nearly die laughing she reaches into the other sleeve and does a similar dance, slowly ripping off the second pad from her other armpit. She holds them both up to us like hard-won trophies.

"What's the next secret?" I ask, wiping tears from my eyes.

She sticks the pads to the wall and takes another big gulp of wine, nearly emptying the glass. "I didn't want my dad to walk me down the aisle. I mean, the man had probably said a hundred words to me in my life, most of them negative. But I didn't have a choice. My family is nothing if not traditional." She closes her eyes and takes a deep breath. "I couldn't just roll over on this one. It was too big a moment. I literally laid awake at night trying to figure out a way to stick it to him on this big day where he's surrounded by all his fancy friends. He always cared more about them than me, anyways. Then the morning of the wedding, as I was getting dressed, it came to me. "

She pulls Liddy up and links her arm into hers. "You pretend to be him," she says, nodding at Liddy. "Sorry to make you play the bastard but you were just closest."

Liddy shrugs, smiling with her whole face, her whole being.

"Okay, picture this. We're walking down the aisle, my dad looking and smiling at all his friends, basically oblivious to me."

Liddy plays her part with flourish, waving erratically and pretending to high five people.

"We get to the front of the church, with everyone who's anyone sitting behind us, and Dad holds my hand out to Garrett."

Liddy just stands there.

Feeney looks at her and repeats, *"Dad holds my hand out to Garrett."*

"Oh! Sorry," Liddy says, complying and handing Feeney off to the nearest victim, which is me. I take her hand, unsure about where this is going.

"And right when he does I turn to him and whisper into his ear. Everyone in the church must think I'm telling him I love him or goodbye dear daddy or something, right?"

We nod.

"I lean into him and I say to my extremely conservative father, very quietly, 'I'm not wearing any underwear.' Then I turn to Garrett and take his hand and never look back."

We are doubled over, hysterical and disbelieving, when Feeney lets go of me, swings around and, in one swoop, flips up the immense amount of fabric covering her rear. What we are all presented with is a glowing naked Feeney moon, surrounded on all sides by lace and tulle, a fluffy ass mane.

None of us can speak as she rights herself, tucking her dress back around her. She smooths out the front of her gown and adjusts her veil and in an instant she is once again flawless.

"For the record, I didn't actually moon anyone on my wedding day, but I really wanted to. My dad's face was red for the entire rest of the day. He wouldn't look at me or talk to me during our father-daughter dance, but to be fair that might have been the case no matter what I did or said."

When I can finally talk again I squeak out, "Are there any other secrets?"

She starts pulling out bobby pins from under her veil, slowly dismantling it. Her expression changes.

"Not unless you count the fact that when my dad died five months later of a heart attack, I was actually happy that those were my last words to him. I should feel guilty, but I don't." She looks up at us and her face is clouded with resentment. She reaches for her wine and kills it in one swig, then holds her glass out for another. Max fills it up and the rest of us watch in silence, waiting for her next move.

"Cheers to a day when I can finally wear this thing in a room with a bunch of people I love," Feeney says, a smile chasing away the clouds. She holds up her glass and we all clink.

"To the world's most lovely bride," Liddy says.

"With the exception of her ass," I add.

"To maxipits!" Max says, and we are all laughing again.

Thank God Liddy lives so close or else I wouldn't have been able to find my way home with my marshmallow eyes. I walk up to my front door just as it swings open to the tall, solid shape of Drew filling the doorway. His eyes are full of concern, love, and pity. It makes me want to hit him.

"How are you, babe? We've barely talked . . ."

I consider how to answer him, but it only makes me angrier. I need my home to be a reprieve from the constant emotional assaults. I need sanctuary. Instead, I'm greeted with naked compassion, which sets ablaze the parched kindling of my grief. I set my shoulders and clutch my purse to my chest. "Are you keeping me from coming inside?'

He steps back with a look of confusion on his face. "No, I'm just . . ."

Before he can finish, I scoot around him, unable to even make eye contact. "Thank you."

"Ali . . ."

"Nope, can't." I rush through the living room and up the stairs. I close myself in Lachlan's room and lie on the bed, clutching his American flag pillow to my chest. I need to be somewhere that feels both foreign and safe. My heart is slamming in my ribs.

It doesn't make any sense, but I hate Drew for being alive when Feeney's not. I hate his hulking presence in the world when Feeney's beautiful slip of a spirit is missing from it. He is everything Feeney is not—male, hairy, and here. All he wants to do is love and care for me, and all I want to do is push him away. Literally.

I've been falling asleep either on the couch or in Devon's bed, then sneaking into my room in the middle of the night, flattening myself as far to my side of the bed as possible. Drew wakes up before me, and it isn't until he leaves the room that I can exhale and unfurl my body. I get my best sleep these days between six thirty and eight in the morning. It's not sustainable.

But how do I explain this to him when I don't understand it myself? He's a strong guy, but I don't think it would go over very well for me to tell him that his mere existence makes me irrationally hostile.

The truth is, beyond my kids, I'm not sure I can love anyone who isn't Feeney. I'm not sure I ever will. It would be a disservice to her—an acknowledgement of a world that goes on.

I don't know if my marriage can survive that world.

I fish my phone out of my purse and call Feeney to hear her voice-mail. I listen to it three times in a row until I no longer want to punch everyone and everything around me.

The Time We Wore Fur to the Airport

Five years before

Feeney, Liddy and I decide to surprise Max by picking her up at the airport. She had been visiting her parents in Florida, and Spence texted us to see if we would do the honors: *Pretty sure she'd rather see you all than me after spending a week with Carol and Arthur.*

Max's parents are loving but terrifying. They have strong opinions about every little thing, from what you wear to how you talk to what you want for dinner. Max always comes home raw from her visits, as if a few layers of skin have been stripped away along with her basic sense of self. Her mental state is often precarious for the first few days until she readjusts.

Knowing this, we've decided to dress up like characters from Dynasty. After all, nothing combats a brewing storm of mental illness like feathered hair, ruched dresses, and faux fur. Max walks into the baggage claim area to see the three of us sprawled across the stiff Naugahyde seats in various shades of Linda Evans, Judy Collins, and Catherine Oxenburg.

She stops short and looks at us with narrowed eyes. She does a complete 360-degree turn, stops, and stares again. "Oh my God!" she finally exclaims, her hands clapping her mouth once she figures out it's just us in odd clothing.

She doubles over laughing, and we clamber over to her to embrace her in all our thrift store glory. Very quickly, however, her laughter turns into deep, wracking sobs. She sinks down onto the carpet of the airport terminal, and we simply follow suit, three 1980s vixens comforting our friend from the future.

We just hold her and let her cry into our synthetic sleeves and bodices. She's emptying out the ick.

Eventually she stops crying, looks around, and says, "We're making a scene."

"What are you talking about?" Feeney says. "This is hardly a scene. If we started fighting and I threw you onto the baggage belt, that would be a proper scene."

"She's right," I say. "Your standards for scene-making are pathetically low."

"Plus nobody's looking at you because Feeney has spectacular cleavage in that dress," Liddy says.

"One hundred percent true," Feeney says.

"I'm going to stand up and get my suitcase now," Max says, smiling and shaking her head. "Before security tases us or something."

We all peel apart, Max heading off to grab her bag and us convening by the exit. I notice that Feeney has uncharacteristic tears in her eyes. "You okay, Feeney?" I ask.

"I just wish I had met you all a lot sooner," she says, blinking fast to keep her tears at bay.

"Us too," Liddy and I both murmur, rubbing her shoulders.

Feeney nods and flicks away her tears, squeezing my hand that's on her shoulder. "I'm okay," she laughs. "Just emotional."

"So, is the white stretch Caddy ready?" Max says as she approaches us, wheeling her suitcase behind her.

"Quite," Feeney says as she removes her white faux mink stole and settles it upon Max's shoulders, planting a kiss on her cheek for good measure.

"Well then, home Jeeves," Max says, and we escort her out of the airport in grand if bizarre style.

We group text Garrett to find out if it's okay to go through Feeney's closet to pick out clothes to wear to her funeral. He agrees it is what Feneey would want and lets us know he's taking Caroline and Hannah out to dinner and ice cream and to come while they're out. I don't know how I'm going to possibly handle a tiny room packed full of things that look and smell like Feeney.

An hour later we are all sitting Indian style, or as Feeney would say "oppressed Indigenous people style," in the alcove outside of Feeney's walk-in closet.

"Who's going in first?" Max asks.

"I'll do it." I say, with a false sense of purpose. I walk to the door and place my head and hand against it, taking a deep, bracing breath. Then I turn the handle and walk in.

It is shocking to see all these clothes, all this Feeney, in one place. A weird anguished sound escapes my chest, and I bury myself in the mixture of cotton and wool hanging in front of me. Her orangey face-cream smell is everywhere. I wrap my arms around as many flat Feeneys as I can hold. I hear Max and Liddy come in behind me.

"Shit," Max says under her breath.

"We can do this," Liddy says, more to herself than to us.

I turn around and the first thing I see is a picture of the four of us, taken many years ago, framed and sitting in the one small window in her closet. We are all in various poses: Liddy with her head thrown back in laughter; Max puckering up for the camera; me with a shoulder thrown forward in what I must have imagined was a sexy supermodel pose; and Feeney at the end, looking down the line of us with pure joy. Her hair is whipping along her face toward us as if it's part of the embrace. I walk to the picture and pick it up. It's the only thing in this closet that still has life in it.

"I don't even remember taking this," I say.

We huddle over the picture, surrounded by what's left of Feeney. "I think it was that Fourth of July that we spent down at the river," Max says.

"No, I think it was Jack's fortieth," Liddy says. "I remember what I wore because it was the first time after Luke was born that I could fit in that dress."

"We were so happy," I say. "Did we realize that? Did we know how lucky we were?"

Max yanks the picture out of my hands and places it back in its window seat. "Enough of this. We have to get this done before they get back," she says.

"Wow, buzzkill," I mutter under my breath as I wipe my eyes with my shirt.

"Explain to me what good it does to sit around looking at pictures and wondering if we were happy?" Max says, swinging around at me and jabbing her finger at the photo. Her voice rises on each word. "Of course we were fucking happy—just look at us!" She storms over to the clothes and starts violently raking the hangers across the bar. They make a reluctant screeching sound. "Are we wearing black or what?"

"This is not how we are going to do this," Liddy says. "Stop it, Max."

Max continues to frenetically slide hangers. Screech. Screech. Screech.

"Stop it. Sᴛᴏᴘ! Iᴛ!" Liddy yells, fists at her side. I'm not sure I've ever heard her voice reach this pitch.

Max does, standing stiff with hangers swinging on the rod above her.

"Jesus, we are not fifteen years old anymore. This is not what Feeney would have wanted, us fighting and yanking clothes around in her closet!"

"Well, she should have thought of that, then." Max turns and storms out, leaving Liddy and me standing amidst the wreckage. Our eyes meet but neither one of us has anything to say.

I turn and slowly start looking through Feeney's wardrobe, running my fingers along all the different textures. Nothing in here isn't beautiful, Feeney had no version of my holey Davis sweatshirt. Even her hangers are those matching black-velvet kind—no wire dry-cleaner hangers in sight. Liddy turns to the other side of the closet and joins in. For a while, the only sounds are of the swishing and billowing of silk, cotton, cashmere, and wool. Everything I touch is a reminder, a memory swathed in fabric.

Eventually the door opens and Max walks back in. At one point she puts on one of Feeney's chunky wool sweaters that's about two sizes too big for her due to their six-inch height differential and stands there, looking like a lost child in her mother's clothes.

I open a drawer filled with gorgeous, colorful silk scarves. I lay my hand on top of them, expecting it to sink, but it's stopped by something hard. I push aside what is most likely an Hermes scarf and find myself face to face with a small linen bound book. I gently open it and riff the margin only to be faced with page after page of Feeney's loopy writing. The blood rushes out of my face.

"You guys," I breathe, turning around and holding up the small bundle. "I think I just found Feeney's journal."

Max and Liddy whirl around and look at me, eyes as big as plates. Liddy drops a striped sweater on the floor and moves toward me, holding out her hand like she's approaching a scared, feral animal. "Can I see?"

I hand her the journal, and she sinks to the floor of the closet with it. She cracks it open and looks at a page, then gasps and snaps it shut, looking up at us. "Oh my God, it *is* her journal. What should we do?"

"We need to take it," Max says. "We need to find out what's in there." She is firm and definitive, everything I am not in this moment.

"But it's private," I say, not feeling it in my heart because of goddamn course I want to know what's inside.

Liddy starts rocking, holding the journal to her chest like a tiny child that needs comforting.

"Listen," Max says, bizarrely calm in this improbable moment. "Garrett can't handle this right now. We'll tell him about it when we know more and when he's in a stronger place. But I believe Feeney would trust us with this. She would know we'd have her best interest at heart."

My mind is reeling. I wish more than anything I hadn't found this emotional holy grail and put us all in yet another situation with few good outcomes. But I did. And here we are with it, whether or not we want to be. "I don't know Max, it doesn't feel right."

"Does anything?" Max widens her eyes and holds out her arms, gesturing at our entire situation. "I mean, nobody's written 'Looking through Your Friend's Closet after Her Suicide and Finding Her Journal for Dummies' as far as I know."

It's not enough to make me laugh, but it breaks me out of my stunned shock. "Okay, okay, let's think about this. If there's stuff in there that should be shared with Garrett, or Caroline, or Hannah, we could be the ones to make sure it is. And if there are things that should never be shared, we can make sure it isn't."

"I don't know—it feels wrong to pilfer her journal and decide who gets to see what and when," Liddy says, rubbing her finger over the nubby linen cover.

"Well, I'd argue that everything about this is wrong and the rules are out the fucking window," Max says. "Give me that thing, and let's finish this up and get out of here."

Liddy hands the journal to Max, who slips it into the functional black backpack she uses as a purse. We go back to the task of picking out clothes, with much more purpose now born from the desire to escape this jail of fabric and grief.

I pick out a grey, sleeveless knit dress that feels like—wait, make that *is*—cashmere. The label reads TSE. I have no idea how to pronounce that. I pull Feeney's blue suede shebooties off their place on her shoe shelf and slip both into my purse. Soon enough, Max and Liddy have also picked out their outfits, and we exit the closet, each of us packing pieces of Feeney—her clothes, her shoes, her innermost thoughts.

Back at Max's house, the three of us sit in an awkward triangle surrounding Feeney's journal atop the coffee table.

"So now what?" I ask, drumming my fingers on the leg of my jeans.

"I want to understand it so bad, I practically want to eat it," Max says, clenching and unclenching her fists.

"I know what you mean," Liddy says. "I keep wanting to open it up and smell it."

Despite it all, I laugh. "Here I am wondering whether or not we should read it, and you guys want to eat and smell it. God, we're weird."

Liddy tucks her legs up underneath her loose floral dress. "I keep journals, you guys. And it's not all pretty in there. But if I died, I would absolutely want the two of you to be the ones to go through them and decide what should be shared with Jack and the kids."

"Okay, so that's one vote for reading it," I say. "I don't keep journals, so it's hard for me to know. Do you, Max?"

"Yes, sporadically. Frankly, my darkest times are when I journal the most. Which is probably why I want to read that journal so damn bad."

"I just keep thinking that this is all we have left of her," I say. "We should do whatever we can to understand and protect her, even if it hurts. And I wouldn't want to hand over anything to Garrett or the girls that could hurt them worse than they've already been hurt. So . . ." I close my eyes and sigh, "Let's do it."

Max picks up the journal with gentle hands and puts it on her lap, then fishes out a pair of readers from her purse. She always has a few pairs on hand, in differing shades of bright. Today they're turquoise.

Ever the lawyer, she starts planning the best course, talking mostly to herself. "Okay. We should start by doing a quick skim through to understand how she used this. Did she write short entries or long ones? Did she date them? How far back does it go? Is this just going to be summaries of her days or will there be more depth?" Then, as if she just remembered we were here, she peers at us over her sea-glass frames. "Are we in agreement?"

I look at Liddy, who shrugs and says, "I guess?" Her response is reflective of my own emotional discord. It's both bizarre and reassuring to have Max acting so businesslike about filtering through Feeney's thoughts. I turn back to Max. "Proceed, counselor."

She purses her lips and opens the front cover. On the inside of it, there is a quote in Feeney's loopy handwriting. Max reads it aloud.

Still, what I want in my life is to be willing, to be dazzled—to cast aside the weight of facts and maybe even to float a little above this difficult world. (Mary Oliver)

All the hairs on my arms stand up and my skin is dotted with tiny bumps. Max turns the page and scans it, then a few more, then a few more. Then she flips all the way to the back, finding the very last entry. It's only a few pages before the end of the book. I am holding my breath.

She snaps the book shut and stands up in one, swift motion. Then she jumps up and down about ten times while Liddy and I watch and wait. When she's spent, she sits back down and looks at us, spots of red high on her cheeks.

"Okay, it looks like this covers quite a few years, it seems she wrote sporadically and mostly about feelings and thoughts. Her very last entry is dated only a few days before she died and all it says is: 'Thank you.'"

The words land hard and solid in my gut.

"What does that mean?" Liddy asks.

Max just shakes her head and blinks hard.

After a few moments of quiet, Liddy stands up and pulls the journal out of Max's shaking hands. "I think we need to get through Feeney's funeral before we really dig into this. Once that's over, we can focus on what we find in here. One emotional roller coaster at a time."

She lovingly props the journal up on the mantel above the fireplace, then looks around and spots a candle across the room, which she fetches and places to its right. Max and I jump in as it dawns on us what she's doing. I go into Max's bedroom and find a framed picture of the four of us from a long-ago Wine Wednesday. Max goes outside and puts together a lovely impromptu bouquet, places it in a jam jar and sets it next to the photo. In a few short minutes, a beautiful shrine has come together at the center of the room. We stand together looking at it, Liddy at the center, holding us both to her.

"Until then, she'll be right here," Liddy says, kissing her finger and touching it to Feeney's radiant face in the photo.

The Time She Sang

Four years before

Every year on Max's birthday, Liddy, Feeney, and I drag her kicking and screaming somewhere to celebrate. Nobody bitches and moans more loudly about celebrations than Max, but nobody ends up having more fun, either. She's an introvert until she's had a couple of drinks, then she's the one bringing down the house.

This year we're at the Buckhorn, a dive bar that looks like a cross between a red barn and a Wild West saloon. The noises coming out of this place right now would be equally at home in either location, as tonight is karaoke night. There's no stage or anything; the bar owners just plop down some speakers and a microphone on the sticky floor in front of their sole pool table, turn the TV from football to song lyrics, and voila, instant karaoke bar. We love it.

Max has just clicked past her second drink and is picking up steam, forgetting that she's mad at us and even flirting with the bartender who may or may not have a glass eye.

"What does it take around here for a girl to get a drink?" She plants her elbow on the bar and leans in, smiling.

He is either unaware or unamused. "Ya order one," he says, all one tone.

Max shoots me a dry look and says, "See? This is what happens when you age. Nothing's cute anymore."

"You're cute," the bartender says in the same drawn out monotone.

It's not even possible to see his mouth move under his untamed, yellowish-gray mustache.

Max's eyes widen in surprise and she laughs. "What's your name?"

"Jasper Red." Not one iota of inflection.

She closes her eyes with satisfaction. "Of course it is. Well, Jasper Red, I would like a draft beer and a shot of whiskey. And my friend here would like a Jack and Diet Coke." It's one of the benefits of knowing someone since high school—you've got their dive bar drink order down flat.

"Yes, ma'am," he says, even though he must be twenty years her senior.

"I think I'm in love," Max says as he shuffles off. "It's settled. I'm swapping Mr. Greene for Mr. Red here. Never mind that I may never be able to find his mouth to kiss him."

"You two would make a handsome couple," I say. "And I'd always know where to find you on Saturday nights."

Liddy and Feeney, who had been in the bathroom, find us at the bar. "What song are we doing next?" Feeney asks. "Journey? Bon Jovi? The Carpenters?"

"Yes! Karen Carpenter, *Looking Down on Creation*. I'll go set it up," Liddy says. "Order me a vodka soda with a twist."

"Not sure this is a twist kind of place but I'll do what I can," Max says. "I'm kind of in with the bartender."

There are only two other groups and one well-served old man sharing the karaoke machine with us, so we're able to churn through a lot of material. And drinks.

At one point I suggest *Footloose*, and Feeney starts shaking her head. "Nope, can't do it. There's only one Kenny Loggins song I sing karaoke to, and I have to do it alone." she says.

"Well, what the hell are you waiting for?" I ask her, handing her the microphone.

"You don't want to hear me sing by myself," she says, waving a woozy hand in front of her face.

"You're damn straight we do," Max says, pushing her out of her chair. "Go! Get out there!"

"The only reason I'm doing this is because I've had too many Manhattans," she says as she pushes her chair back and grabs the mic, heading out to what's currently acting as center stage.

I'm expecting something loud, '80s, and heavily keyboarded, so I'm surprised when the song starts up and it's just a single piano, mostly chords, slow and quiet. I'm not sure I knew Kenny Loggins had this sound in his repertoire.

Feeney closes her eyes and leans against the pool table. She nods and smiles almost imperceptibly, then opens her mouth and begins to sing.

"Home for the holidays,
I believe I've missed each and every face,
Come on and play my music,
Let's turn on every love light in the place . . ."

We, and everyone in the bar, are stunned into silence. Feeney is beautiful, reverent, and riveting. She's in the middle of a dive bar in Petaluma, and she might as well have been on stage at Carnegie Hall.

"'Please, celebrate me home . . .'" The chorus is familiar; I've heard this song before, but not for decades and certainly not like this. I had no idea Feeney could sing.

She keeps her eyes closed the entire time, clearly knowing the song by heart, and sings it with such feeling that I find my throat tighten and soon I'm wiping away tears. I look over and see that Max and Liddy are too.

By the end we are all standing and singing with her, not just us but everyone. The two other groups, the well-served old man, Jasper Red, and us, all singing: "'Please celebrate, celebrate me ho-oooome. Please celebrate, celebrate me ho-oooome.'" Over and over, we're swaying and singing with Feeney.

When it ends she finally opens her eyes to see the entire bar on its feet, staring at her, entranced. There's a moment where everything is just quiet. Then she laughs and looks around as we all start clapping and cheering with all our hearts. She drops into a deep, royal curtsy, then places the microphone back on its stand and sits down.

"I need a drink," she says.

Max gestures to Jasper, who yells out, "On the house!"

"What just happened?" I say. "Who are you? That was unreal."

"Oh, stop. I am just someone who has been madly in love with Kenny Loggins since I was eleven years old. And that song is the one I first fell in love to, slow dancing with Nate Matthews in eighth grade."

"Tell us about Nate," Liddy says, plopping her head in her hand and blinking her eyes like a swooning teen.

Feeney sighs and starts fiddling with her napkin. Drinks appear like magic thanks to our new best friend Jasper. "He was perfect. Sweet, handsome, kind, funny, smart. He was too good to be true. And, impossibly, he loved me."

"Why impossibly? You're very loveable," I say.

"I was a little rough around the edges at that point," Feeney says. "Too tall, too skinny, no boobs. My sisters were perfect and gorgeous, and I felt like a complete freak. Nate could have picked anyone he wanted. But he picked me. It was the first time in my life I had ever truly felt special."

"Is it bad that I'm secretly happy that you actually had an awkward stage?" Max says.

"Oh, it was awkward all right. And more than a stage. It was like I had an awkward era," Feeney says. "From sixth to ninth grade, my parents actually refused to frame my school pictures. So it was like they had two children, at least according to the walls."

"That's messed up," Liddy says, lowering her chin. Nobody messes with Liddy's loved ones.

"So, what happened with Nate?" I ask to re-center the conversation.

"He was my boyfriend for about a year. Those were some of the happiest times I can remember from growing up. We would go fishing, play cards, listen to music. We loved walking in the rain together. One time I was out of town when it rained. When I came back, he gave me a bottle of water. He had caught the rain for me since we hadn't been able to walk in it together."

She looks up and we are all sitting there with our mouths dropped open. Liddy wipes tears from her eyes. "That's the most romantic thing I've ever heard," she whispers, choked up.

"But then his parents sent him to boarding school for high school. I was devastated; we both were. It was one of those stupid 'my father and his father and his father all went to Exeter' things. No matter what your child wants, no matter what would actually make him *happy*," Feeney is getting angrier with each word. "He told his parents he wanted to stay because of me, so they forbade us to see each other before he left. I never got to say goodbye to him. We never kissed goodbye," Feeney says quietly.

"Did you see him at the holidays at least?" Liddy asks.

Feeney looks up, and her face is drawn with pain. "I never talked to him again. He died in an accident the second week of school. He was in a car with a bunch of older kids who had been drinking. He was the only one sober. He was also the only one who died."

I gasp and cover my mouth with my hands. Liddy grabs Feeney's hands in hers. Max sits very, very still. Nobody says a thing.

Feeney closes her eyes. "I don't think about Nate that much anymore. But that song . . . When I sing it, I'm instantly thirteen, dancing in a circle with my head on Nate's shoulder. It's heaven." She opens her eyes and smiles. "Sorry for the buzzkill. Literally," she adds, gesturing to the many empty glasses sitting upon our table.

"That is unspeakably sad," Max says.

"I'm so sorry, Feeney," Liddy says.

"It's okay. Despite how it turned out it's one of the bright spots of my youth. I think Nate was the first person who taught me about unconditional love. Now, I have you guys," she says, smiling. "And Kenny Loggins."

Today is Feeney's funeral. Liddy drives. We all sit in the pale leather interior of her Range Rover in silence, twisting Kleenexes around our fingers into fraught little knots.

Max is wearing Feeney's favorite blazer, a gorgeous blue Armani with gold metallic accents unearthed at a San Francisco secondhand store. Around Max's neck is a gold chain with a tiny gold safety pin hanging from it. Her fingers found it in the pocket when she put on Feeney's jacket.

Liddy has on the dress Feeney wore to her own fortieth birthday party two years ago—a black Catherine Malandrino shift. To counterbalance the funereal black, she topped it off with a fuchsia scarf scattered with vibrant butterflies.

Me, I'm wearing the grey cashmere dress. It still smells like her, as if she's giving me a detached hug. I swing between being comforted and wrenched by this. And of course, there are the blue suede shoes.

We pull up to St. Paul's Episcopal church, a painfully adorable white wooden clapboard structure that's straight out of Laura Ingalls Wilder. This is the church Feeney, Liddy, and I have attended over the years, though admittedly not often and rarely at the same time. Even loud and proudly Jewish Max and Spence have been known to attend a Christmas concert or two at St. Paul's if any of our kids happened to be in it. We're early, but there are already cars lining both sides of the street. Liddy has a handicapped parking pass because of Luke, which she almost never uses. Today she pulls straight into a blue painted spot right in front of the church and exhales loudly. "Ready?"

"Never," I say. My heart feels like it's beating three times too fast on the outside of my body.

"No shit." Max answers. "But I've got a purse full of Kleenex and there's only one way to get rid of it." She opens the passenger door and steps out, slamming it behind her. Her heels kick up puffs of dust as she storms toward the church doors. I think she knows we need someone to be our battle sergeant, that none of us would willingly throw ourselves into this emotional skirmish without someone leading the charge. Liddy and I follow her with much less gusto.

Inside there are already at least fifty people sitting in the pews. Nobody is talking much apart from the steady stream of people approaching Garrett to offer *condolences*. I notice, however, that the conversation pretty much stops there.

"I'm so sorry."

"We're praying for you."

"Let us know if you need anything."

Then the inevitable and deafening *dot dot dot* of unanswerable questions. My heart hurts for him hearing those empty words over and over again. The strain shows on his face and in the tightness of the smile he offers again and again.

"*Thank you.*"

"*So kind.*"

"*I appreciate it.*"

Nobody means any of this.

We walk up and he looks visibly relieved. He knows we're not going to say any of that bullshit. When I give him a hug I more feel than hear a quiet sob escape his chest. I look him in the eye and say, "You got this." He nods but looks like a little kid that's been sent to the principal.

"The guys are coming separately," Max says. "Do you want us to sit with you or with them?"

"I'm saving the rest of this pew for Feeney's family," he says. "I'm surprised they're not here yet."

Feeney's family. As if summoned, Feeney's mother and sisters step through the door. Barbara, Eleanor, and Isobel, respectively. The women are immaculately dressed, beautiful, and pinched. I'm pretty sure Barbara is wearing Chanel. Garrett waves to them and indicates the pew. They stride toward us, all cheekbones and highlights.

"We had to park a million miles away," Feeney's mother says as she leans in to air kiss Garrett's cheek.

"I know, I'm sorry. I should have warned you." Garrett says.

"No, we should have taken a limo. I told the girls that, but they thought it was too much."

"Barbara, these are Feen—Josephine's best friends: Liddy, Max, and Ali."

She turns to us and there are Feeney's striking eyes, the same exact shade of blue, but absent all the sparkle that made them Feeney's alone. I feel a stab of resentment—she doesn't deserve those eyes.

"Thank you for coming, ladies. And for your help, of course."

I open my mouth to respond, but she's already turned back to Garrett. "The church looks lovely, Garrett. Truly," she says.

I can't take it. "We'll see you all afterwards," I say, turning on my heel and shepherding Max and Liddy on. "Oh my God, did she just *thank* us for coming to Feeney's funeral?" I ask under my breath, seething.

"She's acting like she's at a freaking cocktail party," Max fumes.

"Deep breaths," Liddy says as she slides us into a pew in the middle of the church. It had never occurred to me that we wouldn't sit with Garrett and the girls.

The three of us clutch hands, Max in the middle. I can't look around because I don't want to catch anyone's eye. Eventually someone comes down the aisle with the programs we spent so much time designing, wording, and folding. I hope there aren't too many wine stains.

JOSEPHINE BLYTHE FOX SIMMS
October 4, 1973–July 16, 2015

Feeney's beautiful face stares out at me. Despite having seen the photo all week long, it still takes my breath away. The corners of her mouth are curled with the beginning of a deep laugh and one piece of her hair has caught the wind, dancing beneath her mouth. There's so much life in it. So much Feeney.

The organ begins to play.

Over the next ninety minutes, Max, Liddy, and I grab and pinch and twist each other's hands so many times, we're sure to wake up tomorrow purple and blue. But it's the only form of communication we can use to express the bizarreness that is Feeney's funeral, the only way we can silently wage our many and various complaints. There are, of course, the requested hymns and readings per Barbara. But things really take a bizarre turn when Eleanor and Isobel get up and move in lockstep to the front of the church. They stand together in front of one microphone and take turns bobbing their blonde heads down into it while speaking about someone I don't recognize as ever having met.

"I'm Eleanor Fox Ridgeway."

"And I'm Isobel Fox Fleming. Josephine was our youngest sister."

"I would like to start today by reading a poem by William Wordsworth," Eleanor says, unrolling a scroll of paper (yes, a scroll). She then goes on to recite the world's most depressing poem.

A slumber did my spirit seal
I had no human fears:
She seemed a thing that could not feel
The touch of earthly years.
No motion has she now, no force;
She neither hears nor sees;
Rolled round in earth's diurnal course,
With rocks, and stones, and trees.

My hand is white where Max is gripping it.

Isobel follows up with, "And I would like to read a Bible verse." Her voice turns deep and solemn as she intones, "'And you shall know that I am the Lord, when I open your graves, and raise you from your graves, O my people.' Ezekiel 37:13." While Isobel speaks, Eleanor keeps her eyes closed, nodding along to the words. Liddy pushes the pointy toe of her shoe deep into my calf.

For a moment, they simply stand there, looking blankly out at us.

I think, or rather hope, that they are done. But no, Eleanor lowers her head toward the microphone again.

"Josephine was good at everything she ever did. She took up ballet when she was six, and by nine she was Clara in *The Nutcracker.*" She leans back.

Oh God, here comes Isobel's head now, I think. I'm right.

"Then she decided to try field hockey, and sure enough, she became one of the top players in the state by sixteen." Isobel leans back. It's like the Oscars yet even more wooden and awkward, if even possible.

Eleanor ducks down and says, "In college she had a *perfect rush.*" She leans back and smiles, nodding her head with pride. I have no idea what this means.

Isobel leans in and says, "And *Town & Country* gave Garrett and Josephine a *quarter-page photo* when they were married." She locks eyes with Garrett and smiles at him with sympathy. "She was so beautiful and accomplished."

Eleanor puts her arm around Isobel. "Oh behalf of the Fox family, we would like to say how very much we loved our Josephine and how much we will miss her." Then they embrace for the briefest of moments and walk back to their seats, their heels clicking loudly along the wooden floor.

I sneak a look over at Max; she is staring at the pew in front of her and mouthing something to herself. She may be counting, I'm not sure. It's one of the many ways she manages her anger.

There is a screen set up, and as *Walking in Memphis* comes on, a slideshow of Feeney's life cues up. We sit transfixed as we watch a Feeney we never knew flit and flicker in front of our eyes. Feeney as a child, resplendent in embroidered pink and yellow dresses. Feeney as a flower girl, her hair curled into tight ringlets, an equally tight smile on her face. Feeney in various ballet costumes, posing in perfect arabesques. Feeney in uniforms—school, field hockey, Girl Scouts. Feeney wearing crowns on her head as the Homecoming Queen, or Prom Queen, or both. Feeney with Greek letters emblazoned across her chest. Feeney in her wedding dress, posing stiffly with the rest of her family. These photos aren't of Feeney Simms, they're of Josephine Fox, and it's an entirely different person.

I don't even cry because I feel like I'm at someone else's funeral, someone I'm not even sure I even like. I notice that neither Max nor Liddy do, either. We just hold onto each other for dear life until, mercifully, it's all over.

It had gotten hot inside the old building, and the zombie-like mass of people inching toward the doors is insufferable. I shuffle along, careful to leave a few civilized millimeters of space between myself and the humanity in front of me, when all I really want to do is push and scream my way out.

Finally, we're out in the open. Max, Liddy, and I turn into the gravel driveway by the side of the church. We're stunned into uncharacteristic silence by the spectacle we just witnessed.

One by one, our husbands find us. By the time they arrived earlier there were no more seats near us, which was probably for the best. Spence puts an arm around Max. Drew tries to grab my hand, but I move it to my purse strap. Jack sidles up next to Liddy with his jacket slung over his shoulder.

"Feeney was not in that room," Max says with authority. She's pissed.

"At least Garrett played the music we wanted during the slideshow," I said. "He told me the other day that Barbara wanted to change it to another hymn."

"Oh, Lord," Max says.

"Yep. I'm pretty sure that's who she was going for," I say.

"There wasn't one photo of Feeney past about age twenty-five in there," Liddy says.

"I'm trying to think of how many times Feeney even saw her family in the last decade—maybe twice? Three times?" I say.

"I don't blame her a bit," Max says, shaking her head and looking at the ground. "That whole funeral was weird as hell. Feeney would have hated it."

I nod. "That sucked."

"We have to go to Feeney's house, though. No way we can get out of that." Liddy states the obvious, flicking her eyes in my direction.

"Fine. Let's show our faces and then get out of there," I say. "I don't think I can handle much more of Feeney's family today."

"I just want to be there for the girls," Liddy says.

"Oh Jesus, those girls," Max says, shaking her head. Hannah spent the entire service with her face buried in her father's jacket. Caroline sat statue-still, eyes staring straight forward, laser-focused.

"The guys don't have to come to Feeney's. It will just make it harder to extricate ourselves. Why don't you guys go home and relieve the sitters?" I say, flicking my eyes at Drew.

"Can one of you give Jack a ride home?" Liddy asks. "He walked over from his office."

"Happy to," Spence says, and off they go looking like little boys dressed up for church, thrilled when it's over and they can finally go home to change.

Drew squeezes my shoulder. "You okay?" he asks.

"No," I say, avoiding his gaze. I know it's not his fault. But it's not his pain, either. I refuse to share it with him. "See you at home. Tell the kids I'll be there soon."

The Time Wine Shot Out My Nose

Two years before

Smack in the middle of an otherwise normal Wine Wednesday, Liddy blurts out, "Jack is having an affair. No, make that affairs."

For a moment, nobody speaks. I swallow a weird knee-jerk desire to giggle. Max recovers first. "What are you talking about?"

"I got a phone call yesterday from a woman who says she's been sleeping with Jack for years. And the only reason she wanted to tell me now was that . . ."

Her voice breaks. She looks at the ground. Nobody moves or breathes. When she raises her head to speak again, she is transformed. Her long, ropy curls quiver with contained energy, her nostrils are flared, her cheeks are pink and bright. She is a freaking warrior.

". . . was that he's cheating on her with someone else."

"Jesus, what did you say?" I ask, my voice barely above a whisper.

"I said, 'That must be hard. I hope you can get some professional help.' Then I hung up and threw Jack's Rolex in the toilet."

"And what condition was the water in the toilet?" asks Feeney, like she's talking to a caged wild animal.

Liddy takes a big gulp of wine and says, "You mean before or after I peed on it?"

I laugh mid-swallow, snorting and coughing uncontrollably. That gets everyone laughing, Liddy most of all, wiping away the tears streaming down her face. We're laughing because it feels so damn good to laugh when what you really want to do is cry. We do that silent, mouth-open, noiseless laugh that hurts your stomach muscles but somehow helps heal your soul. I can't help but think that when we die, our earthly bodies won't miss great sex or eating delicious food but rather this uncomfortable, slightly painful laughter that reminds you of the existence of joy and suffering at the same time.

Eventually the hysteria dies down. "What are you going to do, Lids?" I ask.

"Well, my first thought was to take a hot bath, shave myself hairless, and start calling my exes in alphabetical order."

"Which would mean starting with Aaron Anderson," Max says with a knowing look. Aaron was Liddy's first boyfriend in high school. He now owns the local hardware store, and we're always teasing Liddy about going in and asking him for a good screw.

Liddy exhales loudly. "Of course. But here's the thing. I'd never do it. I'd never cheat on my husband. Even now. It's just not . . . me."

We're all quiet for a bit. It's one of those moments when you're overwhelmingly thankful for having people in your life who don't feel the need to fill a silence. Liddy has earned the respect of our silence. We know each other in just that way.

Eventually Feeney says, "So now what?"

"I have no idea. When Jack got home last night, I told him I knew. I didn't even have to say what I knew. You should have seen his face."

"Sorry Lids, but I could kill him," Max says.

"Hear, hear," says Feeney, moving to refill our glasses.

"That was my first reaction, too," says Liddy. "But now I just feel sorry for him. After Luke was born, Jack never really recovered. Everything in his life up to that point had always come easy. Then he got thrown a curve ball and it knocked him out of his comfort zone. I think he's lost. Actually I think he's been lost for a long time."

"Why on earth are you being so nice?" I ask.

"Because I know what it feels like to want to escape my own life," Liddy says, putting her head in her hands. "I just don't choose to escape with sex. God, I wish it was that easy."

Feeney scoots next to her and puts an arm around Liddy's shoulder. "What are you going to do?"

Liddy lifts her head and looks at us. "I honestly don't know. I don't want to split up, it would be brutal on the kids. Routine is so important, especially for Luke. I guess I should look into counseling but . . . I don't know. My heart's not in it right now."

"Okay," Feeney says, rubbing Liddy's arm like she's prepping her for a boxing match. "Fair enough. One day at a time. Isn't that what they say in rehab? I just have one question."

"Yes?" Liddy asks.

"Can I piss on his Rolex, too?"

By the time we get to Feeney's house we have to park nearly a block away. Both sides of the street are lined with cars I don't recognize.

"Most of these people are just looky-loos. Feeney didn't have this many friends," Max observes.

"Yeah, but Garrett does," Liddy responds.

"He's about to get a whole lot more," I say. "Of the female persuasion, no doubt."

"Gross," Max says.

Liddy pulls into a spot and turns off the car, shoulders hunched over the steering wheel. "I think I'm dreading this more than the funeral itself."

"Me too," Max says. "But it's equally mandatory."

We make our way to the door and let ourselves in. What greets us stops us short.

Everywhere we look, people are standing and talking, holding drinks. People we hardly know. People who didn't love Feeney. It's like the superficial holiday party Feeney never had.

We're standing there in shell-shocked silence when a lavender-hued presence rushes us full force.

"Oh my God! You must be devastated! I've been thinking about you three ever since I heard the horrible news!" It's Lilibeth Stewart, in all her poufy-haired, lily-scented glory. She gathers us up in her ample bosom and holds us close. It's such a surprise that it takes me a moment to realize that she's crying hysterically.

Above her padded shoulder, my eyes take in the scene around us. Much of the party has halted their conversations and are looking uncomfortably in our direction.

I extricate myself and pull Lilibeth aside with an arm around her shoulder. "Thank you, Lilibeth. That means a lot to us." I look over at Max and Liddy. Max is fuming and Liddy's eyes are closed.

"I just can't believe it," she says as we collapse together on Feeney's navy velvet couch. "Of all people, I can't believe Josephine Simms *committed suicide*," but she says the last part in a whisper, the way racist white people whisper *Black*.

"I know. It's horrible," I say. Why the hell am I sitting in Feeney's living room comforting Lilibeth Stewart? I pat her padded lavender shoulder while she babbles and blubbers away.

Ten minutes later I make my rumpled way into the family room where Feeney's long, antique farm table is laden with cold cuts, fruit trays, casseroles, and a slew of desserts, as if pain could be counterbalanced by calories. If only it were true.

I can't eat a thing, but I can drink, so I pour myself a glass of bad grocery store Chardonnay. Feeney would be mortified. I drift through the crowds feeling like a minor celebrity, the kind that people acknowledge visually but don't want to approach. Lilibeth was a handful, but at least she talked to us. Nobody else knows what to say.

I find Liddy and Max sitting with Feeney's cousin, Jane. She's five years younger than Feeney and the only family member she ever liked. Probably because Jane is considered the black sheep of the family, which was one of the highest marks in her favor in Feeney's book. Jane is gay and outspoken, two major taboos in the Fox clan. She's a family-law attorney who lives in Berkeley. Over the years, she's made a few appearances at Wine Wednesdays and Feeney's birthday celebrations. I make my way over to them and give Jane a hug.

"I feel like any minute she's going to jump out and say, 'Just kidding!'" Jane says. "I keep having dreams where she's alive and I am so relieved. Like the world has started making sense again."

"I've had dreams just like that," Liddy says. "Waking up is awful."

Max and I both say, "Me too." Then we all look at each other in surprise.

"What a shitty thing to have in common," Jane says.

"We also had Feeney in common," I say. "Which is more than we can say for most people here."

"True," Jane says as she surveys the room. Then she levels her eyes at us. "So. Did you guys know that Feeney tried to kill herself in high school?"

Nobody speaks. I feel like the Feeney I knew is receding farther away by the second. I'm also disturbingly jealous of Jane for having this knowledge.

While Liddy and I gape, Max simply says, "No."

"I wondered. It's kind of a big family secret, which is so fucked up. Her sophomore year, she took a bunch of Barbara's valium. Eleanor happened to come home right afterwards and called 911 in time. But everyone was sworn to secrecy, and unfortunately they're all really good at that. Me, not so much."

"Was there a reason?" I ask.

"Is there ever just one?" Jane asks back. She shakes her head. "Sure. Depression. A fucked up family. Hormones. If you're looking for the silver bullet, you're screwed." She looks up and shrugs.

I'm floored; I can't decide whether or not this is helpful information. What are we supposed to do with this now?

"How could we be best friends with someone for a decade and not know she tried to commit suicide?" Liddy voices the reality we are all now faced with.

"How much time have you spent around the Fox family?" Jane says. "These are not people who handle what they consider weakness well." She looks us right in the eyes. "I'm not kidding. They scare the shit out of me, and I'm just a cousin. I can't imagine how it was on a daily basis."

"How many people knew about this?" Max asks.

"Well, her immediate family, then me, only because she told me herself not long after it happened, and that's pretty much it. I doubt they even know that I know. Keeping up appearances is extremely important to this bunch."

"Did you ever ask her about it?" Liddy asks.

"Ah. The golden question," Jane says, looking down and shaking her head. "I actually did, but she blew it off, like it wasn't as big of a deal as everyone was making it. And I was too in awe of her to pursue it. I hate that." She squeezes her eyes shut. "Feeney was a force to be reckoned with. She always seemed above the fray. And even if I knew she needed help, I wouldn't have had the slightest idea how to give it to her."

"Yeah," I say, defeated. We're all guilty of the same thing—believing Feeney when she said she was fine. Because we wanted her to be, we needed her to be. Not because she actually was. The guilt is oppressive. Sharing it only makes it more so.

"I'm sorry if I dropped a bomb—I just thought you should know," Jane says, moving to get up. "I need to go. Call me if you guys need anything. Or if my family gets annoying. All I have to do is show up, and they scatter like roaches." Then she hugs us each hard and gets up and walks off.

I feel desperately sad. It feels like losing a piece of Feeney again. It's all I can do to not rush after her and pull her back to us, if only to sit in depressed silence together.

"Now what?" Liddy asks. I'm unsure if she means it literally or existentially.

Max rubs her forehead hard with both hands. "Let's go check on Garrett and the girls. And then let's get the hell out of here."

Caroline and Hannah are sitting on the lawn together with another girl I don't recognize. Their dresses pool around them while they pick at pieces of grass. Garrett is sitting at an outdoor table nearby with a few men who look vaguely familiar. Max and I sit down with the men while Liddy plops down on the grass with the girls.

Garrett had been sitting comfortably, one ankle balanced on the opposite knee, the Polo symbol on his socks in perpetual pre-strike position. When we sit down, he swings his legs down and sits up straight. I catch his eye and he looks almost afraid. I lean forward and catch him in an awkward side hug. Max gives him a couple affectionate back pats. Like birds on a wire, the men take off one by one.

"How are you doing?" I ask.

He exhales. "To be honest, it's easier with people like that," he says, gesturing to the mens' wide, retreating backs. "It's harder when I see you all." He looks at us apologetically and his eyes fill. He does that cough thing men do when they're trying not to cry and wipes his eyes with one thumb and forefinger.

"We get it," I say. "It's how we feel together too. Unfortunately we're stuck with each other."

"Is there anything we can do? Need help with the girls?" Max asks.

"Thank you. But there are a bunch of school moms who are taking turns picking up the girls and trying to keep things as normal as possible. If you don't want to be here, please don't feel like you have to be. To be honest, I'll be better today if you were not here," he says, looking at the ground.

"Don't have to ask us twice," Max says, giving him a swift hug as she stands. "But we'll be back tomorrow to check on you guys, okay?"

Garrett nods and swallows while avoiding our eyes. I squeeze his shoulder. You forget sometimes that often the ones who look the most put together are putting on an act. It's hard not to wonder how long Feeney had been doing the same thing.

Max and I go over to where the girls are to give them hugs. Caroline is being distant with us, Hannah grabs tight and asks us not to leave. I cup her face in my hands and kiss her forehead, her nose and both cheeks, the way I've seen Feeney do a million times. She closes her eyes and tears stream down her face. I can taste them.

"We'll be back tomorrow sweetheart," I say. "And any other day you want us. Okay?"

She nods, her eyes still closed. I look over at Caroline, and she is watching us like a hawk. "Caroline, whatever you're feeling, know it's okay. If you're mad, if you're sad, if you're confused, it's all okay."

A look crosses her face that looks almost like terror, then she swallows and her face goes blank once more. I keep my eyes on hers while I say, "We love you guys so much." She finally looks down so I stand up and brush off the grass. Max and Liddy follow suit. Together we walk toward the front door, eyes straight forward, as if we don't feel the assault of dozens of unspoken questions bouncing off our backs.

Getting back to Max's house feels like taking your Spanx and heels off at the end of a long night. We sit in our own personal silences for a while, Max with her chin in her hands, Liddy with her legs tucked up underneath her, me picking at the fringe of the soft throw I have blanketed myself in.

"I feel like I was at the funeral of a complete stranger," Max finally says.

Liddy nods. "How is it possible that her family knew so little about her? About who she really was, not just some laundry list of accomplishments from her youth?"

"Frankly I'm starting to feel like we didn't know her either," I say.

"We knew her, Ali. We did," Max says, an edge entering her voice.

"We knew what she wanted us to know, Max. Like it or not, Feeney wasn't entirely herself with us, or we wouldn't be in this situation. At the very least, we should have known she had tried before."

Max exhales and leans forward. "Do you share everything with us? Absolutely everything?"

This stops me. I haven't told them that I can barely look at my husband.

Max continues. "Yeah, didn't think so. Does that make you not entirely yourself?"

I shake my head and try again. "Well, she wasn't honest with us. She couldn't have been, or else we would have known she was . . . suffering."

"Maybe she didn't even understand what was going on," Liddy says. "Maybe it wasn't as sinister as you're making it sound, like she was purposely keeping something from us."

I feel like I'm being ganged up on and it's infuriating. "I'm not making anything sound *sinister*; I'm trying to make sense of the hell that we are going through!"

"For the record, Ali, being suicidal isn't a great conversation starter. And mental illness isn't really something you can 'make sense of,'" Max says, making air quotes with her fingers.

"Since when was Feeney mentally ill?" I snap at Max.

"Most people who kill themselves aren't exactly stable, Ali."

"Feeney wasn't MOST PEOPLE! Okay? Stop trying to put her in some category!" I am standing now. I feel like I could practically lift off with pent-up rage.

Liddy puts her face into her hands. "Jesus, how did we get here?"

Max says, "Feeney was suicidal and none of us knew it. That's how we got here. And you know what? I don't think that's all that fucking unusual."

"Would you stop being the Dalai Lama of mental illness, Max?" I say.

She looks up at me. "That is a really shitty thing to say, Ali."

Liddy springs to her feet, surprisingly catlike. "Will you listen to yourselves? What Jane told us today should make us feel empathy for Feeney, not anger that she didn't tell us! How do you not see that?" Her voice catches and tears fatten her eyes. Max and I look at each other, disarmed in an instant.

"Oh God, Liddy, you're right," Max says and stands and grabs us both. We all hold on tight to each other and really cry. We're lost. We're loud and ugly and none of it matters. All we know is that none of us are complete anymore and never will be again.

The quiet moments after a big cry are not unlike those after sex. Everyone is spent and not much needs to be said. Liddy gets up and brings us a box of Kleenex. We all blow and sniff and wipe and sigh.

I take a deep breath. "Here's something I do know. I can't say goodbye to Feeney like that. It's not right. She deserves better."

Both Liddy and Max nod in agreement.

"Okay, so, how do we do it?" Liddy says, shaking her head with the incredulousness of this question. There's no possible way to say goodbye to someone like Feeney.

"Well, for starters, we need to give her a different funeral," I say with conviction.

"Oh Jesus, don't make me go through that shit again," Max says, shaking her head. "I can't do it."

"Well, what if we just say the things we want to say? It doesn't have to be formal, or at a church, or with anyone else around. I just . . . I can't . . ." I frantically look back and forth between Max and Liddy. "This can't be it."

"We can't let today be the way we honor her. She deserves better," Liddy says, nodding.

Max inhales, then says, "Let's just have a private memorial for Feeney at my house. Just the three of us. Nobody else, no rules, no fucking programs."

"Not even any flowers. Unless it's dyed carnations," I say. I see a hint of a smile on Liddy's lips for the first time in days.

"I'm in," she says.

"Me too," I say. "Thank you, Max."

She nods. "Do you think it would be weird if we ask Garrett for some ashes?"

"No, I think it's a great idea. Let's do it soon," I say. "Before the family scatters them or sticks them in a fancy drawer or whatever the hell people do with ashes."

Max folds her arms and looks at us with a sense of purpose. "You know as well as I do that if we don't go get some from Garrett right this minute, we'll never have the balls again do it."

I swing my head to look at Liddy, who is already reaching for her keys. "Get back in the car. Let's go."

Less than 10 minutes later, we're standing on Feeney's front steps facing Garrett in the doorway. It's only been five hours since we last saw him after the funeral, though it feels like five days.

"What do you mean the ashes are gone?" Liddy asks with an incredulous look on her face. "Where did they go?"

"Barbara took them all to put her in the family crypt. She wouldn't even hear of me keeping any here for the girls. She said it was morbid to spread her daughter out all over the country."

"What's morbid is cooping her up with all those uptight assholes for eternity." Max says. "She couldn't stand any of those people while she was alive, now she has to hang around with them in perpetuity?"

"Believe me, I know. But I am not kidding when I say that Feeney's mom is more terrifying to me than anything I ever dreamed of as a child. There was no arguing with her—there never has been."

"So where is Feeney now?" I ask.

"You mean her ashes?" He looks perplexed.

"Yes, Garrett, I mean her ashes! Where is she?"

"Probably with her mom and sisters at the Hotel Healdsburg. I gave them the box when they left the house a couple hours ago. We are all going to go back to Greenwich next month for an interment ceremony."

"A what? I thought crypts and interments went out with horses and buggies," I say.

"It's still very much a thing in the Fox family, unfortunately. I'm so sorry that I can't help you, but I need to get the girls settled in for bed."

"Can we help?" Liddy asks.

Garrett smiles. "Most of the time, yes. But tonight, I think it's important that it's just us. Thank you, guys." We hug and tell him to give them our love.

Dejected, we turn to leave. It feels like we've lost her all over again. Max stops short in the middle of the street with her hands out at either side, fingers splayed, like a dog at point. We know this stance, it's not a good sign.

"Oh Lord help us," I say under my breath.

"We can still get some of those ashes."

Liddy and I just stare and blink.

"We'll all go over to the hotel to pay our respects to Feeney's family. We'll invite them downstairs to have a drink in the bar with us. One of us, I'm thinking Ali, will need to use the bathroom."

"Me? Why me?"

"Shhh, I'm still working this out. You'll come back and say that there's someone getting sick in there and would it be okay if you ran up to their room super quick? Then you'll go up and get a ziplock of Feeney. This will totally work!"

"Did you just say 'ziplock of Feeney'?" Liddy says.

"That's all we need. Let's go to your house and get a baggie, Ali."

"This seems like a terrible idea for about a million different reasons," I say.

Max turns to face us, shoulders back, nostrils flared. "Listen, Feeney's ashes are less than a mile from us right now and soon they'll be on the other side of the country. If we don't do something about this now, we'll never forgive ourselves. We have to at least *try*."

Liddy and I stand in the middle of the road in paralyzed silence.

She folds her arms. "Okay, let me put it this way: What would Feeney do?"

We instantly move toward Liddy's car.

The Time We Danced at Bouchon

Four months before

We're sitting on the patio in the dazzling sun at Bouchon, one of the best restaurants in wine country. It's Feeney's birthday. In typical Feeney fashion, she had taken the reins and made reservations for the four of us before we even had a chance to plan something for her. "I want to eat at a place where there aren't sponge-off menus," she had said. "My treat."

Out of nowhere, she breaks into song. Somewhat to the tune of *Footloose*.

"'Been working. So hard. I'm punching. My card.'"

She is loud and making a scene and could not care less. We start bopping in our seats along to the beat that's only in Feeney's head.

"'Eight hours. For what? Don't tell me what I got.'"

She slams four sheets of paper on the table, so hard our water splashes. Not our wine, however, because each glass is empty.

"I got these tiiii-ckets. To see Kenny Loggins!"

Max, Liddy, and I start to giggle.

"You're coming with meeee . . . 'we're gonna tear up the town!'"

She stands up and we all join her, doing a wine-fueled, '80s jumping and snapping dance.

"'Cuz we're gonna cut loose! Footloose! Kick off your dancing shoes!'"

Out of nowhere, Feeney sits down quickly and starts picking at her food. We sit down a moment behind her, out of breath, slightly confused. Just then the manager steps into view, Feeney must have seen him coming.

"Is everything all right here?" he asks in a stern, disapproving voice.

"No, sir," Feeney responds. "We've been out of wine for some time now, and no one has bothered to ask if we would like more. And we do. One more bottle of the Fiddlehead Sauvignon Blanc, please." She looks him in the eye and dabs the side of her perfectly glossed mouth. Then she smiles and blinks coquettishly.

He leaves and we start laughing so hard that Liddy puts her head down on the table. We're all wiping our eyes and noses with our starched white cloth napkins.

"As I was saying before I was so rudely interrupted," Feeney says when she catches her breath. "We're going to Kenny Loggins at Rodney Strong Vineyards at the end of the summer, August thirty-first. You guys know about my love for Kenny Loggins and I certainly knew none of you cheapskates would actually pay to see him, so it's my birthday gift to me."

Under her breath, Max sings a guitar lick from Footloose. *"Bow buh bow buh bow buh weah weah!"* We fall apart again.

The Hotel Healdsburg is where the fancy tourists stay—the ones who whisk off to wine country for a casual getaway with designer clothes packed into Louis Vuitton bags. But the lobby bar is a local favorite. Feeney, Max, Liddy, and I have logged many hours cozying in front of the oversized, blazing fireplace, absentmindedly swirling wine glasses while we talk and talk.

Max and Liddy settle on the plush couches across from the fire-place while I step away to approach the front desk, which isn't in the front and is not really a desk. It's more like a sleek kitchen counter with a chipper person standing behind it greeting me with a smile that doesn't make it all the way up to her eyes. My stomach is doing a samba.

"I'd like to call up to Barbara Fox's room, please."

"May I tell her who is calling?"

"Ali Stirling."

I stand and chew the inside of my cheek while the clerk dials the number with one perfectly manicured middle finger. I can practically hear Feeney saying under her breath, *"Who uses the flip-off finger to dial?"*

She speaks quietly into the phone and then hands it to me. I hope she can't tell how badly my hands are shaking.

"Hi Barbara, it's Ali. Feeney's friend? Max and Liddy and I are downstairs at the bar and would love to buy you, Eleanor, and Isobel a glass of wine if you're up for it." My most fervent hope right now is to be turned down. I smile at the hotel clerk with terror in my eyes.

"Oh darling, that's a lovely thought. Let me check with the girls."

I hear muffled talking, all the same refined tone.

She comes back on. "We were actually going to come down ourselves in a bit. Let us freshen up and we'll meet you shortly." Click.

I hand the phone back to the clerk and walk back to the bar, legs wobbly.

"Are they coming?" Max asks when I reach the couch.

I can't talk yet so I nod twice, eyes wide.

"When?"

"Shortly," I squeak.

"Shortly? Is that like five minutes or thirty?"

I shake my head and lift my shoulders. I don't know, I don't speak Barbara.

Liddy signals the server. "Well, let's get this ball rolling. We're going to need some liquid courage. Make hers an extra good pour," she says, pointing at me.

After what seems like an hour but couldn't possibly be as I haven't even finished half my glass, the three ladies breeze into the room. Breezing is probably the only way they ever enter rooms.

We stand up and all exchange cheek kisses like a choreographed routine. "So lovely of you to come see us," Barbara says as she sits down and smooths her hair. "This has been a very difficult day."

"We're so sorry," Liddy says with feeling. "We loved Feeney more than you'll ever know."

"Thank you." She half smiles then picks up the wine list and pulls her reading glasses out of her black quilted Chanel bag. Feeney's sisters follow her lead.

After an awkward moment of silence Max asks, "So . . . when do you head back east?"

Without looking up, Barbara responds, "First thing in the morning. We have heaps to do before the ceremony at home."

I stand up too fast. "Excuse me. I have to go to the bathroom." My heart is hammering hard in my chest. "I have to tinkle."

Max is looking at me with her mouth practically hanging open. *Yes, I realize I just said tinkle but this was your crazy idea and you can't expect me to sit around and make small talk!* (I say this to her with my eyes.)

Barbara flicks her eyes up at me over her glasses. "Certainly, dear. We'll order our drinks."

I scuttle out of the room in a state of both relief and panic. Once I'm in the spring green tiled bathroom I lock myself in a stall and stand with my forehead against the back of the door.

"Damn it, Feeney I wish you were here," I say, my voice echoing off the sterile walls. I exhale loudly. "Please help me do this crazy thing. I'm doing it for you because I love you and I miss you so goddamn much."

A few tears drop from my eyes onto the floor. Splash, splash, splash. It occurs to me that the next person who comes in will probably think my tears are pee, which makes me smile and wish I could tell Feeney about it.

After a few minutes I let myself out and walk to the sink, surveying my face. It's salvageable. There's color in my cheeks for a change and amazingly most of my makeup from earlier has stayed put. A little cold water on a paper towel pressed to my eyes and a quick mascara sweep is all it takes to make me look like I'm not a deranged, grief-fueled person about to pilfer a baggie of my best friend's ashes.

I lift my chin up and say to my reflection, "Let's do this."

Back in the bar I am hit with a wave of adrenaline, and my acting skills honed over two whole years of elementary school theater kick in. I stand over the ladies and shudder as I say, "I'm so sorry you guys but there's someone . . ." I put my hand up to the side my mouth and stage-whisper, ". . . *unwell* in the restroom. Must have been a big day at the wineries!" Big, corny wink. "I suppose I could ask to use the men's room . . . or, say! Would you be so kind as to allow me to pop up to your room? I'll be back in a jiff." I don't know why I'm talking like a housewife in a 1950s sitcom.

"Oh of course. It's Room 111. Do you want one of the girls to go with you?"

For a moment I'm thrown. Who are the girls? Max and Liddy? Hell yes, I want one of them with me! I start to respond then I realize not a moment too soon that she's talking about *her* girls, who don't seem like girls to me and who I definitely do *not* want coming along.

"No, no, I'll be fine. Thank you so much for saving me from that *scene.*" Thumb jerk, more corny mugging. I'm not cut out for acting.

She hands me a room key with a diamond-encrusted, alabaster-skinned hand that's shot through with snaky blue veins and I think to myself, *So that's where the term blue blood comes from.*

"Be right back," I chirp.

I take the stairs to expend some of my frenetic energy. Once I'm at Room 111, it takes me a few tries to get things working as my hand is shaking so hard. But then I hear the melodious sound of the key being accepted and the next thing I know, I'm inside with the door safely shut behind me.

Deep breaths, Ali. Deep breaths.

I walk in and survey the room. Nothing is out of place, the bags are perfectly lined up and zipped, there's not so much as a lip gloss out on the bathroom counter. The room already smells like expensive perfume and something slightly dusty, probably old money.

Hesitant, I venture further into the room. Should I pee in the bathroom to solidify my story? I decide it's not worth the time, and besides, I don't have to go. I can't see anything that looks like it could be ashes—no urn, no box, nothing but designer luggage. Awesome. Looks like I'm going to have to do some rummaging.

I unzip the largest suitcase, thinking while doing so that I've even never touched a piece of luggage this expensive before in my life. I pack in duffle bags from L.L.Bean.

I inhale sharply when I get it open. Not because I found Feeney, but because everything inside is wrapped in its own separate sheet of tissue paper. Is everything in here brand new? Wait, no, it's all the same tissue paper. Holy bejeezus, this is how these people pack! And is the paper . . . scented?

Well, it must be, because I sneeze. With snot. Into the suitcase.

Onto the tissue paper that looks like it's never been disturbed. Except, of course, for my snot that's now smattered across it like a pale crime scene.

"Oh shit!" I say, looking around for something to clean this mess up. I see a box of Kleenex. I slip one from the box and go to work dabbing my DNA gently off of the gorgeous paper. While doing so I have to stifle another sneeze, but there's no way I'm making this mistake twice. After a few minutes the damage is far less visible, and it's going to have to do. I have to find Feeney.

I quickly open the other suitcases, and it's more of the same thing. Shirts, pants, even bras and underwear, all tidily wrapped in delicate, scented paper. If I wasn't in such a rush I'd marvel at the bizarreness of it all.

Nothing in the suitcases. I'm worried about how long I've been in here now. I can't fail, I just can't. It would be too much of a loss in a week where loss has been the overriding theme. I stand up and look all around me.

"Feeney, where are you?" It's a question asked in desperation, hands in my hair, tears burning my eyes. But right after I ask it, something happens. A beautiful moth glides out from nowhere, flits before my eyes, and lands on a the handle of what I thought was the minibar. It beats its wings twice, then flies away.

"There's no way—" I'm saying as I walk toward it. But even as I question it, I know what I'm going to find. I open the door to what turns out to be an empty recess with a medium-sized box inside, stamped *Whitman Mortuary*. With awe and reverence, I pull off the top of the box, open the plastic bag inside, and press my hand into the soft ashes. "Thank you, Feeney," I whisper, bringing my grey-tinged fingers to my lips.

Then I jump into motion, grabbing the small bag from my purse. I didn't think to bring any sort of scooper so I'm frozen for a moment. I turn the bag inside out and simply grab what I can. I close it up and stuff it into my purse. There are ashes strewn about of course, but time is ticking. I close the box, fill up my lungs and blow as hard as I can. Feeney takes to the air in a swirling, twirling cyclone, and I can't help but smile as I imagine her loving it. I close my eyes and feel a few tiny ashes land on my face. It feels like a kiss.

On my way to the door I stop and check the bathroom mirror. I look flushed but fine. On closer inspection, there's a barely visible fleck of ash at the top of my hairline. I leave it and head for the door.

As soon as Max sees me round the corner downstairs, her eyes widen and she slowly leans forward. I wink at her and watch as a sly grin steals across her face. Then she turns back to Barbara, nodding along to whatever she is saying.

I sit back down and grab my glass, taking a deep swallow of the garnet-colored wine. I close my eyes and breathe and let my adrenaline settle to a simmer. For the first time in days, I feel a sense of comfort.

Eventually we say our goodbyes to Feeney's family and walk out into the coolness of the evening. Max turns to me the minute the door closes behind us. "So, what happened?"

I contemplate telling them the whole bizarre story, but in the end I just smile. "Let's just say Feeney likes this plan."

The Time She Taught Me to Starfish

Four years before

I'm driving down Feeney's street around ten at night, on my way home from a board meeting at the kids' school. As I usually do when I drive by the house of someone I know and love, I glance over at it as I pass, but something I see makes me instantly start to slow down. There seems to be a large, white creature on Feeney's front lawn.

"What the hell?" I say under my breath as I turn the wheel toward the side of the street. I park and get out, and only then do I realize that the large white thing is Feeney, lying on her back on the grass in her pale grey pajamas, arms and legs spread wide.

"Hey," I say, a universe of questions in my voice.

"Hey," she replies, as if this was the most normal thing in the world.

"Whatcha doing?"

"Starfishing."

I lower myself down next to her and slowly spread my body out so it matches hers.

"And what exactly is starfishing?"

She laughs. "You should know, you're doing it."

"Good point. But why am I doing it?"

She's quiet for a moment, and I can hear the chirping and clicking of all the nighttime insects I normally tune out.

"Sometimes I just need to feel like I'm planted on this earth. I need to feel connected to it in a way that I can't do while I'm running around on my goddamn feet all day. So I wait until it's night and then I come out here and press my whole body into the ground. It makes me feel like I can breathe again." She tips her head to the side to look at me and I do the same. "You know?"

I'm not sure I know but I nod my head. "And why do you call it starfishing?"

"Because I'm stretched out like a starfish and I'm looking up at the stars. It feels like I'm fishing for them. I lay here until I find one that winks at me. Then I'm able to get up again."

"I take it one hasn't winked."

"Nope. Not yet. But it can take a long time."

We lay there for a long stretch in silence, looking at the vast sky filled with stars. To me, they all look like a bit like they're winking.

"Nobody's ever starfished with me before," Feeney says. "It's kind of nice."

"It is," I say, meaning it. "Thanks for popping my starfishing cherry."

Feeney laughs hard and I start too, and the exaggerated bouncing of our bellies as we lie flat on the ground makes us laugh even harder.

Her hand that's stretched out closest to mind touches my fingertips. We hook our two pinky fingers together and just lie there as our laughter subsides. Then, without warning, she hops to her feet. "Just got my wink."

"Wait, what about me?"

"Stay here as long as you like." She smiles down at me then turns to head inside. I stay, searching the stars for one that seems to be made only for me. I never find it.

As I'm brushing my teeth and getting ready for bed, I hear the door
to our bedroom creak open. It's hesitant, which is unlike Drew, who
bursts through doorways like the Kool-Aid man. I peer out of the
bathroom and see Lachlan and Devon standing in their pajamas,
looking very serious.

"Hey, peanuts." I turn the faucet off and come out to meet them,
drying my hands on a towel. "All good?"

Devon looks at Lachlan, then at me, her hands fidgeting. "How
did Auntie Feeney die?"

I freeze and my mouth goes dry. How had I not seen this question
coming? The day after she died, I sat them both down and told them
Feeney was gone. We had never really talked about death before, at
least not when it came to humans. When Lachlan was younger, he
got it into his head that all people live automatically until they're a
hundred, whereupon they promptly drop dead. I thought it was cute
so I never corrected him.

At the time about Feeney I asked them if they had any questions
and they both said no. Now I realize that of course they must have
had questions but could also sense that I was in no condition to
answer them. Even now I can hear the tentativeness in Devon's voice,
and it makes my heart clutch.

"Sweetie, it's really hard to explain," I say, buying time while
my mind races. I sit down on the side of the bed and they perch
on the end, looking like two scared birds. I look down at the towel
in my lap, not brave enough to meet their eyes as I speak. "To be
honest, I don't know all the details but she was . . . sick and she . . .
tooksomepillsandshedied."

I feel slightly dizzy. My heart is pounding erratically. Is this the beginning of a panic attack? I remember to take deep breaths. I force myself to raise my eyes to my achingly innocent children.

Devon's sweet face is filled with alarm. "Aren't pills supposed to make you better? You can die from taking them?" Oh geez. Oh shit. "Well, you're right—pills do make you better. But if you don't take them correctly or if you take too many of them, it can be very dangerous." I lock eyes with Lachlan. He knows better. The look on his face is stricken and tight.

"How come she didn't know that? Could that happen to you? Or me?" Devon asks, her voice rising higher and higher with each word. I can tell she's scared and trying not to cry. I'm scared and trying not to cry.

Lachlan turns to look at her, placing his hands on her quivering shoulders. "No, Dev. It's not going to happen to any of us." He looks back at me and I can see he's just as unsure, even as he's bravely consoling his sister.

"I promise you that this will never happen to me or Dad. And I will never let it happen to either of you. Got it?" They both nod slightly, with wide, anxious eyes. "I wish I could tell you why Aunt Feeney died, but I don't really know. I'm not sure we'll ever know, and . . . that's really hard for me too." I want to go on, but I know the tears are coming, hot and heavy, and I don't want them seeing me crying yet again. They're freaked out enough.

We all fall silent. I reach out to them and they lean into me, older and bigger than they've ever seemed before. I can sense the childhood seeping out of them. I clutch them to me as tight as they'll let me. I'm sure they have more questions, but selfishly I don't encourage them. Not yet. Not now.

Lachlan pulls away looks at me and says, "I'm sorry your friend died, Mom. She was really cool." Then he pulls Devon up and they walk out of the room together. I hold the towel to my face and let the tears come.

A suicide has so many victims. A single act, carried out in solitude, triggering shockwaves that pulse out indefinitely, in every direction. Friends, family, family of friends, friends of family. Anyone who has been touched by Feeney is now reeling by degrees. Up until this moment my pain had felt like mine alone. Now I understand that it belongs to everyone.

The day of our memorial for Feeney or our celebration or whatever the hell we're calling it, it rains all day. In July. We've decided to write letters to Feeney, telling her what we wish we had told her while she was alive. I spent hours on mine, wrote several drafts, drank several glasses of wine. I still think it sucks.

I pull up to Max's house and sit in my car looking through her window. I can see candles flickering inside. I can't do this. I'm sitting in my dirty car with a shitty letter to my dead friend in my purse. I fire up the car and drive off in a panic.

About two blocks away from Max's house, anxiety turns into self-directed anger. "Ali, you goddamned coward, turn this car around right now. Feeney deserves better from you." I wait a minute. I'm not used to talking to myself, so I'm not yet sure if I listen. I flick on the blinker. Apparently, I do.

I pull up again in the exact same spot and revert back to the exact same panic. I lean my head back against the headrest and take deep breaths. Why aren't I crying? I cried most of the night last night working on my letter, maybe I'm fresh out of tears. Instead I feel jittery and am fighting the urge to throw the car into drive again. At least the distraction of writing the letter and holding this funeral has briefly kept my mind off the journal. Now the knowledge of it comes flooding back, threatening to send me speeding off again.

Max opens her front door and looks at me from the doorway. She nods at me then moves back into the house. Somehow this one obstacle being removed, the life preserver thrown at me of not having to knock on the door, gives me what I need to get out of my car. I trudge toward Max's house with my head down, hands jammed into my raincoat, knuckles tight against the godforsaken letter.

The first thing I see when I walk in the door is our usual set-up: four different wine glasses sitting on a tray on the living room coffee table, ringed around a cold, uncorked bottle of white wine. Max got sick of us always mixing up our glasses so one day she went to Goodwill and bought us each unique ones. Mine is stamped with the ugly logo of a local real estate company; every time I see one of their signs I instinctively want a drink. Liddy's is made out of glass that's tinged a certain shade of amber so it always looks like she's drinking cat piss. Max's is stemless and shaped in just a way that we call it the tit glass. Feeney's is tall and regal, just like her, albeit with a gaudy gold serpent coiled around the stem. And it's here, now, like always.

"Really, Max?" I say, bristling.

"Would you have preferred to come in and only see three?" she says. "I didn't know what to do. In the end I decided we'd pour her a glass, too."

Right then, Liddy walks through the front door, pausing when she sees the glasses as well. She nods. "Good. One for Feeney. As it should be." Then she walks to the table and pours wine into every glass. Max looks at me and sticks her tongue out, making me smile half-heartedly.

I shrug out of my raincoat and settle on Max's lumpy couch, my butt practically molded to this particular seat. There is a fire in the fireplace, the only warmth this room has to offer me right now. Feeney's journal is still holding court on the mantel. The garden flowers must have died because they've been replaced with peacock feathers. Where did Max get peacock feathers?

"How exactly are we going to do this?" This seemed like a good idea two days ago. Now I'm not so sure.

Max says, "Well, first I want to play a song."

She moves to her boom box—she actually still owns a boom box—and powers it on. She holds up a CD case—she actually still uses CDs—and peers at it closely. I can already see that it's a Kenny Loggins CD. Ah, there are the tears.

The piano starts slow and quiet, backed by the distinct hollow sound of '80s era CD quality. Max walks over to us and pulls us up off our seats. She smiles, her green eyes bright with tears, and throws an arm around each of us. "'Please . . . celebrate me home. Give me your number, please . . . celebrate me home,'" she sings off-key along with Kenny Loggins, and we all join in until we're crying too much to sing so we just sway together to the music. That's exactly what we're doing today. We're celebrating Feeney home.

When the song ends, Max stops the music and pulls a piece of binder paper off her desk. She puts on her emerald green reading glasses that match her eyes and says, "I'll go first."

Liddy and I sit, Max stays standing. Liddy puts her head on my shoulder and I grasp my palms together tight under my chin, like a prayer.

"'Dear Feeney, my amazing Feeney, I'll never know why you did this . . .'" Her voice cracks and she looks up at the ceiling and closes her eyes. "Crap."

There are a few long moments of just the quiet rattling of the paper in her hand. She runs her fingers through her hair and nods a few times to herself. Because we know her as we do, we know that this is Max giving herself a pep talk. We wait.

When the rattling stops, she looks back down at the paper in her now steady hand. Her voice is strong as she continues to read. "'But I do know this. I know we all had real happiness together, and that's saying something.'"

She looks up at us with a mixture of hope and dread written across her face. Liddy nods, I attempt a smile. She sighs and continues.

"'You taught me to stop fixating on shadows and start looking for light. You showed me that joy can be found in things like Wednesdays and cheesy music and that love is right here, right now, so why not embrace it? You looked at life and saw it all, the good and the bad, the beautiful and the ugly, and you decided that the best thing to do with it all was to turn up the music and dance.'"

She drops the letter onto the table, removes her glasses and covers her face with her hands, the green glasses standing out straight between her knuckles like a flag. She says in a whisper, "And God, did I love dancing with you."

Liddy and I stand up and put our arms around Max. She leans into us like a child, so unlike her.

Liddy pulls away and grabs her glass of cat piss. Her voice is hoarse as she raises it and says, "To Feeney. We love you."

Max and I each grab our glasses. "To Feeney," we both manage to get out, then I drink like it's water in the desert.

Max and I sink back down into the couch, while Liddy puts her glass down and walks over to the simple canvas bag she uses as a purse. She pulls out a square of folded yellow stationery. She opens it up and starts unconsciously rocking from foot to foot.

"'I'm a letter writer. I write love letters, letters of advice, or silly drawn pictures to my kids; I even write letters to myself. But I have never written a letter like this.'" She stops and nods to herself a few times before continuing on.

"'Feeney, you were the only person I've ever known that I trusted 100 percent.'" She looks up at us, "No offense." At this time, in this place, none taken.

"'I shared things with you I could barely even admit to myself. About Jack, about Luke, about Lily, about me, about life. I could tell you anything and know that I would be heard and not judged. And you shared back, or at least I thought you did. I want you to know this, even though it's too late for it to matter— if you had told me what you were thinking about doing, how you were feeling, I would have tried to understand. I would *never* have judged you. I wouldn't have even tried to talk you out of it. I would have listened, just as you always did for me. Maybe just the very admission of how you felt would have helped you, as it always did for me. It's the only thing I will ever fault you for. Not for doing what you did, but for not trusting me with how you felt. You, of all people.'"

I can't look at Liddy anymore, the pain is so naked on her face, so reminiscent of my own. I stare into the fire while she continues to talk.

"'For the past eight years, I've basked in the light of your friendship. My hurts hurt less, my joys flew higher, even when I wasn't with you I was better because of you. Just knowing you were in the world, my world, made me happy. You were this beautiful, radiant light that never went out. But then . . .'" Liddy closes her eyes for a brief moment, drawing in her next breath. "'But then, you did. And somehow, though I can't imagine it, I'm going to have to get used to the dark.'"

She folds the paper back in two and looks up at us. "I'm not sure I'll ever write another letter again."

We all just sit and look at each other for a moment until Max leans forward and grabs her glass. "To Feeney," she says in a flat, sad tone. We sip wine in silence broken only by the occasional pops of the fire.

"I guess it's down to me," I say. "I'm not standing up. I don't think I could if I wanted to." I scoot my butt forward on the chair and pull my letter to Feeney out of my pocket. I clear my throat to gird myself.

"'This is what I love about you, Feeney, in no particular order,'" I hear myself say. "'Your laugh. Your disdain for technology. Your inevitable high-heeled shoes. Your ability to detect and eliminate bullshit of any kind. The way you made me feel, like I was funny and wise and delicious. The way you treated your daughters like full-fledged individuals. The way you named all the cars you ever owned with first and last names like Betsy Farnsworth. How you baked cookies for the fire station every year and made a big deal about delivering them with Caroline and Hannah to teach them about being charitable when really you just wanted to check out the hot firemen.'"

Max laughs quietly, more like a reverse snort.

"'How you took charge of things. How everything was better when you were there. Your advice, which was always spot on, the only exception being the time you told me I'd look good with bangs.'"

I stop because everything is swimming, blurry and unreadable. I feel like I can't read another word. I put my head into my hands, my palms pushing into my chin. Liddy puts her hand on my shoulder and we just sit like that.

I raise my head and blink a few times, then hold the letter to the side while I look at my friends, talking through my tears. "You know what kills me? I never said any of this to her. How fucking sad is that?

Feeney had to die for me to write a letter telling her what I loved about her? This is so stupid!" They look back at me, blinking and helpless.

I look down at my letter and it's crystal clear now, my vision honed by a mix of sadness and righteous anger. My voice is different too, stronger, yes, but bright with bitterness at the futility of this exercise. "'I love how you sing to your cats. I love the extra squeeze at the end of your hugs and the fact that you never let go first. I love remembering that time Devon broke one of your good crystal glasses and looked at you terrified, so you threw yours down on the floor too.'"

I feel the blood draining out of my head. "'Most of all I loved your heart, Feeney. There will never be another one quite like it. It's one of the only things I'm sure about anymore. And also that my heart will never be the same.'"

I can't look at anyone so I just grab my glass and close my eyes and drink, purposely taking too much so it will burn on its way down. Then I crumple my letter in my hands and stand up with a loud outcry of something—grief, pain, anger, all of it—and throw it into the fire. I watch my words curling and burning and lifting into smoke. And then, and then, I cry.

We are spent. All the wine is gone except Feeney's. Nobody has said a word for the better part of ten minutes when Max suddenly gasps. "Ali, did you bring the ashes?"

I had totally forgotten about them. The bizarre excitement of their procurement felt like a rite in and of itself. But sure enough, they're still in my purse, nestled among tubes of lipstick, stray Tic Tacs and twisted ponytail holders. I fish them out, and we stand together looking at the little bag of what looks like pale gray sand. Nothing at all like our colorful friend.

"What should we do with them?" Liddy whispers.

"Where do you guys think she'd like to be?" I ask, my hand shaking along with the bag.

Max whisks the bag out of my hands. Before I can even register what she's doing, she opens it up, takes a generous pinch of Feeney and tosses it into that final full glass of wine.

"With us," she says.

Her eyes look wild and her voice bordering on maniacal. Liddy and I stand and stare at her, eyes wide, mouths open. We are too stunned to do anything else.

"*This* is what Feeney would want. This is what we're going to do." She's nodding her head and talking more to herself than to us. Then she lifts up Feeney's glass with conviction, ashes and wine swirling together in the light of the fire. "We love you Feeney!" She takes a long sip and then stands there grinning, her mouth glistening, holding the glass out to us with both hands.

She is so radiant in this moment, it's like a hole of sunlight has been punched through our darkness and gloom. I feel a real, honest-to-goodness smile spread across my face, and my heart jumps. For a moment, Feeney is right here laughing along with us. Daring us. Loving us.

As if in a dream, I reach out and take the glass. I hold it with two hands, cupping it and looking down into the swirling, straw-colored liquid. My eyes blur with tears but I'm still smiling as I lift it to my lips. I close my eyes, inhale deeply, and take a gulp.

I'm surprised that it doesn't taste any different. But as it moves through my body I start to feel transformed, my pain buoyed by love and joy and the deep, resonant knowledge of friendship in my bones. I open my eyes when I'm done and hand the glass to Liddy.

Liddy's skepticism melts in the face of our enthusiasm. She smiles as she takes the glass and says with reverence, "To Feeney." She tips her head back and drains the glass, cheeks pink, curls spilling down her back. Then she rears back and throws that glass into the fireplace as hard as she can and it explodes into a million tiny shards of glass and gold.

The Time I Almost Died

Three years before

It doesn't even occur to me to call my husband first. I step out of
the shower with soap still in my hair and dial Feeney. "Hi you," she
answers, as always.

"I have a lump," I say, panicked. Just saying it out loud makes me
double over in fear. "I just felt it in the shower. Oh God, what do I
do?"

"Do not move. I will be there in five minutes."

I drop the phone and start to sob. In my mind I've already lost my
hair, I'm writing letters to the kids for them to open after I'm gone,
I'm wondering how long it will take before Drew gets remarried.
That's about as far as I mentally get before I hear the front door open
and close.

She comes around the corner into my room where I'm hunched
over in my towel, crying. She sits down next to me, putting her arms
around me as I sob into her shoulder. After a few minutes I come
back to myself just enough to use the towel I'm clutching around me
to wipe my eyes, nose, face.

"I'm so scared," I breathe.

She lowers her head so she's looking straight into my eyes. "Which
side?" she asks, her voice calm and steady.

I raise my right arm and point to the right side of my right breast.

"Can I feel it?" she asks. I nod and drop the towel.

I close my eyes as her fingers press into my skin, gentle yet confident. It only takes her a couple of attempts before she finds the lump, a small, tight nut under my skin. I catch her eye, but she just nods calmly.

"Okay. Here's what we're going to do. Dr. Beltran is golfing right now with Garrett. I'll call and make sure you get seen today. I'll be right back, don't go anywhere."

I look up at her and gesture at my get up. Where exactly would I go?

She leaves the room and eventually I hear her talking in the next room, her voice solid and steady. I feel like a kid home sick from school, my mom talking to the doctor. It's immensely reassuring. I get up and put on some clothes, careful not to even brush my hand against the offending lump. It already feels like it has a personality, a tight, festering nugget of evil.

She comes back into the room. "You have a mammogram in one hour. You've heard of Instagram? This is Insta-mam."

My laugh is weak but grateful.

"I'll stay with you all day, okay? I already texted my sitter to pick up our kids after school."

I sigh, big and deep. "Thank you, Feeney."

"No sweat," she says.

She drives me to the appointment. We find cheesy '80s music on the radio and turn it up loud and sing to distract ourselves. Then Beyoncé comes on, and we crank the air conditioning into our faces, pretending we have our own glamorous, hair-whipping wind machines. The result of all this silliness is that when we pull up to the clinic, I look like a terrified, pale version of Tina Turner.

I give my name to the receptionist, who turns and looks at Feeney, a question on her lips. Feeney puts her arm tight around my shoulder and says, "I'm her *partner*. I'm staying with her." The receptionist shrugs and tells us to have a seat.

This is the first moment it occurs to me that I should let Drew know what's going on. I punch his number into the phone. The minute I hear his voice, though, I'm paralyzed with fear and can't find any words. Feeney slips the phone out of my hand and talks quietly into it.

"Hey Drew, it's Feeney. I'm with Ali. She felt a lump in her breast a bit ago and we're getting it checked out. She's okay and I'll stay with her the whole time."

I hear her side of the conversation and can figure out the rest. "Yep, the kids are taken care of. . . . I'll have her call you as soon as we know anything. . . . I'll tell her." She hands me back the phone and says, "He loves you."

"That I know." I say. "But I'm really glad I'm here with you. He would make me much more stressed out. He'd be asking the doctors a million questions and ignoring me completely."

She squeezes my hand. "Sounds like a man in love—which is also to say a pain in the ass."

The next hour is spent having my ample boob squished into the dimension of a Frisbee and taking pictures from every conceivable angle. I've done this a couple times before but, because of the lump, there's an intensity and a scrutiny that's new to me. Every knit of the brow, every shift of the eye—I notice everything. It all feels like bad news.

Finally I'm dressed again and ushered into the doctor's personal office. Feeney has never left my side. Though she's stayed in the background, a very un-Feeney like place to be, her steady, solid presence has been my balm.

He strides in, still pink in the cheeks from the golf course. I can smell the cut grass and sunscreen.

"Hi, ladies. Feeney, you did me a favor by calling me off the course today. Garrett was kicking my butt." He laughs to himself and then looks up at us, realizing a little late that we are not in the mood for golf-related banter. His face settles into a mask of concentrated concern. "Alison, your tests were inconclusive, and we're going to need to do a core biopsy. It sounds worse than it is. We're basically going to go in and take a piece of the lump and test it to see what we're dealing with here."

"So," I croak, barely above a whisper. I clear my throat. "So, it could be cancer?"

"Well, it could be, but it could also be a number of other things. That's why we need to test it. Until then, let's try not to worry. I can get you in tomorrow if you're able to swing it."

"She can swing it," Feeney says, loud and strong. I look at her with a mix of awe and horror.

"Great. Let's get this show on the road. The receptionist will book you on your way out," he says, then stands up and gestures to the door with his hand.

As we're walking to the reception area, I feel like a zombie, lurching in and out of my body. "So, is the 'show' that we're getting on the 'road' the whole cutting into my boob thing?"

"Yes," Feeney says. "You can't dawdle with this shit, Ali. The faster you find out what's going on, the faster you can deal with it."

"I get that but . . . tomorrow? It's too soon," I say.

Feeney swings around and looks me fiercely in the eye. "You can't sit around and worry," she says. "You need to get this off your chest."

Then she catches her unintended pun. Her eyes grow and her mouth turns into a perfectly round lower case o. "Oh my God, I didn't mean . . ."

"Get it off my chest?" I say with a hysterical lilt. "Get it off—"

I start laughing harder than I have in ages, bending at my waist with my legs crossed so I don't pee myself. She's still standing in front of me with hands to mouth, her eyes looming huge. I see her head cocked, fighting laughter, trying valiantly to remain the adult. It doesn't last long. Soon, we are both doubled over and howling with laughter in the aisle between examination rooms. A patient in a blue and white paper gown cracks a door to see what all the ruckus is about.

I lean on a nearby office chair until the racks of hysteria subside; Feeney is propped against a desk. I am laughing so hard that I almost stop breathing. Once I finally inhale again, however, panic sets in for real and I start gasping. I can't seem to get enough air into my lungs. Feeney grabs me to her side, holding me tight while I try not to hyperventilate. She rubs my back up and down, up and down. I am out of my body and numb, but the repetitive motion eventually serves to remind my lungs how to take in air again.

"You can do this, Ali. And I'll be with you." I nod, unable yet to fully breathe, much less speak.

The lump turned out to be benign. A simple procedure whisked it out of my body and I moved on, good as new. Feeney was there for all of it. Now she's gone, and I didn't do a thing to help her when it was her turn to be scared. I didn't do a goddamned thing.

The morning after our goodbye to Feeney, I wake up alone in bed as usual. Drew is a clockwork early riser. I can hear him downstairs, making the kids breakfast. It's Saturday, so I know I have the entire upstairs to myself for the morning while the kids watch TV and Drew reads the newspaper cover to cover. It's a blessed relief.

Ever since Feeney died, it's been all motion and emotion. I feel like I've been beaten up from the inside out. Something you don't know about grief until you're smack in the middle of it is: It's really fucking physical. This is not "I feel sad." This is "I feel like I can't breathe properly, like somebody ratcheted my ribs in by several inches. My eyes are so dry I can feel them move in their sockets, and they burn until they're crying, then they swell almost shut. I'm exhausted all day but can't sleep at night so my bed is both a blessing and a curse. I have pain in parts of my body that were just words before—sternum, cranium, brow bone. After crying, my body hurts in the same way it did that one time I had food poisoning."

I turn on my side and spend several minutes staring out the window. A white butterfly flits by, a hummingbird drops down into the trumpet of a lily, the branches of our oak tree lift and fall to the silent cadence of the wind while a mourning dove call echoes in the background. Nothing I haven't seen and heard a hundred times before, but today I sense Feeney in it all. She is the fragile, improbable beauty of butterfly wings. She is the daring flash of red on the breast of the hummingbird. She is the trusting, open face of the lily. She is the majesty of the tree, arms held wide, hair dancing in the breeze. She is the peace of the dove while I am in mourning.

I don't feel less grief, but my sadness has moved from a black shard in my gut to something that's as much a part of me as my breath and blood. It is in me, as is Feeney.

The first few days were so scattershot, so frantic and confusing, it was like trying to see a finished mosaic through a thousand tiny pieces. I think I'm finally understanding that she's irrevocably gone. It's such an awful shock the body almost refuses to accept it, like a foreign organ.

But when acceptance starts to lap at your ankles, you really don't have a choice. You can stand there until you're underwater in denial, or you can slowly, awkwardly start to tread water. Both options are hard work and far worse than the option you used to have, which was to enjoy your life happily from the shore, eating ice cream and waving smugly at the people trudging through their own pain.

Before this week, the worst thing I ever lost was my passport, on a beer-fueled trip to Mexico after high school. It was a huge pain in the ass, and I had to call my parents in tears and ask them to sort it out, which turned into years of being told I was irresponsible. I thought it was terrible. Now, I think it's downright cute. Before this week, I didn't understand that I could lose an entire person. An entire history together. I pull out a carton of milk from the refrigerator and look at the expiration date. When I bought this milk, my best friend was still alive. All this time, all these memories, and I didn't know Feeney and I were marching toward a day when it would all just up and disappear, wisps of smoke where there once was a roaring fire. It makes me wonder if it was all worth it. But of course it was, the vibrant memories flooding me with proof that we lived and loved and glittered. And yet it makes the dull, gray days that are my reality now all the more brutal and devastating.

I can't help but wonder if our happiness was unsustainable, like there was always some unlucky event in our future, the bill due for our countless days of joy. Were we too happy? Too glib? Too unaware of the daily tragedies of life? But then I get a flash of one of Luke's stays in the hospital, helpless limbs full of wires and tubes, looking up at us with his sweet, unassuming face. And I think of Max, dutifully swallowing multiple pills a day to keep her out of that same hospital, although a different area—the psych ward. Then I think of myself, and I realize that I was the only one of us untouched by the kind of pain that is so close that it burns. And I know that this loss, Feeney's death, is my burn. And maybe I'm feeling it hotter and harder than they are. It's second degree for them, first for me.

My cell phone rings from my nightstand, shaking me out of my thoughts. I see a photo of Max's tortoise Dave flashing on the screen. I answer and slip under the covers.

"Good timing, Max. I was just spiraling."

"Well, that's a topic I'm an expert in. What flavor: Anxiety? Depression? Futility?"

"Um, it's kind of like a combo platter."

"Shit. Those are the worst. Need any pharmaceuticals?"

I chuckle despite myself. "I don't think anything in your medicine cabinet is going to fix this, Max. At least I know I'm not alone in how I feel."

"You certainly are not. Which brings me to why I called."

I flip over as she sighs in my ear.

"Ali, it's time for us to crack the journal."

My stomach seizes and flops at the same time, dread mixed with anticipation. "Today?"

"Well, we've all said what we want to say. It's time to hear from her."

I exhale and pull my legs up into my chest. "I haven't even gotten out of bed yet."

"Well, rise and shine, sister. I'm going to call Liddy and see what time works best for her. Are you busy today?"

What did I used to do with my days, before I spent them in this blind grief wander? I'm sure there are things I should do, but nothing seems important. "Not really."

"Okay, I'll text you after I talk to her." Click. Max never wastes time with greetings or goodbyes.

I stand up and wrap a warm robe around my pajama-clad body.

Ever since Feeney died, I'm always cold, from the inside out. I head downstairs and stand at the bottom of the staircase, watching my family doing their normal Saturday morning thing. I know I need to eventually fold myself back into them, into reality, but I can't figure out how. I feel so apart from these people I live with and love. Every time I look at Drew, I feel skinless, like he can see all the emotions churning inside me, especially the ones I don't want to name. I keep catching Lachlan and Devon sneaking anxious looks at each other, unsure how to reverse the usual dynamic so that I can be the one being tended to.

I enter the kitchen and sure enough, I feel the air change around me. I've become an exotic animal in my own house. I force a smile and kiss the kids on their warm hair. I smile at Drew. "Coffee smells delicious." His eyes light up as I turn away and grab a mug from the cupboard. "So, what's on the calendar today?" I focus, laser-like, on pouring my coffee.

The uncomfortable silence erupts into giddy plans to ride bikes, play basketball, walk into town for ice cream, play video games—all with friends. I watch the swirl of my spoon in my coffee, afraid to raise my eyes and ruin this pure moment with tears. I spackle a smile on my face and nod along to their happy voices. "That sounds super fun!" I can practically see Feeney rolling her eyes.

I'm not fooling Drew. "Kids, whoever makes their bed first gets to decide dessert tonight. Go!" I hear chairs screeching and feet pounding up the stairs along with some mild trash-talking. I deflate, dropping my shoulders and looking up at him, no longer hiding the trail of tears that seems to never abate. He moves toward me, and I shake my head. He slowly sits back down, confusion written across his face.

I clear my throat and take a sip of coffee, fortifying myself. "I want to thank you, babe. For keeping things going around here and for giving me space. I can't explain it, I don't even understand it, but it's what I need most right now."

"I'm happy to do whatever needs to be done. But I wish you'd let me help *you*."

"How Drew? How can you help me? Can you fix it? Can you make it not have happened?"

"I can hold you. I can love you."

I'm a terrible person because I laugh. He is so earnest, but the idea that somehow his arms, as strong and lovely as they are, will be of some kind of help to me is comical. I know I'm being unfair. But what about this entire fucking situation is anything close to fair?

I rub my forehead to center myself. He is looking at me like I might spontaneously combust. I wish it were that easy.

"I'm sorry. It's just that nothing is normal. I can't do normal right now. I don't even know what that means anymore."

"I wish you would talk to me about this."

"I am talking to you right now. I'm telling you what I need. You keep wanting to change the conversation."

"Ali, I'm trying to *have* a conversation."

I close my eyes and sigh. "Remember that movie *The Hurt Locker*? When the solider comes back from war and nothing makes sense? He can't deal with his family, he can't even go grocery shopping. He goes *back to war* because he can't deal with normal life. That is how I feel. But there's no war to go back to."

It's quiet enough for a few minutes that I can hear Lachlan and Drew shuffling around in their rooms upstairs. I take another sip of my coffee and hold it underneath my chin, letting its warmth seep into my hands and heart.

"I'm so sorry, Ali. I wish there was something I could do."

I raise my eyes to his. "That's how I feel every minute of every day.

And there's nothing any of us can do. At least when I'm with Max and Liddy, we have the same scars. I don't have to explain or pretend anything. It's so much easier."

"I know I will never understand how you feel right now, but that doesn't mean I don't want to try."

"I know you do, babe, but I can't help you with that."

We stand across the kitchen island looking at each other, both unsure how to proceed, while the kids tumble back into the room, each insisting that they totally won the bed-making contest.

The Time I Sprung Her from the Pokey

Four years before

I am startled out of sleep by the ring of my cell phone sitting on the nightstand. Mid-sleep phone calls always send my adrenaline through the roof, and this is no exception. I snatch the phone up and see that it's Feeney calling.

I hit the accept button and ask under my panicked breath, "Are you okay?"

"I'm in jail. I need you to bail me out," she responds, in a tone of voice that suggests she's royally pissed.

"Oh God." My mind reels and then catches on something. "It was the van, wasn't it?"

"I snapped. It was parked on our street again tonight. I gave it a major mastectomy."

"With?"

"Black spray paint."

Feeney has been on a rampage about a sexy maid service van that keeps parking on her street. It's Pepto-Bismol pink with giant photos of busty women in French maid outfits plastered on the sides. She calls it "Satan Tits" because the phone number emblazoned on the side is 1-800-666-BUST. She's been talking about how she wants to deface it for months. Apparently it wasn't the idle threat we all assumed it was.

"What did you do?" I ask, cringing.

"I took it from PG-13 to G. Or perhaps I should say from DD to A. Take a look for yourself on your way over here."

"Oh God. Okay, where do I go? The police station downtown?"

"You've lived here your whole life and you've never been hauled off to jail?" she says. "I'm beginning to rethink our entire friendship."

"My bad." I'm hunkered under the covers so as not to wake up Drew, in a cozy tent that only fits myself and my incarcerated friend.

She sighs dramatically at my lack of a criminal past and says, "Yes, I'm in the pokey downtown. Come spring me."

"I'll be there in less than ten."

"I'm not going anywhere," she says, then hangs up.

I sit there for a minute processing everything, then laugh to myself and swing my feet onto the floor. Leave it to Feeney to introduce me to my friendly neighborhood police station.

On my way to the station, I make a side trip down Feeney's street. The van is parked toward the end of the street, I can see the pink glowing in my headlights. As I get closer, I see that every girl is now wearing a black, spray-painted turtleneck. One has black eyeglasses, another has a black bow in her hair. They all look decisively unsexy. I feel a flash of pride for my vandal friend.

I flip the car around and as I do so, my headlights illuminate the windshield of the van. I audibly gasp. Feeney had spray-painted two crude pigs' heads onto it in a way that looks like they're driving. On the hood she had written in big block letters, "OINK! WE'RE PIGS!" My pride grows.

I pull up to the station, a brick building nestled next to the office of the local newspaper and across the street from a restaurant we often go to when it's one of our birthdays. On the same street is the tasting room of a winery we like and a beautiful home decor store we often go into for the sole purpose of ogling. I can't decide if it's wrong for Feeney to be in jail on this street or actually quite wonderfully right.

I walk in and approach the reception area. A bored-looking woman with French braids despite being well over sixty looks up at me.

"I'm here for Feeney . . . I mean Josephine Simms," I say.

The woman breaks out into a wide grin, and her eyes light up. "Darling, that lady is my hero. Come on back," she says, pushing a button that buzzes me through.

The moment I come through, braid lady gives me a big side hug. She smells like potpourri.

"You tell your friend she did a good deed tonight, okay? I hate that goddamned truck," she says while I nod, wide-eyed. "I'm Fran. Follow me." Then she bellows over her shoulder, "Wanda! Cover the front!"

She loops her arm through mine and walks me into the back of the station, where we encounter a tired man in uniform with a nametag that reads "M. FORRESTER."

"This here is Ms. Simm's friend." She looks at me and says, "What's your name, darling?"

"I'm Ali Stirling. I'm here for Fee . . . Josephine Simms," I say. I am always nervous around police officers. I have a weird fear that I will spontaneously and uncontrollably make a grab for their gun.

"You're going to have to post a bond," he says, looking up at me.

"What does that mean?" I ask. "I need to pay money?"

He tries but fails to hide his eye roll when he says, "Yes. This was a Class B misdemeanor. You'll need to pay $150 to get your friend out tonight. And be advised that you won't get it back if she doesn't show up in court."

"Okay. Can I write a check? Or use a card? I don't have that much cash on me," I say, starting to dig around in my purse.

"It's covered," Fran says, patting my hand that's still sitting on her upper arm.

"Wait, what? What do you mean?" I ask, still nervous, now confused.

"A bunch of the gals in the office and I put together a fund. We all think your friend walks on freaking water. Mitch here might not agree, but he's always been a stick in the mud." Fran gives Mitch a glare and says, "Let these ladies go home. Now." Then she turns on her heel and storms off.

I watch as Mitch's cheeks go from peach to a distinct shade of cherry. "Wait here," he says, with as much authority as one can muster after a verbal smack down from an aging woman in French braids.

I sit in a hard plastic chair that's pushed up against the wall. Comfort is not a priority here. I shake my head as I consider everything that has transpired in the last hour of my life. Along with having Feeney for a friend comes the opportunity for a paradigm shift at any given moment.

I hear a bustle down the hall, and soon Feeney walks through the door, rubbing her wrists and smirking. Mitch follows close behind, looking miffed. Feeney is in black from head (an oversized knit ski cap) to toe (trainers wrapped in black duct tape).

"Well, if it isn't my liberator in shining armor," she says, wrapping me into a hug.

"Happy to help," I mutter into her hair.

"And you," she whirls around to face Mitch and surprises him and me both when she grabs his hand and plants a kiss on the back of it like a wooing Casanova. "You were a superb captor."

His cheeks fire up again as he busies himself with getting the paperwork together that we both need to fill out.

"I'll get your things while you fill out these forms," he says and then scurries the hell out of there.

Feeney and I both start laughing, catching each other's eyes with shared mirth.

"Thanks for bailing me out, Ali. I owe you. Literally. I'll drop off a check tomorrow." she says.

"Mitch didn't tell you?"

"Tell me what?" Feeney says, her eyes questioning.

"Feeney, a bunch of women who work here passed the hat to pay your bond!"

"What? Why?"

"They think what you did is heroic. And, for the record, so do I." I smile at Feeney and relish the changing looks that appear on her face. She goes from confused to stunned to touched in a succession of moments. It feels like watching the gradual changing of the sky at sunset, with each new scene as beautiful and captivating as the last.

"Can I meet them?" she eventually says, her voice hushed.

"Well, I can introduce you to Fran. She's the only one I know. She has French braids," I say.

"Take me to French Braid Fran," Feeney says reverently.

An hour later we are still in the small reception area of the police station. It's Fran, Feeney, myself, and four other women who work there. None are police officers. Someone found a warm bottle of champagne, and we all toasted Feeney. I don't know if I've ever seen her so happy. This is a woman who grew up surrounded by famous names and big money, and her moment of truth is here, right now, in a small-town police station surrounded by minimum-wage workers. And me, who makes jack squat. Yet it all feels so right.

Finally, I look at my watch and nudge Feeney. It's almost five in the morning. The sun and our children will soon be up. She nods and then turns to the group and says, "Sadly, we have to go. But I have learned something important here tonight. I've learned that women aren't just creatures that tear each other down. Growing up, that's all I ever knew. Tonight, you all proved to me that women can—literally—bail each other out, prop each other up, and cheer each other on. This is a lesson I wish I had learned earlier, but it's one I promise I will never forget."

I find myself with a lump in my throat. I certainly didn't expect to find a moment of women's liberation in the Healdsburg police station reception area with complete strangers but it's happening, and it's powerful. And it's all Feeney.

We all go around hugging and saying "go, girl" and "love you" and we mean it. I walk out of there with my arm around Feeney's shoulder feeling like I've scored the best human on the planet as my friend.

Right as we're getting in the car, the station door opens and Fran rushes out. She grabs Feeney in a bear hug and says something into her ear. Feeney throws her head back in laughter, then they part. I assume it must be another girl power message. Fran winks at me and strides back into the building.

In the car, Feeney leans back against the seat and closes her eyes. "What a fucking night," she says.

"You can say that again," I reply.

"What a fucking night."

It's the most obvious of jokes but sometimes those are the ones that make you laugh most. Especially in the aftermath of a night fraught with emotion. We laugh until tears trail our cheeks.

"So what was the final straw?" I ask when I get my breath back.

After a few quiet moments, she sighs. "There was no final straw,

Ali. There were just a giant pile of straws that were dying to be set on fire. It was an entire lifetime of anger at the sick objectification of women by men. I mean, it would be one thing if I chose to live in Las Vegas where this kind of thing is everywhere. I specifically chose, to the detriment of two careers, to move to a small town to get away from that shit. And then the bright pink titty bus comes to my street. MY STREET!" She pounds the seat with her fists.

She pauses to look at me sideways, puts on her best Humphrey Bogart accent and says, "Of all the neighborhoods in all the towns in all the world, Satan Boobs had to drive into mine."

I laugh. But I have so many more questions. "When and how did you decide to go ahead and become a fully operational vandal?"

"The first time I saw that van, about a year ago, I went out and bought $150 worth of black spray paint. Which, by the way, is no easy task. You've got to show your driver's license, sign a waiver, sign some other form—it's easier to get a mortgage. But Satan Boobs never had a chance. It just took me a while to work up the courage to do it. Earlier today, as we drove by the van, Hannah asked, 'Why would anyone want someone to clean their house with no shirt on?' I went straight home after school drop off and duct-taped my shoes."

"I totally get it," I say. "If you had asked I would have been your wing girl."

She laughs. "I know. I honestly thought I could do it and get back to my house in less than twenty minutes. But the more I did, the more I got inspired. I just couldn't stop. Keep in mind I was wearing all black from head to toe. I'm sure I looked like a total punk. Apparently one of my neighbors called me in. I was already done when the cop pulled up, but I was taking photos of my handiwork. I had black spray paint all over my hands and a bag full of empty cans. It was, as they say, an open and shut case."

"You were caught black-handed?"

"Ha. Good one. Indeed I was."

"What did they do?"

"They were pretty calm. They got out of their car and approached me with their hands on their weapons and said, 'What's going on here?'"

She shakes her head. "I was not as calm. I started wildly gesturing toward the van and saying, 'Tits are going on! I have young girls that have to drive by the bright pink Satan Tits van multiple times a day. What are you all doing about it?'"

"Then they were like, 'You're going to need to come with us ma'am.' I threw the paint can I was holding at one of the guys and said, 'Fine but you suck.' That did not help my cause at all."

"Wow," I say. Then again, "Wow."

"So then they handcuffed me and took me to the pokey."

"Which is across the street from Barn Diva restaurant," I add.

"And a few doors down from Ridge Tasting Room," she says.

"Toto, I don't think we're in New York anymore." I say, both of us laughing and shaking our heads. When I pull up at her house I level my eyes at her and say, "You going to be okay?"

She looks at me, really takes me in, then she smiles in a way that, now, breaks my heart to remember it. "Yeah. Yeah, I really am. That felt good."

I believe her. "By the way, what was it that Fran said to you outside the station?"

"She told me that Mitch's brother is the owner of the sexy French maid company."

I have just finished getting dressed when my phone chirps. It's a text from Max.

4:00 my house. Bring wine and Kleenex.

Me: *I'm basically being sponsored by both those things right now. See you then.*

The knowledge that I have this plan in place, to be with the only people who truly get me right now, and to have a glimmer of Feeney, if only in handwriting, releases some of the atmospheric pressure inside me. I'm able to do a couple loads of laundry and even play a few games of Uno with Drew and the kids. It's all I can handle. They don't even try to pretend they're not letting me win.

Just before four, I pull a cold bottle of Feeney's favorite rosé from the fridge, stuff a handful of Kleenex in my purse, and head out the front door. My family has scattered to their various friends and activities, and I feel enormous relief not being responsible for their happiness.

Liddy is already at Max's when I walk through the front door. They turn toward me, and their familiar faces, strained with familiar grief, feel so much more like home than the one I just left. My brief wave of relief is followed by an even bigger one of anxiety that I will never feel at home in my own house again. I push that ugly ogre of a thought aside.

Max pops open the rosé and brings us all glasses. We settle in our favorite chairs while she takes the journal down from its spot on the mantel and holds it in her lap. Today her reading glasses are coral.

"It's almost like she's here with us," Liddy says. I close my eyes and imagine it.

"I have a few books of poetry," Max says. "And what I like to do is close my eyes and open to a page. I always feel like I get the right one for how I'm feeling. I propose that's how we go through this journal. It will feel more like a conversation."

"A conversation with Feeney," I say. "What I would give for that right now."

Liddy nods her approval, and Max holds the book in her hand for a few moments and then opens to a page. She begins to read.

"'Caroline and Hannah. Their names are my only prayer. When I feel like I can't go on, I whisper their names, over and over. They are the ones I worry about the most. If I can't do this thing called life, what will become of them? I hope that they never have to know. But, just in case, I'm building a family for them that's different from what I had. People to love by choice, not because they're related. People who genuinely care and love them. If it ever turns out to be too late for me, it won't be for my girls.'"

Max looks up at us. "You guys, that's us. Us and Garrett. We need to be family to those girls. And part of doing that is understanding Feeney better so we can continue to talk about her as they get older. And this journal will help us."

We ask her to read it again and again until the words are tattooed in our minds. Then I ask if I can take a look. I drum my fingers against the cover then open it up and let the pages fall where they may.

"'I heard a story today on the radio about a man who spent over twenty years alone in the woods in a makeshift camp. Somewhere cold and snowy. People were questioning his sanity but I couldn't help but think he must be the most sane person on the planet. To be able to spend that much time with nothing but your own mind? That's absolutely terrifying to me. That's what I loved about New York, it was impossible to be alone. Even when it was just me in my tiny apartment, my antenna was always zinging with street-level noise, neighboring conversations, cars, trains, and helicopters heading somewhere, anywhere. Each a possible escape from myself if I needed it. As a child, I talked to myself constantly. Now it feels silly, so I write instead. Hi, Feeney. Hang in there.'"

I look up in wonder. "I would never have thought of Feeney as someone who hated to be alone. Maybe it's because her personality was so big, she always seemed like more than one person. How can someone like that ever be lonely?"

"I don't think she was lonely, Ali. I think she was scared to be alone, which are two very different things." Max sits back and wraps herself so tightly in a plaid throw that she looks like a large, holiday cocoon. She closes her eyes. "I know what that feels like."

"Scared of what you would do?" Liddy asks.

Max searches the room as if it has answers. "Scared of where my mind might take me. It's like getting on a roller coaster with no safety bar. You might be okay, or you might get horribly mangled. That's how it feels to not be in control of your thoughts. It sounds like Feeney felt that way too."

We sit with this for a few moments until I feel a rush of frustration. "I know I've said this a hundred times, but how did we not know this about her? Max, you've never tried to hide what you deal with in your head. We've never judged you. Why didn't she talk to us?"

"I never tried to hide it, but I also didn't grow up with the crazy standards that she did. Remember what Jane said at her funeral? That her family was terrifying, and they all swept her suicide attempt under the rug? Jesus, can you imagine being so desperate and having everyone pretend it never happened? What do you think a young teenage Feeney took away from something like that?"

"But we're not her family," Liddy counters. "We're her people. We would have listened. We would have helped her."

Max shakes her head. "If there's one thing I know from my prosecutor days, a lot of that shit is hardwired pretty young. By the time she met us, she'd probably been hiding it for so long, she didn't even realize she had options."

The waste of it is staggering. So little done, so late. How were we so happy when she was so burdened? How was she so burdened when we were so happy?

Liddy sighs for us all. "My turn."

"'Two things I'll never let my girls see me as—a burden or a victim. I look at them and I see nothing but freeways of possibility, meadows full of hope and flowers. I will not be a wall. I will not be a raincloud. Hannah looked at me today and said, "I happy." I almost stopped breathing. That's all I want for her, for Caroline. For nothing to mar that pure, innocent happiness. For the adult world to not mess it up, not even teach her the proper way to say it. Leave her alone. Leave them both the fuck alone. If I give them nothing else in their entire little girl lives, I want them to be able to say at the end of the day, "I happy."'"

In an instant, I feel a burning need to look for Post-its. I jump up and head to the kitchen. When I return, Max and Ali are looking at me with question marks for eyes.

"I think we should bookmark pages when they mention the girls or Garrett, so they can read them when they're ready." I hold up a colorful cube of notes.

"Oh my God, did this just become a craft project?" Max says. "If so, I'm out."

"We're the caretakers, right? Well, we're also the historians. We can note pages and passages, that way they won't have to go through the whole thing if they don't want to."

"I think that's really smart," Liddy nods. I scribble "C & H" on a vibrant blue Post-it and press it against the page Liddy just read.

Max gestures toward the journal. "What if this makes them feel somehow responsible? I mean, Feeney not wanting them to be burdened? That's a pretty heavy saddle to throw on those girls."

"But there's so much love in this too. And so much of her. I'm not saying we share this with them any time soon. But someday, they may find some solace within these pages. Doesn't it feel good to hear from her again? Even if what we hear hurts?"

"Shit, I don't know," Max says, covering her face with her hands. "Maybe I can't see it clearly because I'm not a mom. Maybe a part of me wants to shield them from what I know is going to be awful. Fuck."

Liddy reaches out to both of us, one hand on each of our shoulders. "We all need to start seeing Feeney more clearly. We need to fold what we know now into what we knew then. All of us, including eventually her family. It may take years, it may take a lifetime. But we owe this to her. We need to see all of Feeney, and this journal may be the only way we will ever do that."

"Liddy, why are you always so goddamned smart and sane?" Max shakes her head but there's a smile in her voice. "Give me that thing. I want another turn." She gestures for Liddy to hand her the journal.

"'I can't decide if I want to live forever or not at all. I can't determine if the world is stuffed with beauty and magic or loaded with pain. The minute I decide it's one, I feel the other. They are echoes of each other. I laugh, and hear a reverberation of pain. I cry, and somewhere in the shadows there is joy hiding. The only place I can't seem to be is in the middle, which is where it seems most people like to live. The middle is the place where I get lost, where I can't seem to feel anything at all.'"

Max places the journal on the table, depleted. She rakes her hands through her hair. "We just spent an hour with Feeney's journal, and we understand her better now than we did in a decade of friendship. What are we supposed to do with that?"

"I'll tell you," I say. "We're supposed to never let this happen with anyone else we love. We're supposed to stop saying we're fine when we're not. We're supposed to admit when we need help, even if we don't even know what that help might look like."

"Sometimes that's easier said than done, Ali. But it's something we can all work on."

Max looks at us with a look of such grief and understanding that it silences us all. For minutes we just sit and baste in our collective pain.

"Enough already!" Max says, and we laugh, knowing that it will never be enough, but also that life goes on—improbably, insensitively. We wipe our eyes, we blow our noses. We always have Kleenex on hand.

"I have an idea," Liddy says.

"Please tell me it doesn't involve burglary," I say.

"No, those are only Max's ideas. My idea is this. We'll never have a Wine Wednesday again, it would just be too sad. So what if we have Feeney Fridays? Just us and her journal. With or without wine."

"With!" Max says.

"I like that idea," I say in a hushed voice, staring at the journal. "But here's what I can't get over. Feeney had to die for us to know she was suffering. She had to die for us to know how she felt. I'll never forgive myself for that. We can't ever let this happen again. I don't want to have to read either one of your journals to know what's really going on, and I don't even have one, so . . ."

"So let's tell each other now. Let's write the letters and say the things we want while we're alive and well and *here*," Liddy says.

"I have a better idea," Max looks up at us, her cheeks flaming.

"Let's actually have our funerals. Fuck waiting! Fuck death! I want to hear what you guys have to say about me!"

It's so silent in the room I can hear my heart beating. "Like, real funerals?"

"Why the hell not?"

"Okay," I breathe, then look to Liddy, our resident adult, for her opinion of the plan.

"I fucking love it."

The Time She Screamed

One year before

Every so often over the years of our friendship, Max, Liddy, Feeney, and I would go somewhere for a night or two away. San Francisco, usually, or Tahoe. It was unnecessary because we would basically do all the things we did at home, just in a different location. But it was fun, and we were nothing if not always on the hunt for fun.

The last trip we took was last summer, to Point Reyes, a tiny town not too far away by the ocean. We rented a converted schoolhouse that had four bedrooms a stone's throw from the local shops and farmer's market. We were in heaven, or at least I thought so.

We had had a full day—hiking in the hills to view the wild elk that roam the fields above the cliffs, stuffing our faces with pizza washed down with wine for lunch at a local restaurant, picking up just-caught crab to bring home to the schoolhouse for dinner, skinny dipping in the ocean because Feeney said she never had an irresponsible youth and wanted to make up for it, getting caught by a couple of teenage boys and probably scarring them for life with the sight of our collective post-baby nudity.

Tired and sun-freckled, we're sitting in the dining room of our rented house and lazily talking after a big crab dinner with plenty of wine. Max is doing an impression of her heavily accented grandfather who believed in the liberal use of Yiddish. "Whatever you do, *bubbeleh*, don't marry a *goy*, a *klumnik*, or a *faygele*. Your *shmundie* is a *shul*."

"What does it mean?" Liddy asks, laughing.

"Not to marry a gentile, a loser, or a gay guy," Max says. "Because my vagina is a temple. I didn't, either, though I've slept with all of the above. So much for my sacred *shmundie.*"

"My grandfather was a little too interested in my *shmundie* if you ask me," Feeney says. Her words are slurred, eyelids at half mast. She's drunker than I've seen her in a long while. Even drunk, Feeney's never been sloppy. Tonight is a different story.

The warm buzz of the room shifts on an axis. Max, Liddy, and I all look at each other in surprise.

"What do you mean, Feeney?" I ask her, putting my hand over hers.

"What?" she says, looking up at me and blinking slowly, as if she hadn't just dropped a verbal bomb on the entire room.

"Your grandfather. Did he . . . do something to you?" I ask, heart pounding.

She looks confused for a moment, then looks around at us as if she is just realizing we are here. I'm trying to think about how much she had to drink. It didn't seem like any more than the rest of us, but she is very far gone.

"What are you talking about?" she snaps, as well as a very drunk person can snap, and pulls her hand away from me.

"You just said—" I start, but Feeney lurches up from the table and turns her back on us.

"'M going to bed," she says and stumbles to her room, the only one that's located downstairs.

We are left stunned and confused. "Should one of us follow her?" Liddy asks.

"She's just going to pass out," Max says. "How did she get so drunk?"

"I was wondering the same thing," I said. "And what was all that about?"

"I have no idea. But we're not going to get anything from her tonight," Liddy says. "Let's ask her about it in the morning."

We disband slowly, each of us heading upstairs to our rooms with questions churning in our heads.

In the middle of the night I am awakened by a terrible sound. At first I think it is an animal dying outside, but as the fog of sleep dissipates I recognize it to be human—and coming from inside the house. It is loud and relentless and awful.

I run out of the room and run into Max and Liddy, who were just coming out of theirs.

"What the fucking fuck?" Max says. Her hair is sticking up on one side of her head.

Liddy's face is drawn tight. "It's Feeney. Come on, let's go."

We all run down the stairs, and Liddy swings open the door to her room. Feeney is under her covers completely, hunched over in the middle of the bed, screaming. We all approach the bed but only Liddy reaches out to her. Max and I are huddled together, uncertain what to do.

Liddy sits down on the bed and puts her arm around the blanketed Feeney, who starts thrashing like a trapped animal. Liddy starts talking in a loud, authoritative voice.

"Feeney. Feeney. Stop. It's okay. Stop. Feeney. Feeney. Stop." She pulls the blanket off of Feeney, who looks up at us yet somehow through us, as if we are on different sides of a two-way mirror. Her screaming abates and turns into a low, growling moan, and she buries her face into her hands.

The change snaps Max and I into action, and we flank Feeney along with Liddy, sitting on the bed rubbing her back and making soothing noises. I have just opened my mouth to start asking questions when she simply rolls over and falls back asleep in the fetal position. "Feeney?" I ask, jostling her shoulder gently. She is out.

We all slowly stand up and stand over her for a moment, not sure if we should stay or go. Liddy motions for us to follow her into the hall.

We huddle together in the dark and whisper. "This happens to Luke sometimes," Liddy says. "It's a night terror. She probably won't even remember it in the morning."

"Jesus. Shit. Jesus," Max says, shaking her head. "That was terrifying."

"Do you guys think she's okay?" I ask.

"It's Feeney," Max says. "She's always okay. That's what makes it so freaky."

"Try to go back to sleep," Liddy sighs. "We'll deal with it in the morning."

We break up and head to our respective rooms. I lie awake in bed for nearly an hour, listening for Feeney. I want to run to her if she needs me. I'm also legitimately freaked out. Those sounds, coming out of her mouth. It doesn't compute.

The next thing I know, fingers of sunlight are tickling my eyelids. The episode in the middle of the night has taken on the hazy, otherworldly feel of a dream. The memory of it clenches my stomach, but at the same time I have the sense that daylight will make everything better.

I emerge from my room to see that Max and Liddy's doors are still closed. I head downstairs and see Feeney busy making coffee in the kitchen. My stomach tightens again, but then I am filled with an overwhelming need to hug her.

"Good morning," I say. She turns, and I just reach out and grab her, pulling her into my arms. We hug, then I stand back and hold her elbows. "Are you okay?"

"Other than a major headache, I'm fine," she says. "Are you okay?"

I hesitate. I don't know what she knows or what I should say. I didn't expect the question to be turned back around on me. "I guess, I just was worried about you," I start. "Last night . . ."

Feeney stops me short. "I'm sorry I got loopy. I don't remember much after dinner. I've been having trouble sleeping so I've been taking some of the anti-anxiety pills Garrett takes when he flies."

"Since when?" I ask.

"Just the last couple of weeks," she says dismissively, then turns and busies herself again with the coffeemaker.

I stand behind her pondering my next move. "I just . . . you said . . ."

"Please, don't worry," she says. Then she turns around and gives me one of her dazzling smiles. "I promise I'm good." She pours herself a cup of coffee and sits down at the table with her cellphone, scrolling through news and Facebook. "Oh my God, Ali. You have to see the photo Gwen Frank posted. It's her and Jerry smiling like they're the happiest couple on earth while everybody with eyeballs knows he's gay."

Right then Max and Liddy come downstairs. They look at me and I shrug, my eyes wide with zero answers. Feeney swings around and says, "So Ali said I was three sheets last night. Sorry if you had to take care of me."

"Please, Feeney. We don't care," Liddy says.

"You were just saying some stuff . . ." Max starts.

"Yeah. I was just telling Ali, I've been taking some pills of Garrett's to help me sleep. You're supposed to take them with food so I always take them before dinner. I think I just overdid it with the wine. I don't remember anything after we finished eating!" She says this with a self-deprecating and extremely dismissive shrug. "Sorry if I was talking nonsense. Please just ignore me."

We did. We ignored her because she asked us to. We've all had nights we don't want to be reminded about. We all assumed there would be plenty more opportunities to ask the questions we didn't ask then. We were all wrong. One year later, almost to the day, she took her life, parked less than a mile from the beach where we all swam naked.

I get back home, and Drew is sitting at the kitchen table, working on his laptop. I've never seen him on his laptop outside of his office, so I know something's up.

"Hey," I say, though it sounds more like a question.

"I didn't want to miss you when you came home," he says. "Come sit on the couch with me."

He leads me by the hand to the couch, and we sit facing each other. The look on his face is one I'd never seen until recently, like he's afraid he might break me.

"We didn't get to talk much this morning . . ." He does the thing he does when he is nervous, rubbing one thumb hard, over and over, with the other. "I know you're going through something terrible. I understand that you want to be with your friends. I just also want to feel like your partner. And right now, I don't."

"What do you mean?" I say, knowing full well what he means. I just don't have anything by way of a solution to offer, so instead, I stall.

He exhales and scratches the back of his head. "It's just . . . I want to know what's going on. I'm worried about you. But you're either not here or, when you are, you're not here." He taps his forehead with his finger.

I can feel the fury swirling, fueled in part by the frustrating knowledge that he is right. "Okay, Drew. I'm sorry that you're not getting my undivided attention. I'm sorry it's *inconvenient* for you that my friend died."

"Babe, that's not what I said."

"Maybe not but it sounds like what you meant."

"That's not fair, Ali. I'm trying to find out how you are."

"I'm really fucking sad, Drew, is *how I am*. Feeney is dead. If you want to talk about something being unfair, how about the fact that my life is basically falling apart and you're sitting here telling me that I'm not being a good partner to you."

"That's not what I meant Ali, and you know it." His words are starting to sound clipped.

"Yeah you did."

"No, I . . ."

"Yep," I interrupt.

"No, listen . . ."

"Yep. Yep. Yep." I practically sing it.

"Ali, stop." He stands up and holds his fists down at each side.

He stares at me for a few moments, breathing hard. I stare back, challenging him. I know I'm being difficult and putting words in his mouth. I know it. I just don't care. Or rather, I care more than I can allow myself to feel, and fighting is easier than laying myself bare.

"You say your life is falling apart," he says, slow and quiet, talking more to the couch than to me, thumbs moving frenetically. "And I'm sure it feels like that. But I'm here. The kids are here. Your life is here with us. We love you. " He looks up and searches my eyes. But all I can see is red.

"Well, right now, that's not good enough," I snap.

I hear a sound behind me and turn to see Devon standing in the hall with wide eyes. Then she spins around with a sob and runs to her room, slamming the door behind her.

"Dev, wait," I say, though I'm not sure what to follow with.

Drew looks at me with his jaw set and then looks down, shaking his head. "I've got it," he says, heading off toward her door. "But we're not done."

I want to stand at attention, click my heels and say, "Yes, sir!" But I am just adult enough to stop myself. Instead, I grab the pillow next to me and hold it to my chest, then bury my face into it and scream.

The Time We Got Caught on a Stakeout

Eight months before

"You know what I've always wanted to do?" Feeney says, uncrossing her long legs and leaning forward on Max's couch. "Stake someone out." Her eyes burn with excitement. "Like *Lethal Weapon* style."

"Oooh, fun!" Max says, bouncing up and down on the sofa. "Who?"

Feeney leans back and shrugs. "I don't care. I just want to do it. You guys pick the perp."

"Please nobody say Jack," Liddy says, rolling her eyes. "There's no fun in that."

"Not Jack," I say, looking at Liddy and smiling. "But what about Aaron Anderson?"

At the mention of her high school boyfriend's name, Liddy instantly pinkens while we all voice our agreement that this is a terrific idea. She makes a limp attempt to resist us, knowing full well there is no resisting us. She finally just laughs and shrugs. "Well, at least we know where he works."

The next night Feeney picks me up in her black Chevy Tahoe, handing me a fedora straight out of *Bonnie and Clyde* and sunglasses that look like '80s era BluBlockers. Feeney is wearing a straw cowboy hat and aviators. "I have disguises for us all," she says in a very serious tone.

"I see that," I say as I don my gear. There's a price tag dangling from my hat. "Very inconspicuous," I say as I look at her, and we both crack up.

We pick Max up next, and Feeney hands her a hunting cap with earflaps and wayfarers. Max puts them on and gives us a model pose.

"Not fair, she actually looks pretty good," I say.

"Great, I'll hold onto this get-up for date night," Max says.

We pick up Liddy last. When she comes out her front door and sees us in our various disguises peering out the windows at her she starts laughing so hard she has to sit down on the front step.

"What in God's name are we doing?" she says as she slides in next to Max.

"We are staking out," Feeney says. "Or out-staking. I'm not sure what the verb form is." She hands Liddy a red, white, and blue sequin baseball hat and a pair of sunglasses with hearts for lenses. "I saved the prettiest look for you. In case we blow our covers."

Liddy puts on the hat and pushes the glasses up her nose. "How could that possibly happen with such excellent spy gear?"

We are stupidly happy and absurdly silly. Just the way we like it.

We've been parked in front of Aaron's hardware store downtown for an hour. We've gone through a bottle of wine and two bags of Cheetos. "No healthy food on stakeouts," Feeney had said. "Danny Glover called me personally to tell me that's the rule."

Our plan is to follow Aaron home (at a non-discernable distance) to see where he lives. This is the extent of our grand stakeout. Just like everything when it comes to us, the journey is way more important than the destination.

Liddy is in the middle of a story about the art class she teaches at Luke's school, something about how all the kids kept eating the dried macaroni they were supposed to be gluing to paper, when there's a knock at the passenger window and we all scream. Cheetos fly everywhere.

Feeney rolls down the passenger side window, which happens to be mine. I find myself nose to nose with a policeman.

"You ladies need help with anything?" he says, looking around the car, taking in our outfits and the (thankfully) empty bottle.

I open my mouth to say no when Feeney leans over me and stage whispers, "We're on a stakeout, Officer . . ." She glances at his badge. "Officer James." Then she smiles and winks.

"Isn't that kind of my job?" he asks.

Liddy jumps in from the back seat. "It's not actually a real stakeout, sir."

He raises his eyebrows. "You don't say." His radio crackles with unintelligible chatter. "While this is certainly interesting, I have to run. I'm going to leave you in good hands, though." He stands up and steps aside. Only then do we realize that none other than Aaron Anderson, the subject of our stakeout, has been standing behind him the whole time.

"Oh shit!" Max yelps, while Liddy just closes her eyes and looks like she wants the interior of the car to swallow her whole.

Aaron walks up to the car with his head tipped to the side, trying to discern who exactly we are and what exactly we're doing there.

"I suppose this is why stakeouts are supposed to happen in the middle of the night," Feeney says under her breath while rolling down the back window to reveal Liddy.

"Well, this is a surprise," Aaron says, peering in at us, a smile playing at the sides of his mouth. "The last time a suspicious occupied car was parked across the street, we had a bunch of copper pipe stolen. I wasn't expecting to find some of my high school classmates in . . . colorful headwear."

He leans his forearm against Liddy's window. "Hey Lids, good to see you."

She opens her eyes and peers up at him. "Hey," she gets out.

"Do any of you need any hardware?" he asks.

"Liddy needs—" Feeney starts, but I elbow her hard before she can say what I know she's going to say.

Liddy shakes her head, smiling despite herself and opens up the door. She pulls herself out and gives Aaron a quick hug, closing the door behind her. We all look at each other with wide eyes and lean closer to the open window so we can hear their conversation.

"Sorry if we freaked you out, Aaron. We're just bored housewives being weird. Actually, that's kind of my job description these days."

Aaron laughs. "Swap 'teenagers' with 'housewives' and you'd pretty much sum up how I remember you from high school. Wait, that didn't sound like a compliment, but it was supposed to be."

"Everything good? Business? Family?" Liddy asks.

"Wow. The two things in my life that aren't going well. Couldn't you just ask about something easy, like politics in the Middle East?"

"Oh, sorry," Liddy says.

"No, no, it's fine. Sarah and I got divorced last year. She lives in Petaluma with the boys. I still see them all the time, which is all I care about. Business is as bustling as it can be for a hardware store in wine country." We can hear the smile in his voice. "You?"

"All good," Liddy says, a little too quickly. "Okay, well, we should probably go. Sorry again." They hug awkwardly, and she whooshes back into the car.

He leans down to the window once more. "No problem. Come back anytime." He says it to all of us, but looks right at Liddy as he adds, "Really." He pats the window once, then turns around and crosses the street.

"Damn, that's a fine ass," Feeney says. "Was it that good in high school?"

"Yes, it was," Liddy answers. Her cheeks are rosy, and she has a dreamy smile on her face.

"You do realize what you look like, right?" Max asks.

Liddy gasps and looks in the rearview mirror, only to be reminded that she has a patriotic sequin hat askew on her head and Summer of Love sunglasses perched on her nose.

"Oh my God," she groans as we all laugh.

Feeney puts the car in gear. "Stakeout over! We've been made!"

"I'm sure it had nothing to do with the terrible disguises," I say, shifting my eyes at her.

"It had everything to do with it," she says, giving me a wink. "Thanks ladies, one more think I can cross off my bucket list."

"That's got to be some list," Max says.

"It is," Feeney says. "And you're invited to all of it."

We drive off trailing Cheetos and laughter, thinking we were ready for whatever Feeney threw at us. We were wrong.

The next day, I get up and make everyone eggs and bacon. It's as far as I can go right now by way of an apology. I feel like a human magnet pushing away all the living things around me. I'm actually grateful for the mechanics of family life; they keep me plodding along a moving sidewalk where I don't have to think or feel too deeply. Make the beds, put in a load of laundry, drive the kids to camp, tell Drew I love him without making eye contact as he heads into his home office for work. When everyone is off in their corners, I can finally breathe.

I call and make an appointment with Reverend Peter from St. Paul's church. If we're going to do this funeral thing, we're going to do it right. I invite him to meet me at Oakville Grocery, home to Feeney's pearlwiches, for coffee. When he arrives, I'm sitting at a table outside, my leg bouncing a mile a minute despite the fact that I'm drinking decaf. I jump up and give him an awkward hug. Once, I hugged him in the greeting line after an especially inspirational sermon, and ever since I've felt like I can't go back to the simple handshake.

"Thanks for meeting me," I say, taking a deep breath to muster nerve. "There's something I want to ask you about."

"Is it okay if I get some coffee first?" he asks, and in his eyes there's both a smile and a question. He's handsome in an endearing, sweet way, with wavy auburn hair and persistently pink cheeks.

"Oh, right. Yes, of course!" I laugh, it occurs to me that I'm acting like a nervous girl on a first date.

I sit back down and close my eyes. Sometimes it's hard for me to believe that I'm a grown up. I don't feel much different than I did as a teenager—a little more confident yes, a tiny bit wiser, but other than the waistline differential, there's not much separating me from my teenage self. I still even have the same friends, for heaven's sake. When Lachlan was about two he announced, pointing at me with a chubby finger, "I'm a kid and you're a grown nut!" I told the story at Wine Wednesday, of course, and from that point on, Feeney adopted the phrase. "Life's tough when you're a grown nut," she'd say.

Tears spring to my eyes with zero warning. I never used to be a crier, now it seems I'm constantly dripping.

It centers me, though. I remember that I am indeed a grown up, and my best friend has left this earth. That's about as grounding a reality as one can have. When Reverend Peter emerges with his cup of coffee, I'm ready for him.

"I have a somewhat unusual request," I say, meeting his kind, gray eyes over his coffee cup.

He puts it down on the table and clasps his hands together on his lap. "Shoot," he says. His entire body language says *I'm open.* This must be something they teach in reverend school.

"Feeney's funeral was lovely," I start with hesitation. "But it wasn't her. I'm not sure if you know this but she was pretty . . . untraditional."

He closes his eyes and smiles a sad smile. "I do know that." Then he looks at me directly. "Do you know that she came and talked to me fairly regularly?"

"What?" I sputter. "Who, Feeney?"

"Yep. She would drop in to the church every couple of months and we would talk. She'd usually start the conversation with, 'Forgive me, Father, for I have sinned.' When I told her that I wasn't a father and that was a Catholic thing, she said, 'I know, I just always wanted to say that.' It was like our little routine."

I laugh and gasp at the same time. "What did you talk about?"

"Anything and everything. She had a lot of questions about faith, and we would wrestle with it together. But sometimes we'd just shoot the shit."

I'm not sure what's more shocking, this information or the fact that I just heard Reverend Peter say *shit.* I'm still taking it all in when his voice breaks into my reverie.

"The last time I saw her she asked me how I knew there was an afterlife. She wanted scientific proof. So I told her that science has proven that energy can't be destroyed. It simply takes on other forms." He opens his palms to the sky. "And what are we all if not energy?" He sighs and his shoulders lower as he closes his hands again. "I've thought a lot about that conversation this past week."

We both sit and stare at the table, brains swirling with the burning question that is Feeney. "Sorry, you said you had a request?" He looks at me and I see true sadness in his eyes.

"Max, Liddy, and I loved her so much," I start, closing my eyes as they brim over. "And we wish we had told her more. We wish . . ." I shake my head with futile grief. "We don't want to wait until we all die to celebrate each other. We want to hold our own funerals now. While we're alive and well. At St. Paul's."

I look up, and his eyebrows are making for his widow's peak.

"I know it's weird," I say. The back of my neck starts to prickle with sweat.

He puts his head back and closes his eyes, then smiles with tears sparkling in his eyes. "It's the best kind of weird. How I can help?"

I will always hug him now.

The next out-of-body experience comes that afternoon when Max, Liddy, and I sit down with our collective calendars spread out in front of us, trying to schedule our own funerals. We want to try to do them all in one week, figuring it will be good to keep the momentum going. This isn't exactly the kind of thing you drag out.

"What about the week of August tenth?" I throw out.

"I'm getting a crown replaced on that Tuesday," Max says, frowning over her iPhone screen. "And I already cancelled it once, so I've used up my get out of jail free card."

"And I've got some doctor's appointments lined up for Luke that week. It would be weird to be working them around our funerals." Liddy says.

"I'm pretty sure this will be weird no matter what," I say. "Just saying."

"True, but I want to be focused. The following week is better.

Other than Lily's dance schedule, I'm free. And I can get the sitter to take her if need be."

"I'm getting highlights on Monday, but the rest of the week looks pretty open," I offer.

"And you'll have hot hair for your funeral," Max says, looking at me over her reading glasses, royal blue this time. "I can do that week too. Are you guys okay with me going first? I'm afraid my anxiety will shoot through the roof if I don't."

"Works for me," I say. "Here's a question—are we inviting the guys?"

Max takes off her glasses and chews on the tip of the earpiece. "I'd like to, I think."

"You okay with that Liddy?" I look over at her, and she's lost in thought. "Lids?"

She raises her eyebrows. "I mean, I can invite Jack, but I doubt he'll come. We're not talking much these days."

"Maybe he'll surprise you," I venture.

She shakes her head and sighs. "I'll go second. Ali, you okay being the grand finale?"

"Sure. So, Tuesday, Wednesday, and Thursday, then? August eighteenth, nineteenth, and twentieth?" I look at Max and Liddy with my pen poised.

"Ink it," Max says, and we do.

The Time She Made Us All Dogs

Seven years before

"So I have a theory," Feeney says. "Do you guys ever watch dog shows?"

We're holding Wine Wednesday at Feeney's house for a change as Max's house is currently tented and being sprayed for termites. We're settled into Feeney's plush velvet couch that's a color somewhere between blue and green. Feeney's taste in decor is like her: quirky, colorful and fun. Sitting on the table in front of me is a full-sized antique diving helmet, a mini statuette of Mr. Peanut, and a bowl of colorful marbles. Feeney likes to absentmindedly play with the marbles while talking. She's doing it now.

"Not on purpose," Max says.

"You're such a party pooper, Max," Liddy says. "I love dog shows."

"Did you just call me a party pooper?" Max asks. "Is it even possible to be an over forty-year-old party pooper?"

"Speaking of poopers," I say. "I've seen a couple of dog shows on TV. I can never decide who to look at more—the humans or the dogs. They are equally fascinating."

"Okay, good," Feeney says. "So, here's my theory. I think all humans should be categorized like dogs. I mean, think about it. Why do dogs get all these categories and we just get a few? I personally know at least three human Chihuahuas."

"Ooh, this is fun," Liddy says. "What am I?"

"Okay, I've already pinpointed you all at least to your categories. We'll need to debate your actual species. Liddy, I think you are a herder. Max, you are a terrier. And Ali, you're a worker."

"Worker? That sounds like work. Also boring," I say, pouting.

"So now who's being a party pooper?" Feeney says. "Wait here, I'm going to get the book with the descriptions."

She exits and the three of us look at each other. "You are totally a terrier," Liddy says, pointing at Max. Max growls and we all laugh.

"Okay, here are the descriptions," Feeney says as she plops back on the couch with a book about dog breeds in her hands. "Terrier," she looks up and points at Max. "'These are feisty, energetic dogs. Terriers typically have little tolerance for other animals, including other dogs. Their ancestors were bred to hunt and kill vermin. Many continue to project the attitude that they're always eager for a spirited argument.'"

"Oh my God, you're right," Max says, her eyes wide with recognition. "Little tolerance? Check. Attitude? Check. And vermin are being professionally killed back at my house right this minute."

"And now Liddy, the herder," Feeney says, smiling over the top of the book at us. "'Herding breeds are able to control the movement of other animals. A corgi, perhaps one foot tall at the shoulders, can drive a herd of cows many times its size. Pure instinct prompts these dogs to herd, especially when it comes to children.'"

"That's totally you!" I say to Liddy.

She laughs and shrugs. "What can I say? You all need herding," she says.

"Okay Ali, now you." Feeney shifts her body toward mine and looks down at her book. "'Most working breeds are robust, intelligent, and headstrong, often unsuitable for novice owners. Made up of guardians of livestock and property, police dogs, sled dogs, and rescue dogs, these workers come in all shapes and sizes, but for the most part, these are powerful dogs.'"

"Huh," I say. "I suppose I am headstrong."

"You're also unsuitable for novice owners," Max says, which makes us all laugh.

"You're the dog we'd all want in an emergency," Feeney says.

"That's a pretty good compliment," I say. "What about you, Feeney?"

"Well, I'm a little unsure. My size puts me in a sporting category. But the description that fits me best is toy. Listen to this: 'The main function of this group is to embody sheer delight. Don't let their tiny stature fool you, though; many Toys are tough as nails.'" She looks up at us. "Tough as nails but meant to embody sheer delight? I mean, I'd be perfectly happy if that was on my gravestone."

"Yep, you're a toy in a sporting body," I say. "Do you need therapy for that or something?"

"I think I'll manage," Feeney says. "It's the least of my problems."

"Let's figure out our breeds," Max says, bouncing in her seat. "This is fun!"

"Says the dog show hater," I raise my eyebrows at her. She rolls her eyes at me in return.

Feeney flips back to the terriers and runs her finger down the pages. "Okay, hmmmmm . . . aha. This is you. Upbeat, mischievous, comical, with terrier fire and fearlessness. Max, you are a miniature bull terrier." She flips around the book and shows Max her dog.

"I may need one," Max whispers, her tone reverent.

"Okay, now Liddy." She flips through the book to the Herder section and begins her perusal. "Oh, this one is easy. You're a collie. Graceful, devoted, and proud. And look how pretty you are!" She flips the book around for all of us to see Liddy the dog.

"Ohhhh . . ." we all say at once.

"Great hair," I add.

"Ali, my worker. Let's find you." She narrows her eyes and flips a few pages. "Yep. Here you go. Brave, affectionate, and loyal, the bullmastiff will always have your back."

She turns the book around, and I can't help but smile at the sweet dog looking back at me with big, floppy lips.

"Okay, give me the book. We need to nail your breed, Feeney." I grab it from her and huddle with Max and Liddy. Feeney sits across from us sipping her wine with a bemused smile on her face. I point to a page and say, "Got it. Silky terrier. Friendly, vivacious, and cheeky!"

I show her, and she throws her head back and laughs. "Silky and cheeky, I love it," she says. "Well, I don't know about you all, but I like being a dog. It's better than being a human. Although I do love all the humans in this room."

"I thought we were dogs?" Liddy asks, with such earnestness that we all laugh.

Max flashes us a wicked grin. "We're bitches."

"So, how are we actually going to do this? I mean, are we going to lie down on the ground and act dead during our funerals?"

We are sitting on our favorite bench in the town square, discussing our impending funerals. Attending your own funeral is yet another thing there is no handbook for. A couple of days have passed since we scheduled the funerals with Reverend Peter, but it's hard to think about or talk about much else when we are together.

"I want to say that that sounds morbid but I suppose that's true for all of this," Max says. "Morbid is the new black."

"Maybe we should walk over to St. Paul's to check out our options," I say. "If Reverend Peter is there we can ask him what he thinks." We all decide this is as good a plan as any.

We locate him in his office, working on his laptop. I'm surprised. I always pictured him typing his sermons on an old-fashioned type-writer, the kind that dings and has to be manually reset.

He looks up at us and smiles. "Let me guess—you're here to talk about a funeral."

"Or three," Max says.

"Thanks so much for being so understanding about this, by the way," Liddy says.

He shrugs. "The church is here to help people deal with suffering. Not to tell anyone how to do it."

My heart swells with gratitude for him. "We're not really sure how to make this happen," I say. "Like, where do we put the . . . quote, unquote, dead person?"

"Good question," he says. "Why don't we go into the chapel and look around."

He grabs his keys and strides off. We follow behind him like obedient sheep.

I haven't been back inside the church since Feeney's funeral. Some of the flowers are still here, barely even wilted. It feels like months since I stood in my doorway, attempting to register Feeney's suicide. It's startling to be reminded that it hasn't even been two weeks. It's like dog years. Every day without Feeney is longer than one before.

The church is old and made entirely of dark wood, the only color streaming in through stained glass windows. I've never been inside when its empty; it feels like a room that's holding its breath. The wood creaks as we walk around, and I find myself on my tiptoes.

"Reverend Peter?" I whisper.

"You don't have to whisper," he says, turning around with a grin. His voice makes me start. I clear my throat.

"Right. Sorry. Um, can I look around up there to see if there's a good place for the, uh, guest of honor to sit?" I gesture at the front altar of the church.

"By all means," he says. "Look anywhere you like."

I walk down the aisle to the front of the church, the same aisle I walked down fifteen years ago in ivory duchesse satin, the same aisle I walked down twice holding unsuspecting babies about to have holy water dripped on their downy heads, the same aisle I walked down days ago in a fog of grief. Churches bear witness to our best and worst moments. I'm not sure which one this is. Both, I guess.

Without the people, music, candles, or pomp and circumstance, the room is oddly normal. The organ sits off to the right, the pews for the choir to the left. I motion for Max and Liddy to join me. They come arm in arm down the aisle and stand in front of me. I can't help myself.

"I hereby pronounce you husband and wife. You may kiss the bride."

"But which is which?" Liddy asks.

"If anyone here has a dick, it's me," Max says.

"You can't say dick in church!" Liddy looks at Max aghast.

"I just did."

I flick my eyes up to see if Reverend Peter has overheard this lovely repartee. I don't see him anywhere. Most likely he realizes the situation is weird enough for us to require a few moments alone.

"I feel like the person whose funeral it is shouldn't be visible," I say.

"I agree. Open caskets are creepy as shit. I don't want to see you dead, even if you are still alive," Max says.

"But we have to be able to hear and see everything," Liddy adds.

"Agreed. So I guess we could lie down in the pew over there." I gesture to the choir pew.

"That doesn't seem very dignified, to be lying in a pew," Liddy says. I have to agree. "Look at this amazing chair," she says, walking over to an elaborately carved wood chair with a needlepointed back and seat. "This looks like something that a guest of honor at her own funeral should sit in." She runs a hand over the seat. "Someone spent so much time on this." She settles into the seat, bouncing a couple of times for good measure.

"How do you feel?" Max asks.

"Not dead," she responds. We laugh together. It's a welcome moment of relief.

"We could move it into the corner so we can't see each other but you'd be able to hear everything from there," Max says.

"I see you've found Constance's chair," Reverend Peter says, reappearing in the doors of the church. "That's the chair I sit in during services."

Liddy springs up.

"No, no. Please sit. It's a perfect place to put the funeralee. And I can vouch that it's quite comfy."

"Who is Constance?" I ask.

"The story I heard when I first arrived was that Constance was the wife of the reverend who was here in the early 1900s. She sat in the front row of church every Sunday, wore a hat and gloves, and was the picture of respectability. She needlepointed all the kneelers as well as that chair. Then her husband had a heart attack and died. She attended the funeral but then immediately skipped town and became one of San Francisco's most successful whiskey runners during Prohibition. Whenever we're low on wine for Communion, we say 'Looks like Constance paid us a visit.'"

"Oh my God, it's perfect," I say. "Oh my gosh, I mean."

Reverend Peter laughs. "All is forgiven."

We have our dates. We have Constance's chair. We don't have Feeney, but at least for now, we have a plan.

The Time She Broke

Nine months before

My cell phone rings and I look to see who it is. There on the screen are Feeney's lips, huge and close up, puckered into a kiss. This is a habit of Feeney's; she steals our phones when we're not around and changes the photo of her that comes up when she calls. Eyeball, nostril, cleavage, armpit, we've seen it all. Once it was one of her cat's butthole. I sincerely hope hers never pops up.

"Hey," I say.

"So, I need a ride to the hospital," Feeney says, in a calm voice that is at odds with the nature of her request.

"What happened? Are you okay?" I sit straight up, synapses firing on all cylinders.

"I think I broke my arm. No, it's definitely broken, I just don't know how broken and that's why I need to go to the hospital. If it was minor I'd just wrap an Ace bandage around it."

"Okay, I'm grabbing my keys. I'm on my way. What did you do?"

"I tried to move the girls' bookcase to the other side of the room."

"And . . .?"

"And it was not amenable to being moved. Especially not while full of books."

"Are you in pain?"

"No, it's shits and giggles over here, Ali. What do you think?"

"How bad is it?"

"Well, I already fainted once."

"Jesus, okay, I am already driving. Hold tight."

"Tightly holding." Click.

I get to Feeney's house and let myself in. She is sitting on the couch in her living room, pale as a sheet, holding her arm that's in a right angle facing the wrong way. I go woozy just looking at it.

"Okay! Okay. Let's go." I'm trying desperately not to react to what I'm seeing.

I help her to the car, and we drive in silence, both of us in a state of shock. She continues to hold her right angle of an arm up high in front of her like a platter of hors d'oeuvres. I keep my eyes on the road.

We get to the emergency room, and the admitting nurse takes one look at Feeney and orders a wheelchair. I stay to work on paperwork and tell her I'll find her when I'm done. I'm frankly relieved when she's no longer in eyesight. That arm, I'll never forget it.

A nurse returns and tells me they are going to do X-rays so I should just wait. I gladly take a seat in the sterile hospital waiting room and go about reading three-year-old magazines I wouldn't have wanted to read even if they were current. *Popular Mechanics*? *Redbook*? There's not a *People* to be found on the rack. God, I'd even take *Martha Stewart Living* if it were offered.

A couple of hours later I hear Feeney's voice from down the hall. She's got the orderly pushing her chair in hysterics telling him about the time she stitched up her own finger after cutting it while cooking. She couldn't find any thread so she used mint-flavored dental floss. If I remember correctly, it got horribly infected and she had to have a giant shot in the ass. To this day she can't stand the smell of mint.

She comes around the corner and she's smiling ear to ear, her arm wrapped in a peacock blue cast and nestled in a sling. "Hi Ali!" she

says like she's greeting me at a party. She leans forward conspirato-
rially. "You should break your arm. They give you some really good
shit."

I drive a hopped up and exceedingly chatty Feeney to the drug-
store so we can pick up more pain meds. Percocet, the strong stuff.
What I didn't know then is that she never took a single one. Until the
night she took them all.

When I walk in my house after being at the church, there sitting on
my couch is Caroline Simms in the flesh, looking so much like Feeney
that I don't even know what to say or do.

We lock eyes and she stands up, rubbing her palms nervously on
the front of her white jeans.

"Caroline . . ."

All I want to do is to gather her up into my arms and hold her tight,
but I also need to respect her space. Unlike Hannah, who runs to me
and buries her face in my chest every time I see her since Feeney died,
Caroline has been keeping us all at arm's length. I walk toward her
with my arms wide. I figure the worst she can do is rebuff me. Or, I
suppose she might hit me. I wouldn't really blame her.

She wraps her arms around her torso and drops her head. I get to
her and grab her shoulders, gently pulling her toward me. She doesn't
resist, so I wrap my arms around her and we settle into the couch in
tears. Mine are soft and silent. Hers come from a place I didn't even
know existed until Feeney died, that depth of pain that only a terrible
grief can touch. I know that place intimately now.

I sit and hold her while she holds herself and cries. I rest my cheek against her hair that smells of sunshine and shampoo and try to imagine what it must feel like for Caroline to need most desperately the one person who has most hurt her. My heart breaks in a million pieces all over again. If my pain is awful, hers is relentless.

Eventually I lean back, and she rests limply against my shoulder. I play with her hair. Every once in a while she hiccups and another wave of tears comes, but the force of them is weakening. I know to wait. I've come to learn the different rhythms of grief.

"I've been so angry," she whispers.

"I know. That's okay, honey. I have been, too."

"You have?" She looks up at me, her deep blue eyes so familiar it makes my throat hurt.

"God, yes. Also confused and sad and a lot of feelings I can't even describe."

"Why did this happen?" The look in her eyes is so tormented. She needs an answer so badly. I don't have one for her.

"I don't know, Caroline. But I do know how much your mom loved you, and Hannah, and your dad, and us, and life. She was more alive than anyone I have ever known. I think . . . I think that she was going through something really hard and didn't know how to talk about it. But I believe with all my heart that she wasn't thinking clearly when she died."

"She didn't say goodbye," Caroline says, and buries her head into her hands, wracked with another wave of grief.

I rub her back, searching for the right words before realizing they simply don't exist. "No, she didn't. I'm so sorry."

When the latest round of tears subside, I turn to face Caroline and put my hand under her chin, lifting her eyes to meet mine.

"I'm so sorry your mom is gone. But I can bring her to you. Anytime you want. I can tell you all about how amazing she was, I'll tell you stories about all the things we did together. Just because she's not here doesn't mean you don't have access to her."

Somehow it's easier being vulnerable with her than with the very people I live with. We are living on a different level of grief than most others, a very deep place with no escalators.

Caroline nods and I hug her to me again. When we pull apart I ask her, "Hey, how did you get in here?"

She reaches into her back pocket and pulls out a key on a chain with a piece of masking tape stuck to it. On the tape "Ali" is written in Feeney's familiar writing. "I found this in the junk drawer, and I decided to walk over." She holds it out to me.

"Keep it. You are welcome here any time."

Just then, we hear a hubbub of noise in the front yard, and Drew flings open the front door and stops short. Lachlan and Devon fall against each other on their way in.

"Oh, hey," Lachlan says to Caroline, and then I watch as his cheeks turn flaming pink. Devon walks over to us and puts one arm around Caroline in an awkward hug. Nobody seems to know what to do or say.

"I think we all need some ice cream, pronto," I say.

Devon looks up at me in surprise. "Really? Before dinner?"

"Even better. Ice cream's going to *be* our dinner tonight."

Devon's face lights up, and Lachlan whoops, "Right on!" then runs into the kitchen with Drew not far behind.

"Stay for dinner?" I ask Caroline. "I'll call your dad and tell him you're here and that it's meatloaf and broccoli."

She smiles and nods. As we're both standing up from the couch, she grabs my hand. "Thank you, Aunt Ali."

I kiss the top of her warm hair. "Please don't thank me. I'm so glad you're here."

As I sit at the table and watch the kids giddily slurp down their ice cream, laughing and talking together about everything from soccer to Harry Potter, I find myself studying Caroline. I try to imagine me at her age, just starting to figure life out. What would have happened had the rug been pulled out from underneath me as it has her? How would it have changed me? Caroline has always seemed like she has the world by the tail, but now her world has snapped back to strike her down. I feel a rush of protectiveness for her and anger at Feeney so strong I actually gasp.

"What's wrong, Mom?" Lachlan looks at me, a thin line of chocolate above his upper lip.

"Cold rush," I say, then I stand up and go into the kitchen, where I close my eyes, run the water, and wait for my breathing to return to normal. I stare at the drain, my mind circling along with the water.

I've been angry at Feeney for leaving me, sure. And for not talking about her pain. But this is the first time I'm angry at her for leaving her family. It flares hot and hungry, fueled by Caroline's pain and innocence. Within moments, however, the anger shifts, away from Feeney, to this whole damned fucked-up world that takes things like addiction and infidelity and even abuse in stride while judging people whose minds don't toe some sort of invisible line.

For the first time, I understand that it could have been me. I have been so full of "how could shes" and "I would nevers" that I hadn't considered the fact that, given the perfect storm of circumstances, I may have made the same choice. I'm sure the guy that sawed off his own arm when it was stuck under a boulder never thought he'd do that either. Sometimes your options are horrible. There's no sanctimony left in me.

"I'm sorry I failed you, Feeney," I say, to the drain in my sink. "But I won't fail Caroline or Hannah. And I won't fail anyone else. I will listen closer, pry harder, and not let up. I will stay vigilant. I won't shrug something off or think it's too awkward to talk about. I will ask the hard questions. Because I know now that the worst conversation is the one you wish you had once it's too late."

Later as I'm driving Caroline home, she turns toward me in the dark interior of the car. "My whole life I'm going to be the girl whose mom killed herself. People are going to feel sorry for me." Her voice thickens. "I hate that."

I take a deep breath. "Caroline, you are so many things. Your story isn't predetermined. You are a beautiful, strong, independent young woman who has gifts that truly boggle my mind. Your mom and I used to marvel at how amazing and sure of yourself you always are."

"You did?" she asks in a quiet, small voice.

"Yes, we did," I say. "Don't let what's happened take anything away from you. And don't let it define you. And for the record, I don't feel sorry for you. Because you had the best mom in the whole world. You didn't have her for long enough, that's true, but she will always be a part of you. Nobody can ever take that away. Many people, myself included, didn't have anything close to the kind of mom Feeney was."

We pull up in front of her house and sit quietly in the car together for a few minutes. She takes a deep breath and unbuckles her seatbelt. I feel like I need to give her something else in this moment, a bridge to somewhere, but I'm completely at a loss. But the minute she opens the car door, a thought pops into my head.

"Sweetie, did your mom ever take you starfishing?"

"What's that?" Caroline says, her brow furrowed with confusion.

"You're about to find out," I say, patting her on the leg. "Hop out."

We lie on the grass for a few minutes in silence. I hear Caroline sniff quietly, and I look over at her lovely profile. It shouldn't be me here with her, I realize. I am a poor substitute.

"My mom used to do this?" Caroline asks. "Like, a lot?"

"I don't know. The only reason I know about it is that I was driving down your street one night and found her mid-starfishing session. She said it helped her feel grounded."

"Yeah, like, literally."

Her unexpected wit forces a laugh from deep inside me. This girl is going to be okay. Not now, not maybe for years, but someday, she's going to be okay.

I roll over to face her and reach out my hand. She rolls toward me and takes it.

Tick, tick, tick. It's getting to the point when I can't think of anything else but the funerals. Everything else is just filler. I'm either in the land of Feeney, full of impossible possibilities like planning and attending my own funeral, or I'm in the land of mom/wife, where I do mundane yet necessary things like spray bleach on mold and check for lice.

Drew has been giving me a wide berth. I know I need to reconnect with him, but my energy is all focused on these funerals. When I told him about what we are doing and asked him to come to mine, a look of concern flicked across his face before he said, "Of course I'll be there, Ali." He even smiled a little as he said it. It's a start.

Finally, it's the day before Max's funeral. I call her home phone; Spence answers.

"Are you calling for the soon to be deceased?"

"The very one."

"I'll let her know. You okay, Ali?"

I catch my breath. These are the moments that gut me, the kind words, the empathetic questions. When I answer, my voice is high and tight, full of tears and pain. "Not really. Okay as any of us, I guess."

"I'm so sorry, Ali. Feeney was so lucky to have you, and you were all so lucky to have her."

"Agreed. Now stop being so nice and get your wife or I'll never stop crying."

"Yep. Hold on."

"Wait, Spence?" An idea had just flapped its wings inside my brain, as if a sent from Feeney herself.

"Yes?"

"Can I come pick up Feeney's journal tonight? Without Max knowing? I'm wondering if she may want to be heard from tomorrow as well."

A throaty "hmm" crackles across the line, and when he speaks, I realize it may be through tears. "Absolutely, Ali. I will put it on the bench on the front porch. Max is so manic with this funeral tomorrow I can't imagine she will notice. I'll get her and then I'll sneak it out."

"Thank you."

I spend the seconds waiting breathing deep and rubbing my forehead with my fingers. I feel halfway back to normal by the time I hear Max's voice.

"I'm not going to lie, Ali; this is pretty weird. I'm going to sleep tonight knowing that my funeral is being held tomorrow. It's a first, that's for sure. And hopefully a last."

"I'm actually jealous that you're first," I say.

"Oh, please. It's like pancakes. The first one is always messed up. We'll be in fine form by the time yours rolls around."

"I'm worried about what happens after."

"After my funeral? We'll come to my house and drink. What did you think?"

"No, I mean after this week."

"Oh."

We sit in silence on the phone for a few beats before Max talks again.

"We're going to have to get used to the fact that nothing will ever be the same. And I imagine it will take the rest of our lives to do that."

"That's not intimidating at all," I say.

"Listen, you're talking to a woman who is going to her own funeral tomorrow. Don't talk to me about being intimidated."

"Good point. Okay. I'll see you tomorrow. Or rather, I won't see you tomorrow. Or both, I guess."

"I'll see you when I'm dead, Ali. I love you."

The day is blazing hot. Liddy and I drive together to St. Paul's. I'm a mass of anxiety and nervous excitement. My legs are crossed and I'm bouncing my foot a mile a minute when Liddy reaches over and puts one warm hand on my leg and leaves it there. I stop fidgeting and start to, if not relax, at least calm several notches down. She keeps her eyes on the road and her hand on my knee. We arrive and park, then finally turn look at each other.

"This is crazy," I say.

Liddy says, "Yeah, but it's good crazy."

I bite my lip. "I'm nervous."

"Oh really? I hadn't noticed." She smiles at me with love. "Ali, if nothing else, this is a step. Forward momentum. Ever since Feeney died, we've all been churning. Maybe this can be a step towards healing."

"Do you ever feel like it would be wrong for us to move on?"

"Completely. Moving on will be terrible. But we don't have a choice, do we?"

"No. But Feeney did."

There. There it is. I hate that I said it aloud.

"Maybe. Maybe not. We'll never know, Ali. It's fine to be angry, but we can never pretend to know what Feeney was thinking."

I hit the back of my head against the headrest a few times to clear my brain.

"I hate it."

"That makes two of us. Now let's go get Max's funeral on," she says, opening her car door to the waving heat.

As we approach the church I catch my breath. I don't remember talking about music, about hiring an organist, but there is a swell of organ music coming from within the doors. It takes me a moment to place the song because of the instrument, but then it hits me: "With a Little Help from My Friends," by the Beatles. Reverend Peter appears in the doorway, and we look at him with question marks in our eyes.

"My treat," he says with a smile. "I happen to be dating the daughter of the organist." Then he opens the door with one hand and gestures us in with the other. I'm already crying.

It's cool inside the dark church. Spence is already inside. He's crying too, of course he is, being that he's most emotionally evolved man on the planet. I'd roll my eyes with envy except I'm happy for Max. She needs this. She needs him.

Spence smiles at us and pats the empty pew next to him. We slide in and listen to the rest of the song.

When it ends, Reverend Peter goes up to the front of the church.

"We are here today to honor and celebrate the life of Maxine Greene. Let's start with a prayer.

"Those who are worn out and crushed by mourning, let your hearts consider this: this is the path that has existed from the time of creation and will exist forever. Many have drunk from it and many will yet drink. As was the first meal, so shall be the last. May the master of comfort comfort you. Blessed are those who comfort the mourners."

We didn't expect Reverend Peter would even be here, much less officiate the event. It settles a reality over the surreal. Imagine that—a reverend embracing the irreverent. I love a world in which this could happen. Feeney would too.

"Now we will hear from Maxine's loved ones." He steps away from the lectern and sits in a regular wooden chair behind it. Constance's chair with Max seated in it is tucked away somewhere where we can't see them.

We all look at each other; we hadn't discussed the order of our commentary. Spence says under his breath, "Okay for me to go first?" Liddy and I both nod, and I'm filled with relief that I don't have to kick this thing off.

Spence stands up and strides to the front of the church. He's dressed in a black linen button down and dark wash jeans, a perfect not-real-funeral outfit. How again is this man not gay?

He looks out at us and smiles. It's a smile so full of naked love and empathy that I have to look away. I feel a pang of longing for Drew, the first since Feeney died, a stab of feeling coming back through the frostbite.

"My first impression of Maxine was this: There is nobody on earth like this woman. She is the only one of her. And it has only ever been true—I have only ever been proven right on that particular front. Now, some may say that's a good thing."

Liddy and I laugh our assent.

"But I believe wholeheartedly that the world is a better place for having Max in it. More colorful, more alive. I certainly am better because of her. I met her, and it was like I had been wandering in a desert. Here was not just water but a wild, rushing river, complete with flying fish and waterfalls. Max was always so unapologetically, ferociously herself that it gave me permission to be the same. I can say with total certainty that there has not been a day when I took this for granted. I have woken up in the morning for the past nine years with a single thought: *This is another day I get to spend with Max*."

His voice gets thick and he holds his hand to his heart. "How lucky am I?"

He looks down. "Life without her is unthinkable to me. It's the eclipse of my sun. My love for her is as constant and as necessary as my own heartbeat."

Liddy and I are barely breathing. Spence is gripping the sides of the lectern so tightly I can see the veins in his hands and forearms. He is quiet for a long time.

"I will make sure that every single day, I will honor the life force that is Max. I will sail the ocean of her with both hands on the wheel, full steam ahead. I will never take a second, a beat, a drop for granted. Never." He nods a couple of times to himself, then walks back to our pew and slides in.

How lucky is Max?

Without warning, I feel myself float out of my seat and head toward the space Spence just vacated. I can't really feel my feet. The lectern is somehow getting closer and closer. I stand at it and turn around and stare out at the empty church, save for Spence and Liddy blinking back at me. I look at Reverend Peter, and he gives me a reassuring smile. I look down and my notes are in my hands, which are surprisingly steady. I hear someone say, "Max" and I realize with a start that it's me. I close my eyes for a minute, and I imagine Feeney standing behind me with her hand on my shoulder like Liddy's hand on my frantic knee. I feel a calm settle over me. I open my eyes and look down again.

"Sorry. Max. I met Max when I was an awkward fourteen-year-old with both boobs and braces. I was afraid to make any wrong moves— or rather, I didn't even know what the moves were. Max was fearless from the start. I have a distinct memory of being dragged up the front walkway at Jimmy Pillmeyer's house freshman year to a party we were definitely not invited to. We walked in, and there was that moment where everyone looked at us . . . I'm sure it didn't, but it felt like the music stopped, like time stopped, but then she made a face and said, 'Ew, freshmen.' It made the kids laugh and then promptly ignore us completely. But we were there! At a cool kid party! At fourteen! She always did that—addressed the elephant in the room like, 'Hey elephant, nice trunk.'"

I hear Spence and Liddy laugh. I'm not sure but I might have even heard Max.

"From the moment I met her I knew she was different. She was a fighter. What I didn't know right away was that she had to be. She was dealt a mind that was brilliant, but brilliance never comes easy. Nobody's that lucky. So she fought. She fought herself, for herself. It's part of what made her so irresistible. Because that's the thing about a fighter. You always want them on your side. Max would take on a rabid lion for me. I'm not even sure I can say that about my own mother. But Max? I'm 100 percent certain she would."

"Max has given me the ability to stand up for myself, to embrace my imperfections, and to speak my mind, and the courage to face the hard stuff instead of pretending it doesn't exist, which was what I had always been taught. These are gifts I'm able to pass along to my children. My children are better humans because of Max. *Their children* will be better humans because of Max. Like Spence said, this whole world will be better because Max Greene came into it with shoulders back and nostrils flared, ready to take it on."

I look up at him, and he is rapt, unchecked tears running down his cheeks.

"I don't think I ever told her this, but she's my biggest hero. I always find myself channeling her when I'm unsure about something. *What would Max do?* I'll ask myself. There's always an answer. And it's never half-assed. *What would Max do about this mom that's being rude to me? She'd march right up to her and ask her what the hell her problem is.* I sometimes tone down my versions of Max, but her responses are always spot on and completely fearless.

"Nobody fought as hard as Max, nobody loved as hard as Max, and nobody hugged as hard as Max. In fact, the only thing easy about Max was loving her."

I fold the paper in half and pull my fingers across the crease, centering myself. Then I walk back to Spence and Liddy. This time I can feel my feet.

Spence puts an arm around my shoulder and squeezes it as I sit down. What a community there is in loving someone.

Liddy stands up and begins her walk down the aisle. She is regal and composed. I want some of whatever she's on.

She smiles out at us, and that's when I see that her face, too, is slick with tears.

She pauses for a moment, looking down at her notes. Then she raises her lioness eyes to us.

"If I were a spider, I'd live in Max's head."

It's such an unexpected sentiment, yet such a perfect one, that I laugh once, loud and hard. My laugh echoes off the empty church walls.

"There would be so much to explore. So many nooks and crannies for me to fill with my sticky webs. So much interesting stuff to capture. I would dine on her thoughts and never go hungry. I would catch her fears and suffocate them then devour them whole. I would be the gatekeeper of her mind, her personal dreamcatcher spun of spider silk."

I'm barely breathing. I never realized Liddy had such a gift with words. She has always been an artist, weaving creative magic with pencils, paint, glass, clay, sand and pretty much anything else she could get her hands on. Now I know she is also an artist of words. I am as choked up with awe of her as I am with love for Max.

"Unfortunately, I'm not a spider inside Max's head. I'm just someone who loved her, from the outside looking in. But that didn't stop me from wanting to protect her from herself sometimes. I also wanted to bask in her energy. It's complicated, having a friend like Max.

"When Luke was born, it changed the way I thought about the malleability of humans. I understood under no uncertain terms that there were limits to what we all can do. Luke may be an extreme example of this, but he's also an extreme example of love. It's almost like his limits have been replaced with pure love, like love is the wave that rushes in to fill the void. Max was beyond intelligent, but she struggled with her emotions and her thoughts. Maybe that's where her love flowed in. Because Max loved so fiercely and so freely, at least to those of us who knew her best, it's almost like she was pulsing with it. Yes, she might rage at you about something, but when it was over, she'd rush in with so much love that you'd almost be grateful for the rage. At least she was real. So very few of us are."

She turns her face to the side for a moment, blinking, and I can tell she's thinking about Feeney. I am too. The horrible truth is that Feeney wasn't real with us. Not at the end. Not when it mattered.

"Max lived and Max loved. She was a verb. Max maxxed. She did it perfectly, and she did it imperfectly. And everyone can learn from that."

She looks up at us, and I give her a nod. She walks back to our pew. I look up to see Reverend Peter starting to stand. I bolt up with my hand in the air.

"Wait! Sorry. I have one more thing."

He gestures towards the lectern and sits back down. I make my second trip down the aisle. This time, I've brought my purse. I pull Feeney's journal out of it.

"Last night, I fanned through Feeney's journal and Max's name jumped out. Apparently, Feeney wants to speak."

I open the journal up and set it on the lectern, my hands planted firmly on either side of Feeney's unmistakable handwriting. I take a deep breath, then start speaking.

"'What I wouldn't give to be like Max. I have never met someone with more ownership of themselves. God, I don't feel like I've ever owned myself. Maybe I did, when I was young, but then I gave away so many pieces of myself over the years that I'm like a slice of Swiss cheese. And what do I have to show for it? A mind that rails at me, a body with memories I can't talk about, a soul that's as lost and unfettered as a piece of ocean debris. Max, however, is a fucking lighthouse.'"

I look up in apology for swearing to Reverend Peter, but he is staring back at me with tears in his eyes. He looks scared and riveted and not at all like the man that confidently delivers sermons every week. I quickly look back down.

"'I envy her; I worship her; I will never be as strong as her. But I can try. I tell myself that if I only have a piece of that I'll be okay. And I do. Because she is my friend.'"

I close the journal and walk back down the aisle to my seat, keeping my eyes on my feet as I go. I know I just dropped a bomb, but this particular one needed to explode. We needed to hear this, here, today. I believe that wholeheartedly.

As I take my seat, I hear Reverend Peter speaking. "Let's close today with a prayer." His voice is low and quiet.

Still looking down, I reach out and grab Spence and Liddy's hands. I close my eyes.

"Lord, give us the strength and power to love each other the way you love us, which is unconditionally. Give us the ability to see each other as you see us, which is transparently and without judgment. Give us the courage to live in a way that serves you, which is in love and forgiveness. And bless the life of Maxine Greene, now and forever. Amen."

The three of us say amen loudly and then fall against each other in what is partially a hug and partially a way to hold each other up. We are spent with tears and emotions.

Spence pulls away and says, "I'm going to go grab her. Do you guys want to come?"

I hadn't thought about this moment, but I find that I really, really want to see her. Right now. I want to know she's alive and here in flesh and blood. I nod through my tears. Liddy does too.

Our little huddle, led by Spence, nudges forward just enough so that we can see Max, who is sitting in Constance's chair in the front left corner of the church. She has her arms wrapped around her tucked up legs, with her face pressed against her knees. She hears us and looks up, shaking her head and sobbing. "Oh my God you guys," she says, opening her arms to us.

We rush forward, and Spence pulls her into a bear hug. We wrap ourselves around her back, and the four of us cry together for everything—what we love and what we've lost, who is here and who is gone. It could have been two minutes, it could have been twenty. It doesn't matter.

Eventually we have moved apart and are wiping our eyes, our noses, removing various amounts of snot and mascara. We are taking deep breaths and composing ourselves. Liddy pulls Kleenex out of her purse and passes it around.

"You guys will come back to the house, right?" Max asks in a wobbly voice.

Liddy and I nod, unable to speak, and we all slowly disperse. I wanted to thank Reverend Peter, but I don't see him anywhere. Maybe he's wondering what he's gotten himself into. I certainly wouldn't blame him.

When I climb back into Liddy's car, it feels as if a week has passed since our drive to the church instead of an hour. I'm reminded of the feeling I get when I go to the movies in the day-time only to emerge to the night. It's disorienting for things to change so drastically so quickly. Being on the other side of our first funeral makes me feel deeply changed, though I'm not even sure I can say how.

"Your writing was magical," I say to Liddy. "Why don't you write more?"

"I used to. I just haven't spent time on it in so long." She starts the car and adjusts the temperature.

"Why not?" I ask. "It's obviously something you love, like painting."

"I stopped when the kids were born. I don't know why."

"Because life," I say.

"Yeah. Because life."

"Well that's the same exact reason why you should get back to it.

We're alive, Liddy. You have a gift. Don't ignore it. You need to write and paint and put beauty back into the world."

We're just sitting in the running car, letting the cool air blast our faces.

"Maybe . . ." Liddy says distractedly.

"No, damn it! Not maybe, Liddy. Yes! Okay? You will write and paint, do you hear me?"

I've grabbed her shoulder, and my voice is rising with an anger that came out of nowhere on every word. She faces me, and her voice matches me with equal anger and fierce.

"Okay, Ali, I will write and paint, are you happy?"

"Yes!" Then I huff and slam myself back into my seat.

Then Liddy puts her head down on the steering wheel and eventually starts quietly laughing, and the absurdity of our fight, of the whole entire day, hits me. I laugh too, shaking my head.

"Sorry."

"Don't apologize. You're right. Thank you."

I shrug. "You know what? We would never have done something like this if we hadn't known and loved Feeney. We are different because of her. Weirder. Better. More . . . I don't know . . ."

"Alive," Liddy says with conviction.

It's a truth that's also a gut punch. Here we are, alive at our own funerals, in some ways more alive than ever, and it's all because of our friend who is dead. It's almost too much to wrap our heads around.

At Max's house there is already a giant assortment of bagels on the table with a tray of every possible topping and cold wine waiting in a large silver bucket. "We're Jewish. This is how we do death," Max says when she comes to the door. She has changed from a black suit left over from her attorney days into a soft, gray V-neck T-shirt, jeans, and sneakers. She looks ten years younger.

We all settle down into various chairs with plates and glasses filled.

"I'm glad you read from Feeney's journal, but holy hell, Ali," Max says.

"I know. I kept thinking about what Feeney would want to say today. I remembered that we have access to Feeney, at least a part of her, with her journal. So I asked Spence if I could borrow it, and I swear, when I opened it up last night it went right smack to that page. It was like she led me to it."

"I believe she did."

"Me too."

"Well, Feeney always did have a flair for the dramatic," Liddy says.

"You guys can't even begin to imagine how surreal it was to hear all that today. But incredible too. I'm starting to think everyone should throw themselves a funeral," Max says. She pulls one leg up and rests her chin on her knee. "You know, I've always felt less than. I've always thought of my fucked up brain as a handicap. I mean, I have to take three pills every single morning just to say relatively sane. But today I heard the people I love most in the world saying that they admire me because of it. My mind is officially blown."

"I suppose that's the gift of doing this," Liddy says. "It's so hard to see yourself objectively. But today you got to hear how we see you. And you are amazing, Max." She reaches over and grabs Max's shoulder.

Max tilts her head to the side and rests her head on Liddy's hand. "Thank God I'm still alive to hear it," Max says. "I mean, if I died and

I haunted my funeral, which I totally would, and I heard all that stuff I'd be like, 'What the fuck? How come nobody ever told me that when I was alive?'"

"Yeah, it's not like we don't give each other compliments, but a funeral is different," I say. "It's like you have to sum up a person's entire being. Nobody ever comes up to you and says, 'This is what is amazing about you as a human.'"

Max jabs her finger toward Liddy with a small grin on her face. "You're next, lady."

"Don't I know it," Liddy says. "I doubt I will be able to sleep tonight."

"Here, let me help," Max says and refills Liddy's glass with a generous pour.

"Is Jack coming?" I ask.

Liddy rolls her eyes. "He's not sure. He 'may have a conflict.' Or so he says."

"He's still not sure whether or not he has a conflict the night before your funeral?"

Liddy shrugs and sips her wine. "Lay of the land these days, ladies." She fiddles with the fringe of a tangerine-colored alpaca throw.

We sit in silence for a few moments, giving Liddy's pain space.

"A spider in my head," Max says, looking sideways at Liddy, lips spreading into a smile. "That may be one of the best things I've ever heard."

"The thing is, I've thought it so many times," Liddy says. "I've just never thought of saying it to you. I thought you'd think I was weird."

Max tips her head back and laughs. "I do, and I love it. You make my brain sound fun instead of scary. Thank you for that, Liddy. And you, Ali. You called me your hero! I'll never forget it. Thank you both." She grabs each of our hands. "I feel really blessed today."

"We are blessed," I say. "And we were blessed with Feeney when she was here."

"Amen," Liddy says. And there's nothing more to say.

I arrive back at home from Max's, and the house is strangely quiet. "Hello?"

"In here," Drew says from the kitchen.

I come around the corner and see that Drew is cooking. This has happened maybe three times in our marriage.

"It's nothing fancy, but it's comfort food," he says, holding up an empty Kraft Macaroni & Cheese box. "I added edamame to make it more gourmet."

I set my purse down on the ground and settle into one of the seats at our banged up kitchen island. "I've been eating cheese and drinking wine like it's my job," I say.

"Well, it's not quitting time yet," Drew says, filling a glass with my favorite red wine. A black and white checked dishtowel is thrown over his shoulder.

"Where are the kids?"

"Both farmed out at sleepovers. I thought it was probably good for us to get some time alone."

I exhale and choose my words carefully. "Babe, I am so drained. I don't want to fight. And I really don't want to defend my need for my friends." I look up at him to gauge his reaction. He is looking at me and nodding. I look back down and forge ahead. "Mostly I don't want to be told I'm doing things wrong when just trying to get through the day feels like an epic battle."

"I don't want to fight either," he says, putting each of his hands on the side of my head, his large thumbs stroking my face. "But here is what I do want. I know you are going through the hardest time of your life right now. And I want to go through it with you."

His hands on my cheeks feel like home. I lean into his touch. He's always been able to close the gaps between us so swiftly. I toddle, he leaps. "Why?" I ask. "Why would you want to do that?"

He puts his forehead to mine. "Because I love you. And I don't know if you remember, but I said 'for worse.' You've given me a lot of for better. This is for worse."

For a moment, I feel nothing. Then the dam breaks, and I feel everything rushing at me all at once. The anger, the shame, the pain, the shock—it's all right here, right now, and there's nothing to do but cry. I lean into his hands as the tears come.

The force of my crying is so strong that I can't continue to stand. I lean into Drew until he is holding me up, then we both sink to the ground. Drew wraps his whole body around me and I cry from the depths of my being. "Oh my God," I cry into his chest. "Oh my God." I throw my hand against his shoulder as he whispers soothing sounds into my ear. I grab his T-shirt and twist it in both hands as I cry. I've been falling apart since Feeney died, but this feels different, more like hurtling off a cliff.

He holds me and we rock together on the floor of our kitchen, the plastic smell of macaroni and cheese all around us. We're there until the sun starts to set, dimming the light in the room minute by minute. I cry. We rock.

When the tears stop, I feel different. Flat. Empty. But also solid, like a vessel. There's something else, something missing. It takes me a few minutes to realize that the knot of fear that's been twisting in my gut ever since Feeney's death has disappeared. It feels like a kicking, raging animal has been put down. And in its place is silence. Not peace, not by a long shot, but simply the absence of its frenetic energy.

And that's when I understand that I've landed. My free fall of grief has found its bottom. It's my kitchen floor, at 8:11 p.m., and it smells like Kraft macaroni and cheese.

I also realize something else. I haven't just landed, I've been caught. Drew is the reason I could hit this place without more wreckage being wrought.

I'm not sure Feeney had anyone there to catch her.

Max picks me up for Liddy's funeral. I climb into her Subaru and lean over to kiss her cheek.

"Is it okay if we don't talk?" I say.

Max opens her mouth to respond and then closes it, gives me a knowing look, and nods slowly twice.

I mouth but don't say, "Thank you."

I close my eyes as we drive. I'm afraid that the tears will never stop spilling out if I keep them open. I'm not nervous like yesterday—I am steeled like a seasoned soldier heading into battle.

Max fiddles with the radio until it lands on jazz. It's perfect. Every emotion, note, and chord thrown in a pile, to a beat. It's how I feel.

When we get to the church, we get out of the car, and Max immediately grabs my hand and holds tight. The organ is playing again. We stand there for a moment together, listening. It's Leonard Cohen, "Hallelujah." Even with my eyes closed the tears are streaming.

We enter the darkened church and see that there are tea lights flickering. Liddy must have put them here. The effect is beautiful and comforting, just like Liddy herself.

Reverend Peter is seated at the front of the church as yesterday. He has his head down and looks like he's praying.

We sit and listen to the rest of the song. I keep expecting the door to open and Jack to walk in, but it remains firmly shut. It's just Max and me, glued to each other's side, sitting in the fourth row of an otherwise empty church.

There are a few moments of silence after the last chords of the song drift away, then Reverend Peter stands up and moves to the lectern.

His voice is thick with emotion as he speaks. "We're here today to celebrate the life of Liddy Nash. Liddy and I talked yesterday, and she let me know she wanted 'Hallelujah' played today. I had heard the song but had never listened carefully to the lyrics, so I looked them up last night."

He pauses and lowers his head. "Here is the final stanza of the song: 'I did my best, it wasn't much / I couldn't feel, so I tried to touch / I've told the truth, I didn't come to fool you / And even though it all went wrong / I'll stand before the Lord of Song / With nothing on my tongue but Hallelujah.'" He raises his head and looks right at us.

"What more? What more can we desire than to feel, at the end of our time on earth, nothing but gratitude and love? Even if our lives weren't perfect, even if things go wrong, thank God we were given the chance to be here. To live. To love. I want to thank Lydia for the gift of reminding me of that. May this day be blessed for her and all who love her."

He turns to sit, and Max says, loud enough for us all to hear, "Hallelujah."

I squeeze her knee, then turn to stand. As I walk toward the front of the church, I feel oddly calm.

Once again, I pull Feeney's linen-bound journal out of my purse. I open to a page with a lavender Post-it note stuck to it.

"I'm going to start with Feeney's thoughts today, if that's okay." I look down at the page and begin to read.

"'Just came from Liddy's house. Here's the naked, sad truth—nobody ever loved me the way Liddy loves her kids. Watching her with Luke is transcendent. She has nothing but patience, wants nothing but to help him grow and learn and work through his disabilities. My disabilities, while neither physical nor mental, were only ever highlighted and spotlighted by my parents. Love was a word to them, not an action. Liddy is all love; it shines out of her, and her children thrive in it. Lily visibly blooms every time Liddy compliments her, which is often and deservedly so. As a child I died inside with every criticism, of which there were so many, internalizing them until eventually I didn't even need my parents to disapprove of me as I can do it quite well on my own now, thank you very much. But that love of Liddy's for Luke and Lily, as much as it pierces my heart and makes me hurt for what I never had, it heals me too. I see that it's possible. I see in her love for me that I'm worthy. And I am just so fucking grateful.'"

I don't even bother with the apologetic look to Reverend Peter this time. This is Feeney in her own words. Many of them are expletives.

I close the book and slip it back into my bag, pulling out a piece of paper in its place.

I open it up and smooth out the folds on the lectern. "Now for my part."

I look up at Max. She gives me an encouraging nod and wipes her eyes like she's annoyed at her tears.

"It's funny. I wrote this before I found what Feeney had written in her journal. But I feel like we're both saying the same thing in our own words. I have to say, it feels good to feel in sync with Feeney again, even if it's just for a moment." I look back down at my hand-writing. Inhale, exhale, begin.

"Liddy Nash was put on this planet to love. She was so generous with her love that sometimes you'd feel unworthy of it. Here's this beautiful, wise woman radiating love at you and you'd think, 'Are you sure you've got the right person? I'm Ali, remember?' But Liddy made you feel worthy. Even more than worthy—valuable. There was a period during college when I was feeling really alone and depressed. I called Liddy and we talked for a few hours and I hung up feeling better than I had in weeks. But then, the letters started coming. Liddy wrote me a letter every single day for a month. She would fill them with these amazing quotes and poetry and drawings and musings. It was like I had my own personal life guru. Every morning I'd wake up and have the strength and energy to face my day knowing that Liddy was right here with me, literally, in the form of her letters. I don't know if she knew how much I needed her. She gave me my life back. I really think I might have dropped out of school without her."

I take a moment to peer around the church to see if Jack has shown up. I look out at Max and mouth, "Jack?" She shakes her head. I shake my head with anger and look back down.

"Liddy has always given of herself so easily and so readily. Lily loves to dance. So what does Liddy do? She drives her into the city so she can work with the ballet. She lays in bed with Lily every night and listens to the music Lily's dancing to, and they talk about what she's working on. She is her daughter's tireless teammate. I, who can barely wrap my head around my kids' homework, am so inspired by this."

"Luke loves art? Well then, Liddy volunteers to teach classes twice a week at the Down Syndrome Association in Santa Rosa. She brings her talent to these beautiful kids that thrive with her help. And she'll research therapies, talk endlessly to doctors and scientists, but at the same time she'll love her son to the moon and back and never see him as anything other than 100 percent the way he was supposed to be."

I take a moment to balance out all the things I'm feeling right now. Love and admiration for Liddy. Righteous anger at Jack. Gratitude for Max. Grief for Feeney. Then I take another breath; I'm almost there.

"In all of what she gives of herself, my greatest hope for Liddy is that she got enough love in return. Because nobody on earth has ever been more deserving of it. Nobody."

God, I had wanted to stare at Jack while I said that. Instead I give Max a quick nod and then head back to my seat. She gets up and passes me in the aisle.

Max stands in the spot I just vacated, head high and shoulders back. In her hands are a few pages of paper haphazardly torn from one of the many legal pads that are always strewn around her house, relics of her former life.

"Here's the thing about Liddy. She was better than the rest of us. She just was. She was a better friend, a better mom, a better wife. Basically a better human. You'd want to hate her for it but you couldn't. Instead you'd just sit at her feet and bask in her. The minute you'd leave her side you'd wish you could run right back. Because her goodness rubbed off on you. It made dark places lighter. I should know because I tend to hang out in dark places. Liddy would just take my hand and light the way out."

Max stops and closes her eyes, gripping the sides of the lectern. She tucks her chin to her chest and stays like that for several moments. Then she raises her head and steels herself.

"One time I was bitching to her about something or another, something that seemed hugely awful at the time but now of course I can't even remember what it was. Right in the middle of my rant, Liddy grabbed my hand hard, looked me right in the eyes and said, 'Think of all the beauty still left around you and be happy.' I was so confused and annoyed. I think I said the non-abbreviated version of 'WTF?'"

This time I actually hear Father Peter chuckle.

"Then she said, 'That's an Anne Frank quote.' Well, shit fire to save matches, if that's not the needle on the record player. She didn't lecture me, she didn't dismiss my feelings, she just gave me a dose of perspective that knocked all my self-righteousness right out. I still say that to myself when I am getting riled up about something unimportant, which is basically daily."

Max smiles to herself and moves on to her next page of sunshine yellow legal paper.

"I have learned so much by simply watching Liddy live her life. She was an excellent teacher, though she didn't even realize she was teaching me anything. Like a baby animal that watches its mother and mirrors their behavior, I would try to match my inner strength to hers. I followed along behind her on shaky baby legs, but I got stronger and better because I learned from the best. This is how I know how amazing her kids are going to be. Imagine having Liddy as your actual mother, oh my God. If there's such a thing as reincarnation I want to come back as Liddy's kid."

Max stops and looks down, swallowing hard. She is fighting herself, I can tell. Her voice is hoarse when she starts again. "So, yeah. Liddy was better than all of us. But anyone who has ever known her is better for having been loved by her. And that is the gift she has given us all."

Max comes back and sits down next to me, bracing herself with her hand on my knee. Reverend Peter moves to the altar. "The guest of honor wanted me to let you know that she'll see you back at her house. Let's end in prayer."

We lower our heads.

"Lord, make me an instrument of Your peace. Where there is hatred, let me sow love; where there is injury, pardon; where there is doubt, faith; where there is despair, hope; where there is darkness, light; where there is sadness, joy. In Your name we pray, Amen."

I've heard that prayer a million times, but today I realize that it sounds like it was written for Liddy. It's what she does. She is an instrument of peace. Peace and love.

We file ourselves out of the pew and walk toward the car. "So, can we talk now?" Max asks.

"Yes, sorry. I just wasn't sure I could hold it together."

"If anyone gets it Ali, it's me. I'm just not very good at shutting up."

"You did quite well, thank you."

"Do you think Liddy knows that Jack didn't show?" Max asks, looking at me and raising an eyebrow.

"We'll find out soon enough," I say. "Let's go see our girl."

We're walking up to Liddy's front porch when she opens the door and opens her arms wide. Her makeup has been cried off, her eyes are puffy, but her smile is full of love. We move together into her arms and group hug. As many of these as we have had in the past couple of weeks, we still need more. It's a reminder that we're all still here, solid and alive and together.

"I love you guys," she says into our collective hair.

"We love you too," we say back with muffled voices.

We move apart and wipe eyes, sniff noses, fix hair. "Come on in," Liddy says.

The wine has already been poured, there is a board on the counter full of cheese and nuts and olives. A sapphire blue glazed bowl full of crusty bread sits next to it.

Max and I sit directly across from the food and dig in. Max looks over at Liddy, and with a mouth full of bread she asks, "So, how was it?"

Liddy shakes her head and opens her mouth but nothing comes out at first. "I'm not even sure what to say, other than I'm still taking it all in, I think."

I hesitate, but then go for it. "Where was Jack?"

She looks right at me, a picture of coolness. "I don't know and I don't care."

My eyebrows shoot up. "Really?"

"Really. I'm sitting at my own funeral, hearing you two talk about my capacity for love, which I had never fully considered before, and the person who is supposed to love me most in the world can't even be bothered to show up." She nods her head slowly and looks off into the distance. "Yeah. I think I'm over it."

Max and I look at each other. "What are you going to do?" Max asks.

"I'm going to tell him exactly that. There's really nothing more to say."

"When?" I ask.

"Whenever he decides to grace us with his presence."

As if summoned, we hear keys in the door. A wave of panic rises up in my belly. I swallow my food and shoot a glance over at Liddy, but she is as calm as a statue of Buddha.

Jack walks in the front door and stops short. "Oh, hey ladies." He looks like a sheepish child as he deposits his keys in a rustic wooden tray in the entry.

"Where have you been?" Liddy says, her head tilted to the side, so calm, so scary.

"Oh, here and there. Meetings. You know," he says.

"No, I don't know," she says.

Max and I are looking back and forth between them like we're at a match at Wimbledon.

"I've been busy babe, you know that," he says, flipping through the mail, clearly on the spot and annoyed.

Liddy watches him like a predator waiting to pounce. She's

completely still, but every muscle in her body is spring-loaded. If she had a tail it would be slowly flicking, just at the tip.

"You didn't come to my funeral."

He glances up in surprise. Then he looks back down at the mail and guffaws. "Jesus, Liddy, it wasn't even really a funeral."

I see a beautiful, determined hint of a smile on her lips but her eyes are deadly.

"You're right. It wasn't. And this isn't really a marriage."

He goes white and drops the mail onto the hall table. He looks between her and us, her and us. He is trapped and I'm glad.

"What are you talking about?"

"You heard me. I'd like you to leave. We'll talk later about what happens next."

"You can't be serious, Liddy."

"Leave."

"This is ridiculous."

"Leave."

"This is *my* house."

"Leave."

"Where exactly am I supposed to go?"

"I don't care. Just leave."

"Oh, this is real cool, Liddy. You know what? You know what? I'd love to go. I've been wanting to leave anyway!"

"Is that so?"

"All you care about is the kids and your friends. When was the last time you even paid any attention to me?"

"You don't need attention from me. You get that from plenty of other women."

He starts to flush. I can see a vein starting to stand out on his forehead. I am barely breathing.

He inhales, then spits out, "Maybe that's because I don't like *what you've become.*" The way he says this, eyes narrowed, nose flared, is so revoltingly condescending it makes my scalp prickle.

"What I've . . .?" All the air has gone out of the room. Liddy is suddenly gaping, grasping, trying to gain a foothold in the face of a slimy argument. Her hands fly up to her temples, and she closes her eyes and digs her fingers in deep. She breathes out, then starts talking in a low, calm, threatening voice. "What have I *become*, Jack? A wife? A mother? Forty-four years old? One hundred and sixty pounds? This isn't what I've become, this is who I *am*. Maybe you should take some of that judgment and take a good hard look at yourself. Are you proud of who you are?"

Jack just stares at her, the muscles in his neck taut with fury.

"If there's anything I've *become*, Jack, it's sick and tired of your bullshit. And I really don't care if you don't like it." At this point she sounds simply resigned and tired. But she is definitely the victor in this battle.

Jack turns on his heel with a disgusted look on his face and walks right back out the door, slamming it behind him like a petulant child. Max and I sit, frozen, eyes huge. Right as we start to turn towards Liddy, the door opens and just his arm snakes in, grabbing his car keys awkwardly and slamming the door yet again.

Max and I look at Liddy in stunned silence. She takes a sip of her wine and closes her eyes, breathing in deeply through her nose. The sound of a clock ticking is coming from somewhere within the house.

"Liddy. You are my hero," Max finally says in a breathless voice.

Liddy exhales and opens her eyes. "That was a long time coming."

"I wish Feeney had been here for that," I say.

"God, me too. What do you think she would have said?" Liddy asks, eyes wide, as if she's just now processing the scene.

"I know," Max says. "She would have instantly broken out in 'Hit the Road Jack.'"

Liddy and I laugh weakly, and we all start singing a wobbly rendition of the song. "'Hit the road Jack and don't you come back no more, no more, no more, no more / Hit the road Jack and don't you come back no more!'" We're slap happy with shock and adrenaline.

"I still can't believe what just happened. You were so strong," I say, gripping Liddy's shoulder.

She takes a deep breath, centering herself again. "I've been trying to keep it together for so long I don't even know what to do next," she says. "I didn't want a broken family for the kids. But this family has been broken for a very long time. What I need to give the kids is a strong mother. And I can't do that when I'm being walked all over every single day."

"Amen," Max says.

"I think what you do next is call a divorce attorney," I say.

"That's the first thing I did after coming home from the church today," she says, looking at us with a righteous, self-satisfied glint in her eye.

"Oh my God, Liddy, who are you?" Max says.

She closes her eyes and smiles, then opens them and shrugs. "I guess sometimes you need to die in order to wake the fuck up." Then she drains her glass. We fill it right back up for her.

Today is my funeral.

Drew surprised me and booked me a room last night at the Hotel Healdsburg so I could have some time alone before it happens. It's a huge splurge. I had just witnessed Jack be so oblivious to Liddy's feelings, and here is my husband handing me a gift basket full of empathy. He packed me off with a chilled bottle of my favorite wine and told me he'd see me at the church. I think I loved him more in that moment than on the day I married him.

I'm lying in the sumptuous bed playing with the million-count sheet with my fingers. There is a steady stream of tears making their slow way down my face, rushing from a place of every possible emotion—grief, love, anger, gratitude, pain, and things I can't even place.

I left Max and Liddy with the journal yesterday. I have no idea if I will hear from Feeney today or not.

How exactly do you prepare for your own funeral?

Turning on the TV seems inappropriate; I can't concentrate enough to read; if I try to write I'll break down sobbing. I could go for a walk but I'm afraid I'll run into someone I know and I have no clue how I'd react. For all I know I'd give them a hug and then punch them in the face. That's how wide the pendulum of my emotions is swinging right now.

I get up and pad into the bathroom to pee. At least that's one activity that's not fraught with feelings. I glance over at the giant concrete bathtub and immediately I know there's no place I'd rather be.

I fill it with the hottest water I can stand and slowly ease myself in, relishing the sting on my skin, needing the pain to take away my thoughts. I sink down as far as I can, leaving only my eyes and nose exposed. I am surrounded, comforted, floating, crying. I am back in the womb, I am afloat in a lake, I am the whole freaking ocean. I am the stars, I am the air, I am Feeney, I am me.

I am me and today is my funeral.

I sit up with a start, gasping for breath, wiping water out of my eyes. I get out and stand naked in front of the mirror, pink as a piglet, steam rising off every inch of my skin. I see myself, not, per usual, as someone who could stand to lose a few pounds, who is searching for a new wrinkle, who probably needs to pluck, but as a full-fledged person. A person who has lost something irretrievable but who has found something, too. Herself. I lean forward and press my lips to my lips. I rest my forehead against the glass, close my eyes and say a silent prayer of thanks to be alive. Alive and well and here. On the day of my funeral.

I move through the stages of getting myself dressed and made up as if I'm in a dream. I so rarely go through this process by myself, in silence, and my quiet solitude adds to the surreality of it all. Everything makes what seems like amplified noise—the slide of the wand out of my mascara tube, the rustling of the crepe of my dress, the pulling of bristles through my wet hair. When I blow my hair dry, I can barely stand the scream of the air in my ear. My senses are turned up to eleven.

Finally I am ready—or as ready as I'll ever be. I look at myself one last time in the mirror. I put my shoulders back. Then I turn and walk out the door, duffle in hand, eyes finally dry. That said, I made sure to use waterproof mascara.

I pull up to the church and park on the side street. Reverend Peter comes out to greet me. He pulls me into a warm hug. He smells like a mixture of Old Spice and old church. It's comforting.

He pulls back and looks at me, still holding me at the elbows. "Ready for this?"

I smile and say, "Yeah. Actually, I am."

"Okay, let's get you settled."

"I have some flowers in the back of the car that I'd love to put on the altar," I say.

I open up the rear door of my car and pull out a huge arrangement of green carnations. Devon and I spent two hours dying them yesterday after I got back from Liddy's. My fingernails are still a distinct shade of lime.

"This is a first," Reverend Peter says as he takes the hideous arrangement from me.

"All of this is a first," I say as I follow him into the chapel.

He places the flowers on the altar, where they practically glow. He takes me over to Constance's chair, which has remained in the same hidden spot for the past three days.

"Need anything else, Ali?"

I shake my head no; I don't trust my voice right now. I give him a small, grateful smile. He smiles back and says, "Have a good funeral."

I sit back and close my eyes. Eventually I hear the organist settle herself on her bench. Reverend Peter had emailed me a couple of days ago asking me what song I'd like her to play. I chose Kenny Loggins, "Celebrate Me Home." For Feeney, for Max, for all of us. Over the past two weeks, Mr. Loggins has gone from being a cheesy '80s artist to a masterful poet in one fell swoop. I was concerned that the organist might not know any Kenny Loggins, for obvious reasons, but Reverend Peter wrote me back that not only did she indeed know the song, her cousin once dated Kenny Loggins. Of course she had. Feeney would be so jealous.

The organ starts to play. I hear the doors open, people moving about in the church. I don't move a muscle.

The music stops playing; someone blows their nose. Reverend Peter stands up and says beautiful words, all of which wash over me and through me and if you ask me to remember any of them tomorrow, I promise I won't be able to. It's as if he is singing in Latin. But it leaves me blanketed in calm. Ready for what's next, whatever that is.

I hear footsteps come up the aisle. They are strong, heavy. I hear Drew clear his throat, then start talking.

"What I wish my wife knew, more than anything, was that I saw her. I saw who she was, who she wanted to be, what made her afraid, what made her strong. I saw her struggle, I saw her soar, I saw her brush Devon's hair with a tenderness that brought tears to my eyes. I saw her put herself aside for her kids, for me, for her friends. I saw her get angry about injustice, about Planned Parenthood shut downs, about my inability to take out the trash before it got smelly. I saw her teach Lachlan how to throw a curveball because I didn't know how and she did. I saw her cry; I saw her kick ass. I saw her want more for herself; I saw how I wasn't always enough for her but I also saw her be grateful for what she had. I saw her love her friends and her family with a fierceness and a loyalty that I didn't know was possible. I saw her break open. I saw her doing whatever she could do to heal. I saw everything. That's what I wish she knew. I wish she knew I saw her. And that I loved everything I saw."

His voice breaks as he finishes. I am barely breathing. I didn't even realize I was crying but there are salty tears on my lips when I lick them. Then I see his face come into view, he is tall enough that he can just barely see me when he turns. Very quietly, eyes full of love, he says to me, "I see you." Then he turns and moves out of view.

Marriage is odd. You filter through a sea of people and pick one, one human being, to tether yourself to for the rest of time. You pick for a variety of reasons—love, lust, compatibility, religious preference, takeout food preference, lack of too many annoying habits, nice fingernails—it's an unending list of vague checked boxes. And you start off on the ultimate high, an enormous party where you are the center of attention and affection and everybody wants you to succeed. Imagine if that was how you started a job, say, or any lengthy endeavor. Suffice to say at some point you're going to look around and think, oh. This is it? Grocery lists and taxes and toothbrushing and making sure to always, always use the bathroom spray. You're happy, you're content, but there's no question that the vast majority of it all is lodged firmly in the mundane.

But then there are moments when you are so moved by this person you spend so much time meandering about with that you can hardly breathe. You are moved in the same way you can be when you see a breathtaking piece of art or hear a beautiful song sung by a pure voice. It doesn't seem possible to feel so profoundly touched by something manmade, but you are—by some gesture made by this man, whose life is so attached to your own that you don't remember what it used to be like to do all those mundane things alone. And you are so grateful that he chose you and you didn't do anything too terrible to fuck it up that you close your eyes and thank the universe, the gods, the random friend, whoever and whatever is responsible for your togetherness. This is one of those times. And you think, *I'll take it. I'll take it all.*

I hear a small, muffled cough, and I know immediately it's Liddy coming up the aisle of the church. I let my head rest back against the chair and close my eyes.

"I met Ali the summer between eighth and ninth grade. I had just moved here from Arizona, and I was terrified to start at a new school. I had grown two inches and two cup sizes in a very short amount of time and was extremely uncomfortable in my newly voluptuous skin. My mom was constantly telling me to cover myself up in front of my father, so I took to wearing clothes that were a few sizes too big. I was in hiding basically every minute of every day of my life. I had no friends and no self-confidence and no idea how to get either one.

I used to go to the library a lot to escape my house and my anxiety. It was my safe spot.

"I was sitting there with my nose in a book one day when a shadow came over me. I looked up and there stood Ali. I remember my first impression of her was that she was very blonde and very tall—in retrospect I think it was just the lighting and my vantage point. She said, 'Hi, I'm Ali.' Three words. 'Hi, I'm Ali.' But with those three words, Ali changed my life forever. She sat across from me and asked me about myself, making me feel interesting. She wanted to know about me, what I liked to read, what music I listened to, where I lived, why she had never seen me around before. With every answer she handed me back a small piece of myself, burnished and polished and newly twinkly. She laughed when I made a dumb joke; she told me about her friend Max; she invited me to a movie with them that weekend. *She invited me to a movie that weekend.* Such a small thing. Such a momentous occasion. We saw *The Naked Gun* and laughed until we peed our pants.

"I feel like everything that's good about who I am is because of Ali. I often think of what would have happened if she didn't come up to me in the library that day. It would have been very easy for me to stay lost. But Ali found me. And when Ali found me, I found myself. I found my voice, I followed my passion for art, and I got my first real boyfriend, much to my mother's chagrin. I wore clothes that fit; I stopped hiding. This was all because Ali made me feel like I had something to offer the world. She helped me see myself, and, for the first time in my life, I actually liked what I saw. It has been one of the greatest gifts of my life."

Liddy's words simmer inside me. I remember meeting her that day, of course I do, but my memory of it is far less meaningful. I was simply curious about her. Having grown up with the same group of kids my whole life, she was like a shiny new object that I wanted to inspect from every angle. I remember being afraid that I was bugging her. These are the things you would never know, would never think to ask. The knowledge of Liddy then and Liddy now fills me with a warm, happy, spreading sensation, like I just drank brandy. I realize that I'm deeply proud of her, proud of my fourteen-year-old self, and proud of our nearly thirty years of friendship. I had never fully thought about it before.

I hear one set of feet retreating and another coming towards me. There is some muffled self-arranging at the lectern, then Max's voice comes through in all its gravelly glory.

"Ali Stirling was my rock. She was the first person I told about my rages, how scary and uncontrollable they were. We were barely fourteen, I think, at the time. It had been happening for a couple of years at that point, and I had just started seeing the first of many psychiatrists. I felt damaged and weird. 'What if I'm crazy?' I asked her, legitimately terrified. She grabbed my hands and looked me in the eye and said, 'Then I love crazy. Because I love you, Max. And I will always be here for you.' I will never forget it. Not even my parents said that to me at the time. They were scared; they wanted to fix me. But not Ali. She just told me she loved me and that I couldn't shake her. And she was true to her word. Lord knows I tried to scare her off over the years, as I have with everyone in the small group of people I truly love, but if I'm being totally honest, Ali was the first one I wholeheartedly believed could not be chased away. Because she was the first to accept me for who I am, whether or not it's who I wanted to be."

She pauses. Then she sniffs, exhales, and keeps going. "The other thing I should say about Ali is that she was fun as hell. I took the absolute worst school photo junior year in high school, and that thing has shown up somewhere odd at least a couple times every year. It's been in Spence's underwear drawer, stuck to my rearview mirror, slipped into a pocket of one of my jackets, sent anonymously to me in the mail. God knows how many copies of it she has and when she made them, but it makes me laugh until I cry every time it shows up. She's someone you know you'll have fun with doing absolutely nothing, which has always been one of my favorite things to do with her. Absolutely nothing. Because she would always make it something. I am thankful every day to have had someone in my life that could make me feel less bad crazy while bringing out my good crazy. Now, that's a friend."

There is silence for several seconds. I am basking in the echoes of Max's voice, her words. I feel languid and outside of my body. Hearing myself talked about in third person and past tense, I get the feeling that I'm not actually here, just kind of floating. I look around to ground myself, bite a hangnail until it bleeds.

"I have one more thing," Max says. I sit up, suddenly my every cell on alert.

I hear the riffing of book pages, and I know I'm about to hear from Feeney. My heart races, my palms break out in sweat, and I feel lightheaded and a little nauseous. I grip the arms of Constance's chair to steady myself, the bead of blood bright on my thumb.

"'My sisters suck. When I was young, I would look at sisters who were close and kind to each other with a longing that was borderline obsessive. It was so very close, just the next bedroom over, and yet so very far. I hoped that one of my sisters would turn a corner and turn into a human being that I would want to share my thoughts and feelings with. But the opposite happened. They older they got, the less they cared about me and the more they cared about themselves and material things. I saw a nature show once about flamingos, and it was like I suddenly understood my own family. Garish birds that clump together and stand on one leg for no apparent reason? Yep, sounds like the Fox sisters. I have had more out-of-body experiences sitting in a room with them thinking to myself, *How is it possible that I share genetic material with flamingos?* When I met Ali, it was like I had found one of my own species for the first time.

"'Ali is the sister I always wanted but never had. She gets me and I get her. It was so easy to get close to her that it makes me even more perplexed about how odd my sisters are. I already feel like I've known her my whole life, whereas the people I have known that long feel like utter strangers. I'm jealous of Max and Liddy that they've had her longer. It's not fair. But I am comforted in knowing we'll be friends until we're old and saggy and wearing tracksuits. Fuck that, I'm never wearing a tracksuit.

"'I have days when I feel like I'm alone on the planet. Anxiety, terrible thoughts, frightening memories that I can't tell are real or something I dreamed. On days like that it feels like me against the world. Very little can bring me any comfort except the thought of Ali, knowing she's on the same planet with me. I can close my eyes and picture her face and I will start my slow, winding descent back to reality. It's going to be okay. I've got Ali and Ali's got me. It's my mantra. I've never told her this. I think she'd think I was insane. I just need her, it's as simple as that. They way I need things like air and water, things that are easy to take for granted but without which I'd be a desperate, clawing animal.'"

I hear the soft thump of the journal being closed.

I sit for a moment, stunned and immobile. I am in a state of numb shock. As it starts to wear off however, I feel a spreading of real, physical pain. I gasp as if I've been hit in the stomach and double over. I feel like I've lost a piece of myself, a limb or a vital organ. I don't know how I will even stand up from this chair much less move on with my life.

Then I feel a warm hand on my back, and I look up to see three blurry faces I love peering down at me. A hand, I don't know whose, reaches down and pulls me to my feet.

"I didn't do enough," I say, sobbing into someone's shoulder. It smells like Max. "I didn't do enough." I can barely get the words out.

I am enveloped by arms and hushed words and a circle of love. I lean into it until I am basically being held upright. I feel like I'll never stop crying. I cry and cry and our huddled mass sways and sways.

And then, after several minutes, I stop. It's as if a faucet has been turned off, like I'm fresh out of tears. I'm breathing as heavily as if I just stopped running, but I'm not even bearing my own weight. I lean back until I'm back on my feet, back in my body.

Max reaches over and pushes wet hair out of my eyes, tucking it behind my ear.

"I knew that would be hard," she says. "But I also knew you needed to hear it."

I nod, not yet sure I can speak. Drew has one arm wrapped tight around my back and shoulder like a brace.

"I wish I had done more," I say quietly. It's the saddest, smallest thing to say. But it's all I have.

"We could all 'I wish' ourselves to death, but it won't do any good. I think those two words need to erase themselves from our minds and mouths. No more I wishes. Only I wills," Max says.

"I will never leave you," Drew says, bending his head to look me in the eyes.

"Me neither," Max and Liddy say at precisely the same time.

I laugh quietly, it's a relief to feel at least a tiny splinter of happiness. "I love you guys. Thank you," I say. I lean in for one more group huddle. "Now get me the hell out of here."

We pull apart and turn toward the front of the church. Reverend

Peter is standing off to the side. He smiles at us. "Can I say a final prayer for you all?"

I smile and nod and he holds his hands out to us. Before I know it we are in a tight circle holding hands. He lowers his head, we all follow suit.

"Lord, there is so much we don't know. That is the weight of the earthly world we carry around with us. It causes us to feel fear, anxiety, pain, grief, anger—all our burdensome negative human emotions. We don't know why Feeney is gone. We don't know what pain she wanted to escape. We don't know how many days we have here, either. And the hard truth is, we won't know until the moment You bring us home.

"But You ask us to have faith. You know it's the hardest thing to ask, but You ask it anyway. Our faith will be constantly tested, but if we are able to hold fast to it, we can find grace. I see Max, Liddy, and Ali all searching for something, tossing caution and the status quo and their fragile emotions to the wind in order to find a foothold. I pray they find it. And I have a feeling that if they do, they'll also find strength in faith. And most importantly, that they will find Feeney again.

"Lastly, I want to thank You, Lord, for the gift these women have given to me this past week. I am a different person than I was one week ago. I preside over weddings all the time; it's one of my favorite parts of my job. But no act of love and commitment has moved me more than these three women celebrating and honoring each other in the face of such great pain. I have a lot to learn, Lord. I thank You for sending me these incredible teachers. Amen."

Nobody moves or lifts our heads. There is a small pool of tears on the church's dark wood floor beneath me. I haven't wanted to let go of the hands on either side of me to brush them off my face.

Finally Max, who is to the left of Reverend Peter, drops his hand and throws herself into him in a full body hug. He looks startled at first but then he smiles and hugs her back. Liddy and I move in and practically push the poor man to the floor. "Thank you, thank you," it's coming from all of us over and over. When we pull back there are mascara marks all over his white button down shirt.

"No, ladies. Thank you," he says in a low voice. Then he turns and walks out of the church.

Drew is standing back, watching us with his head cocked to the side and a smile dancing on his lips. "You guys are something else, you know that?"

"Yes, we do," Max says. "We're just not sure what."

I blow every ounce of air out of my lungs. "That was the best and worst thing I've ever been through in my life. I'm completely wrung out."

Liddy puts her arm around me. "I'm pretty sure there isn't a human emotion we haven't experienced in the past week. Let's go back to your house, kick off our shoes and pop a bottle."

"Yes, please," I say, and we walk out of the church doors together, me holding Drew's hand, Liddy's arm around my shoulder, Max marching a few steps ahead of us.

Back at my house, the first thing I do is head to the bathroom to assess the damage to my face. The face that looks back at me from my mirror is my new one, eyes puffy, skin blotchy, lips plumped up and bruised looking. It's like a Picasso painting of my regular face. They're all the same features, they're just blown up and more colorful than usual.

I don't mind that I don't look like myself because I don't feel like myself. How exactly is one supposed to look after attending her own funeral? I look like I've been through something, which I certainly have.

I stare into my own eyes for minutes on end, the water running the whole time. There's a water crisis in California—what I'm doing is horribly irresponsible. I don't care. I'll conserve water tomorrow. Everything goes back to normal tomorrow. The new normal, whatever that is.

There's no more makeup on my face left to fix. I open my makeup drawer and stare absentmindedly into it. I close it and simply run my fingers through my hair. I turn to leave and get hit with a sudden, powerful wave of grief. I press my hands into my eyes and cry silently until it passes, just a few minutes but they feel interminable. I take another look in the mirror. There she is, I know that girl. The Picasso me.

I open the door and walk out to my living room. Liddy and Max have arrived while I was in bathroom self-exile. Liddy is nestled in the crook of my navy velvet sofa, the one Feeney talked me into buying. Max is sitting oppressed-Indigenous-person style on my zebra-striped ottoman, which Feeney always pronounced "zebra" in a way that made it rhyme with "Deborah." She said that's how they said it on safari, though she'd never been. Will never go.

The new normal. I'm not ready for it to start yet.

Liddy pats the seat next to her on the sofa, and I sink down into it, right as Drew rounds the corner with a bottle of wine in one hand and three glasses held by their stems in the other like an abstract glass flower.

"Hi," he says to me.

"I love you," I say back.

He flushes, and I realize that I don't say that very often to him in front of other people. How stupid of me. I make a mental note to fix that.

I will never forget a moment I had when Lachlan was an infant. We had only been home from the hospital a couple of days, and as I was sitting in bed nursing him, our mangy and beloved one-ear-up-one-ear-down rescue terrier, Scooter, nosed her way in to the bedroom. I looked over at her and my first thought was, "Oh my God, she's a dog." Before I had an actual human child, I pretty much thought she was one. But now that I had this beautiful baby boy in my arms, as beloved as Scooter was, she didn't even come close. I've been reminded of this lately as I look at Drew. With the light of Feeney no longer shining, I find myself seeing him and thinking, "Oh my God, you're my person." It makes me feel guilty on both sides. Like, was I giving Feeney more of myself than I was giving my husband? And then, does that mean I miss Feeney less?

As if to highlight my newfound gratitude for him, Drew sets us each up with a glass of my favorite rosé then bustles out of the room.

Max raises her glass and says, "To the weirdest and most wondrous week I have ever had."

There's not much more to say so we all clink. Then we sit and sip in silence for several minutes, which is not very much like us.

At some point Drew comes in with a huge tray of cheese and deli meats and grapes and crackers and plops it down in front of us. We lunge at it like we haven't eaten in weeks, though it seems that all we've been doing lately is eating and drinking. That and crying.

He starts to leave, but I grab him by the tail of his shirt and tug on it. He smiles at me, sits down, and starts to load up a cracker.

"Listening to you guys today, it was so incredible." I'm not so much talking as simply thinking aloud. Whatever is popping into my head is coming right out my mouth, I don't have the energy to filter. "The things you remember, the things that stand out, I remember them all, too, I just didn't know how meaningful they were to you. It made me feel proud deep down, of myself and of what we've sustained all these years. I mean, loving people isn't easy. But losing them is way worse. And it's a reminder to hold tight to the ones you've got. So consider this fair warning. I'm holding onto you all tight. I'm barnacle-ing myself to you guys for life."

"I'm cool with that," Drew says, his mouth full of meat, cheese, and cracker. "I think it's time for me to go do man things." He winks at me and hustles off.

"I don't want this day to end," I say. "I don't want to wake up tomorrow facing the rest of our lives without her and nothing left to distract me. All this crazy speech writing and flower-dying has been keeping me sane."

"I know. Every time I think about all this coming to an end I feel like I need to breathe into a paper bag," Max says.

"Can I ask you a question, Max?" I ask.

"You just did. But of course."

"What's it like? What happens when your mind betrays your ability to control it?"

"Oh man." Max sits for a few moments looking off into the distance, her gaze soft yet troubled. "It's like you're two people, or sometimes even more, and everyone's at war. You can't get any perspective because you're both sides of the war, you're the offense and the defense at the same time. You don't know who to root for because they're both you. You're winning and losing every minute of every day. And there's never a break—there's never a moment to take a break, wave a white flag, retreat to get some rest. It's just a silent, exhausting, never-ending battle. But somehow you're expected to go about your day, have inane conversations with strangers, drive normally, put on two shoes that match. You're in hell, and all you want to do is put your head down and kick and scream, and instead you have to go grocery shopping and not forget the flour tortillas."

We are quietly processing this when she adds, "And when you're in the middle of that, killing yourself sounds like a complete fucking relief."

"What kept you from trying?" Liddy asks.

"Who says I didn't?" Max locks eyes with Liddy, who brings a hand to her mouth and audibly gasps.

"Max . . ." I whisper. "When?"

Max rakes her hands through her wild hair and stares at the ground as she talks. "I was so fucked up. It was about six years ago. I took too much of my Valium and drank a bottle of wine. The minute I started to fall asleep, I panicked and called Spence. He rushed me to the hospital, and they pumped my stomach. I was mortified when I got out and made him swear not to ever tell anyone." She looks up at us. "I'm so sorry I never told you," she says, then she puts her face in her hands and starts to cry. Actually, it's more like heave-sobbing.

We draw to her like magnets. Liddy rubs her back while I basically drape myself across her back. After several minutes she reaches up to grab a napkin and blow her nose.

"It's been weighing on me so much ever since Feeney died," she said. "I couldn't decide if her death made it better or worse to tell you now."

"Max, there's never a bad or good time to tell us something like that." I give her shoulder a Max-strength grip. "We love you. We need to know when you're hurting. You have to give us that."

"If there's anything we need to take away from Feeney's death, it's that we can't keep things from the people we love. Especially the hard stuff," Liddy says.

"I feel like an asshole for not telling you before. But when Feeney died it was a total slap in the face. Not being honest with you is not being honest with myself. I didn't want to admit what I had done. But I did it. I did it. I did it and I have to live with it. Or rather, I get to live with it because I didn't die, and for that I am thankful every single day. More now than ever before."

"I'm so thankful for that too," I say. The idea that I came so close to losing Max, too, sends an ice-cold trickle down my spine. Two of my best friends have been suicidal, and I never had a clue. How is that possible?

Later, after Max and Liddy have left and Drew has gotten the kids settled in bed and is reading in his favorite overstuffed plaid armchair, I climb into his lap. I curl myself into him and snake my arms around his warm, soap-scented chest. I turn my face to the side so my ear is pressed against his heart and its steady beat is a mantra.

"Well, hello," he says.

"Shhhh," I say.

It's the only place I want to be. Eventually when he goes back to reading, he just extends his arms out further to compensate for the human in his lap. He rests his chin on my head and we stay like this for the better part of an hour.

I'm going over the day, the week, the month, my life, in my head in no particular order. It's like a slideshow carousel that got mixed up in a move. Feeney and I playing gin rummy in a rainstorm and inexplicably talking like old-timey gangsters. Me as a teenager overhearing my parents talk about the suicide of a friend's son; my dad calling

him a "selfish asshole." Drew bringing Lachlan to the hospital after
Devon was born, his tiny spirit crushed when he finally understood
that she was not a puppy. Max, Liddy, Feeney, and I emptying our
coin purses out with wishes in the town fountain after several glasses
of wine. Max and I rearranging Feeney's Christmas lawn reindeer
into compromising positions under the cover of night even though
Liddy didn't approve. Caroline and Hannah sitting in a church pew
listening to people they're related to yet barely know talk about their
mother. Me staring at lime green carnations while listening to my
husband talk about me with so much love in the third person. It's like
acupuncture with emotions instead of needles.

Eventually I turn my head and look up at Drew. "Take me to bed."

And he does.

The Time I Saw Her Again

Five days after

We're in Max's living room again, together. I can't figure out why Feeney is here, but I'm so flooded with relief I don't care. Max and Liddy are talking with their heads together, lost in a conversation Feeney and I aren't part of.

"I thought you were dead," I say, reaching for Feeney. "Oh my God it was awful." I pull her into a desperate hug, and she is solid and smells like she always does, a mix of face cream and the signature perfume she orders from Paris.

When our hug ends, she does her standard extra squeeze and then pulls away, moving her gaze to Max and Liddy. She still hasn't said anything, which is unusual.

My senses tune into their conversation.

"Ever since Feeney died I've been having horrible dreams," Max is saying.

I lunge toward them, frantic with news. "She didn't die! You guys, look, she's right here!"

Max looks at where I'm gesturing with a bewildered look on her face.

"What the hell are you talking about, Ali?"

"I thought she died too, but we're wrong, see?" Some part of me knows this is insane but it's throttled by giddy relief.

Liddy looks at me like I've grown a third head. "Are you okay?"

Feeney speaks, her voice is clear as a bell. "They can't see me, Ali."

"What?" I'm standing in the middle of Max's living room and nothing in the world makes sense.

Max and Liddy have turned back to their tête-à-tête. I spin around and look at Feeney.

"I did die." Her crystal blue eyes are full of sadness and pity and something else, a knowledge or understanding of something I can't touch.

"But you're here talking to me." My eyes are wide with fear and I'm shaking my head, relief turning into a slow spread of dread.

"I'm always here," she says. "I'm here all the time. I can see you but you can't see me. It took me a while to figure that out. You were all talking about me like I wasn't there, and I kept yelling, 'I'm right here!' Finally I understood what was going on."

"So you really are dead," I say, already recoiling from the terrible answer.

"Yes. But did you hear me? I'm still here."

I close my eyes. I have so many questions for her. I need to find out why she killed herself, if she suffered, what to tell her girls, what happens when you die. I need to know if we're all going to be okay. I'm sorting through every question in my brain at warp speed, my mouth a few frustrating seconds behind. I open my eyes to look her and she's gone.

I spin around. Max and Liddy are gone too. "No!" I shout. "No!"

I sit straight up in bed with a gasp, one hand squeezing the sheet, the other holding my chest, feeling my heart thrashing around in my chest like a caged bird.

I look around my bedroom at the dark shapes around me, of Drew, of laundry, of books and magazines. It's all so earthly and present. I tip my head back against the headboard and try to will myself back to the place I just left, but I already know it's fruitless.

But there's something new in me, a seed of understanding, a layer of pain that is starting to close over like a scab—irritating and raw yet alive with the tacit assurance of eventual healing. I can't tell if I welcome this or not. The only thing I know for certain is that I will tell Max and Liddy about this dream tomorrow. And that I feel the tiniest bit less alone.

The day after my funeral, I do nothing friend- nor funeral-related. I drive the kids to their various camps and take a yoga class I've been meaning to take for months. I sit in a café drinking cappuccino and people watching. I go home and clean out my bathroom drawers. I pick up the kids and take them to get frozen yogurt. At home, I goad and poke at them to make their beds, already. I make meatloaf. I hum.

When Drew gets home, I kiss him multiple times on the lips in front of the kids and tell him how much I love him. He blushes and the kids say "ew." We eat dinner as a family, and I listen to the kids bicker with a lazy, detached smile. Drew catches my eye and mouths, "You okay?" I stretch my smile a little wider and nod slowly, two times. I don't think about Feeney or Max or Liddy at all, for the first time in weeks. I am present, here at my nicked and well-loved table, surrounded by piles of things I need to deal with and the detrius of a life with kids, forms to fill out, bills to pay, magazines to flip through and then toss, crumbs and pencils and barrettes and stray coins. I am home.

That night I want Drew inside me like I did when we first started dating, when I called up Max and said, "I don't want to eat, I don't want to sleep, all I want to do is have sex with Drew Stirling. Is there something wrong with me?" Knowing, of course, that Max would green light this behavior. I can't get enough of him, can't get close enough, can't absorb him enough. We writhe and sweat and make the odd body noises we once were self-conscious about and now no longer hear. I come and come and I still want him inside me. When he finally peters out, reluctantly, apologetically, after performing valiantly for over an hour, I tuck myself into his belly so I am practically enclosed by his sleeping body, even though it's hot and I don't like to cuddle.

For the first time maybe ever, I think about what it's like to die. Where do we go? I've always believed in some kind of afterlife, but I've never given much thought about what that means. Where is Feeney right this minute? As I lie there pondering the unponderable, I become aware of a glow across the room and turn my head. The moon is huge in the window, bigger and brighter than I've ever seen it. It looks like it's peeking in at me, a mother at the door of her baby's nursery. A wave of peace washes over me, pushing away the cold grip of fear in my belly, making my eyelids heavy. I sleep and dream of nothing.

The Kenny Loggins concert is tonight. The one Feeney bought us tickets to mere months ago, though it feels like a lifetime. The one she'll never go to.

We've been nervously preparing for it like teenage girls readying themselves for a high school dance, with the same ambivalent feelings about what we're heading into. The question of what to wear was debated and decided based mainly upon weather considerations—jeans, boots, layers. The question of who would drive was batted about rhetorically because it's always going to be Liddy—she has the best car and drinks the least. The question of how much we involve Feeney was the biggest cause of angst because both her presence and absence will be overwhelming. In the end, we tucked the photo of the four of us from her closet into Liddy's canvas mom bag and brought it with us.

At the amphitheater, we sit parked in Liddy's car with an open bottle of wine and the photo. We're drinking a $30 bottle of Sauvignon Blanc out of red plastic cups.

"I can't believe we're here right now," Max says. She fingers the side of the photo where the edge is slightly bent.

"Without Feeney," Liddy adds.

"It's the first of so many things we have to do without her," I say. We all sit with that for a moment.

"Tomorrow will have been a month," Max says, looking up at us from the photo. Liddy and I slowly nod our awareness. "Jesus, that's hard to believe."

"A few summers ago Feeney and I had conflicting vacation schedules so we didn't see each other for something like six weeks," I say. "When we finally got together we were giddy with excitement and talked for three straight hours to catch up." I inhale sharply, the enormity of days looming without her catches me like a kick to the ribs. I have to close my eyes to physically reorient myself the same way I do when I get off a quick-spinning ride.

"Where do you think she is right now?" Liddy asks.

"Nowhere," Max says at the exact same time that I say, "Everywhere." Our eyes meet but, uncharacteristically, we leave it alone.

"Remember when Feeney made us swear we'd outlive our husbands so we could all live together in old age?" Liddy says. "That was the first thing I thought of when Garrett called that night. I know it's crazy, but I kept thinking he must be wrong, because Feeney would never kill herself while he was still alive."

Max chortles, a noise without mirth that acknowledges the absurdity of it all.

We huddle together, Liddy in the driver's seat and Max and I smashed into the front passenger's. It occurs to me that we never would have sat this way if Feeney were here.

We get to our row of seats and it's still daylight out. I hate that about outdoor venues. There's something depressing about sitting down for a concert and being able to see the chewed up gum stuck underneath the seat in front of you.

We stand together above our seats and silently take them in. Four empty seats, spitting distance from the stage. Nobody wants to be the first to sit down. Max finally rips the purses off of Liddy's and my shoulders and plops all of our stuff onto one of the seats. Then she shrugs off her sweater and covers all our purses with it, smoothing it out and patting the lumpen mass as if it were a restless child. "There," she exclaims.

We file into the three remaining seats. I'm in the middle, as I now seem to always be. One of the many of millions of things that was great about there being four of us was that there was never any middle. Or rather there was, but you always had company.

We sit and stare at the stage. Our collective mood is wildly at odds with everyone around us. Everywhere I look I see girlfriends laughing, leaning on each other, sharing stories and jokes and togetherness. There aren't many men. Apparently Feeney was not alone in her passion for Mr. Loggins.

Max turns to us, all nervous energy and verbs. "I'm gonna go get . . .

food or drinks—I don't know—I'll get us some stuff. I'm going to go."
She's up and out before we even open our mouths to respond.

Max and her frenetic energy being gone gives me an emotional
reprieve I didn't even know I needed. I sink into my seat and lean
my head on Liddy's shoulder. In return, she rests her head back onto
mine. Absentmindedly, I reach out and lay my hand on the lump of
personal items that is Feeney's seat. I close my eyes and will everything to be okay, this once, for tonight.

Max comes back and soundlessly hands us each a glass of wine.
We take them and put them in the little wine holders attached to
the backs of the seats in front of us. Uncharacteristically, none of us
drink.

The lights dim and the crowd is whipped into a frenzy. We are
lifted to our feet by the sheer energy of the crowd around us. The
excitement is catching, we look at each other in happy surprise as we
find ourselves enjoying the mounting buzz.

By the time Kenny Loggins walks onstage, our dread has been
transformed into exhilaration, like it's been flipped on its head. Being
here because of Feeney, without Feeney, we've gone from apathetic
participants to instant diehard fans. I find myself screaming for him
in a pitch I haven't attained since a Bon Jovi concert in college. I feel
like one of those girls in the Beatles documentaries.

The very first song is "Footloose." It knocks both the joy and wind
out of me, and I sink into my seat for the whole thing. Liddy and Max,
too. If there were an overview shot of the theater, we'd be the only
ones sitting for three full minutes.

But the next several songs are vaguely familiar and blessedly not
painful, and the three of us grab each others' hands and pull each
other back up and get back into the energy of the crowd. After a

certain point, maybe halfway in, we're just three more middle-aged women indulging a guilty pleasure together.

After a loud, fast-paced version of "I'm Alright," a song I didn't even realize I knew almost every word to, there is a distinct change in the tone of the music. The lights change from a vibrant blue and green to a mellow orange. A spotlight comes on, shining straight down on him sitting at a piano in the middle of the stage. He is playing some chords that haven't evolved into a song yet. He leans down into the microphone.

"I usually only play this song around the holidays, but I woke up this morning with it stuck in my head. It's really messed up when you get your own song stuck in your head."

Laughter ripples among the crowd. The spotlight shining on the stage captures swirling specks of dust that remind me of Feeney's ashes.

"Anyways, indulge me," he says, then launches into a lyric.

"Home for the holidays,
I believe I've missed each and every face,
Come on and play my music,
Let's turn on every love light in the place . . ."

We freeze and find each other hands. He's playing Feeney's song. The one she sang to us that night that feels like decades ago, when she was alive. So very alive. It's all I can do not to buckle but I stand and honor this moment for her.

It is surreal and beautiful and unexpected, exactly like our friendship with Feeney was. The three of us stand together and sing "Celebrate Me Home," tears streaming, voices wobbling, wiping our eyes and noses while smiling with the disbelief of it all. It's joy and pain and the deep knowledge that only Feeney could create such a moment, even now.

I look around at the crowd, a sea of unfamiliar faces, and I know that Feeney is in them all. They are singing along with our pain, because they have pain of their own. I miss her and love her, achingly, all at the same time.

"I was wrong," Max says into my ear. "She *is* everywhere."

The First Feeney Friday

We decide to meet at my house. Our funeral for Feeney at Max's house, the ashes, the broken glass, the journal—it all felt like the exclamation point at the end of the meandering, beautiful run-on sentence that was our foursome. Going back there for this would seem as if we were trespassing on hallowed ground. I asked Max to bring her throw blankets, though. I knew we'd need the security.

We told Garrett about the journal. He had no idea she kept one. We asked his permission to continue to learn about Feeney, with the understanding that we would return it to him whenever he wished, and that we would help him share it with Caroline and Hannah when they were ready. He seemed relieved—both that it existed and that he didn't need to deal with it anytime soon.

I pour us each a cold glass of wine, in matching stemless glasses. Eventually, Liddy picks Feeney's journal up from the table in front of her and holds it in her lap like a child. "Ready to dive in?"

"Feeney, take the wheel!" Max says. Then, under her breath as she takes a sip of wine, "Jesus, what is happening to me, I'm in a book club with a freaking ghost."

Liddy smiles and looks down at the journal. "Okay." She closes her eyes and rests her hands on top of it for a few seconds, then takes a deep breath and fans the pages with her left hand. With a jolt of satisfaction, I notice that her wedding rings are gone.

The pages slow and come to a stop. Liddy reads to herself for a few moments, her curls falling around her face, hiding her emotions. Max and I lean forward in anticipation. Then she starts reading, her voice slow and steady.

"'This was supposed to be my safe place, my happy place. New York is the only place I've ever felt at home, Garrett is the only man who has made me feel safe. They were both home.

"'Now I'm homeless.

"'Garrett came to me in shambles, fucking shambles, to tell me he lost his job. Why? Not because he wasn't doing well, NO, it was because he has been paying for a stripper on the company time for a year—A FUCKING YEAR! During which I had our SECOND CHILD!

"'If he wants to stay in finance he is blackballed from working in New York. I don't know what feels like more of a betrayal. It's not just our marriage he gambled, it's my one and only safety zone. If I didn't have the girls, I'd gladly stay while he figured his shit out somewhere else.

"'The worst part is, he's saying and doing all the right things. He is miserable with guilt. It's like the one bad thing he's done in his entire fucking life and I know I should have that perspective but all I can see is what he's taking from me. Garrett was supposed to be my reprieve. I should have known better.'"

Liddy puts her finger on the page and closes the journal. We all meet each other's widened eyes.

"Oh, shit," Max says.

"Okay, okay, we knew something like this could happen," I say.

"Wait, can we talk for a minute about the stripper? Who uses company money to pay for a stripper?" Max puts her hands to her head as if she can protect her brain from the information.

"Garrett, apparently." Liddy talks into her wine glass as she takes a deep sip.

"Feeney once told me that she wasn't sure she would be with Garrett for the long haul. She said something like she could promise fun but not forever. It stunned me a bit at the time, but of course I didn't know anything about this." I am racking my brain to think of more ways to make what we just read make sense.

"That fucker! What is the thing with men and their fucking peckers?" Max stands up and looks around wildly, like she wants to kick something. It's a good thing for him that Drew isn't home.

"Hold on," Liddy says, grabbing Max by a belt loop and coaxing her back down to the couch. "Let's all take some deep, centering breaths."

"I'd like to put something deep into the center of Garrett's breath," Max says, shoulders hunkered, arms crossed on her lap.

"I know you two haven't dealt with this in your marriages, but infidelity isn't always a deal breaker," Liddy says. "I would have forgiven Jack if it had been once, maybe even more than once if he had been truly sorry. Family is more important than feelings. People make mistakes."

"But it's a mistake that changed the course of her life," I say.

"Yes," Liddy looks at me with a sad smile. "And one that brought her into ours."

Max pulls the journal from Liddy's hands and flips forward a few pages.

"'Caroline came to us super serious tonight, asking what the Acropolis was. I started to talk about ancient Greece, and she looked at me like I was insane. The Acropolis, Mom! When the world ends! She wanted to know about the apocalypse! Garrett and I both laughed so hard, and it popped her anxiety bubble and we were able to all just snuggle and not talk about ancient Greece or the end of the world. It was a good day.'"

"I think I know what we need to do," I say. I go into the kitchen and return holding an Exacto blade. "This journal needs a little bit of surgery. Maybe about a page's worth."

The sun has gone down. I can hear the beginnings of crickets stirring outside. We sit together as the room darkens with ever-increasing shadows.

"Did Feeney ever take either of you starfishing?" I ask.

"What's starfishing?" Liddy asks while Max shakes her head.

I smile at them. "Follow me."

We make our way out of my house, me in front and Max and Liddy following behind. I flop myself down on the grass and stretch my arms and legs wide.

"Do what I'm doing."

Though I see them catch each other's eyes, Max and Liddy hesitantly make their way down to the ground on either side of me and follow orders. I crook my pinky fingers around each of theirs. We all stare up into the vast, purplish dusk.

"This is what Feeney called starfishing. We have to stay like this until a star winks at us."

"This is weird," Max says.

"Totally," I say.

Liddy snort laughs, which gets Max and I laughing, and we lie on the lawn and laugh until our bouncing tummies hurt.

"Weird but amazing," Max says. "Like Feeney."

"Yep," I say.

"I miss her," Liddy whispers.

And right then a shooting star sears across the sky. We all gasp, and I tighten my grip on their fingers.

"I believe we just got our wink," I whisper. A tear creeps out of the corner of my eye, slides down the side of my face and pools in my right ear.

Twelve Feeney Fridays Later

Now, every Friday, we gather at my house. There's usually cold wine and always soft blankets. We read from Feeney's journal, we laugh, we cry, we starfish. I like to think Feeney can see the three of us lying on my lawn from wherever she is. Three friends, bound by love and loss, looking for answers and stars.

The journal is starting to take on the look of my favorite books from college. Post-its stick out at odd angles, pages are dog-eared and the pristine ivory cover now has a slightly grey hue from our sticky, curious fingers. We haven't encountered any more need for surgical procedures. Yet.

So, do we have more answers? No, only more questions. But little by little, we are coming to understand that this is the legacy of losing someone you love to suicide. There's never an aha moment. Just lots and lots of wishing you could go back and do things differently, with zero certainty that it would change a goddamned thing.

Sometimes reading her thoughts brings her to life in a way that's so acute it's physically painful. Sometimes it's beautifully reassuring, like she's quietly sitting next to us as we read. We never know what we're going to find or feel. Like walking through a minefield that might just as likely erupt in flowers.

I open up the now familiar book and scan through the pages until I'm stopped by the unusual picture of stanzas. "There's a poem in

here." I scan to the end. "By Anne Sexton." I clear my throat, as that's
what I assume one must do before reciting poetry.

For John, Who Begs Me Not To Enquire Further

Not that it was beautiful,
but that, in the end, there was
a certain sense of order there;
something worth learning
in that narrow diary of my mind,
in the commonplaces of the asylum
where the cracked mirror
or my own selfish death
outstared me.
And if I tried
to give you something else,
something outside of myself,
you would not know
that the worst of anyone
can be, finally,
an accident of hope.
I tapped my own head;
it was glass, an inverted bowl.
It is a small thing
to rage in your own bowl.
At first it was private.
Then it was more than myself;
it was you, or your house
or your kitchen.
And if you turn away

because there is no lesson here
I will hold my awkward bowl,
with all its cracked stars shining
like a complicated lie,
and fasten a new skin around it
as if I were dressing an orange
or a strange sun.
Not that it was beautiful,
but that I found some order there.
There ought to be something special
for someone
in this kind of hope.
This is something I would never find
in a lovelier place, my dear,
although your fear is anyone's fear,
like an invisible veil between us all...
and sometimes in private,
my kitchen, your kitchen,
my face, your face.

We all sit with these words, they swirl around us like ashes. Then Max whispers, "Anne Sexton killed herself."

"Oh," Liddy recoils as if she's been bitten by something.

Max continues, as if to herself. "I've read a lot of her poetry. It actually makes sense to me. She was bipolar, too, back before they even really knew much about it."

I close the journal and level my gaze at Max. "Promise us, Max. Promise us you will talk to us if you ever feel suicidal again." My heart is thrumming in my throat, anxiety rising like the tide.

"Yes, I will," Max says. "As terrible as it sounds, losing someone to suicide has taken all the seduction I've always felt about death away. I never want the people I love to go through this, no matter how desperate I'm feeling at the moment. And that's saying a lot."

"Thank you," I say, reaching over and grabbing her hand. My body relaxes and the anxiety drains away. "Thank God."

"Maybe this is a good time for me to show you guys something," Liddy says. "I think we could use a little emotional break."

"Amen says the Jew," Max says, smiling at Liddy.

"Okay, hold on a sec," Liddy says as she grabs her considerable canvas purse and starts rummaging around in it. "I know it's in here somewhere. Ah." She gets a look of supreme satisfaction on her face as she pulls out something small and glinting.

Max squints and leans closer. I see what it is but it takes a moment for me to understand its significance. Then, in a clarifying moment, I get it loud and clear.

"Liddy! You didn't!"

"I did." She looks like the cat that swallowed several canaries.

"What? I still can't figure out what it is!" Max says, fumbling for her glasses.

"It's a screw! From Aaron Anderson!" I am bouncing up and down in my seat.

Max gasps and hits Liddy hard on her arm. "Liddy! I'm so proud of you. Spill it!"

Liddy is giggling and radiating pure joy. "I was walking by, and I just felt compelled to turn and walk in. Almost like I was being pushed. Aaron was at the front and thank GOD nobody else was around. I did it just like you guys always said, I waltzed up to him and said, 'I'm looking for a good screw. Can you help me?'"

Max falls against me in shock and laughter. I prop her up and say, "And?"

"He turned beet red and didn't say anything for a minute. I almost spun around and walked out. But then he smiled and said, 'Do you want a short one or a long one?'"

"No!" Max is undone. I am laughing as much at her reaction as at Liddy's story. We haven't been this happy together in a long time. I don't know if the tears in my eyes stem from joy or sorrow and God, who cares?

When I catch my breath I manage, "What did you say?"

Liddy looks down and holds her hand over her mouth coquettishly. Then she flicks her eyes up at us sheepishly and says, "I said I wouldn't mind a few of both."

As Max and I gasp and stamp our feet and lean against each other, Liddy pulls out a small brown paper bag and proceeds to dump out a collection of screws of differing lengths onto the coffee table. They bounce and twirl around.

"We're going to dinner at Scopa on Sunday," she says, cheeks pink, eyes dancing.

"Somehow I'm not sure you'll even make it there," Max says.

"It's just nice to have something to finally look forward to. It's been a long time. No offense," she says.

"No, you're right. It's great. And Feeney would be the happiest of all of us, maybe even happier than you," I say.

Liddy laughs. "I think you're right. You know, if it hadn't been for that stupid stakeout, I probably never would have reconnected with him."

"So what you're saying is that Feeney is getting you laid," Max says.

"Pretty much," Liddy says, nodding.

"In that case, I'd like to win the lottery, Feeney, if there's anything you can do about that," Max says, raising her eyes to the ceiling.

"I'd like a live-in chef," I say.

"I'd like you back," Liddy says, her voice breaking.

"Oh, shit. Me too," Max whispers, all of her bravado gone.

"We miss you, Feeney," I manage to get out, and we put our glasses down and hold each other until the wave of grief subsides. We've all become extremely competent surfers.

Thanks to the combined power of grief and Google, I've learned things these past few months. I've learned that there is a complex network of nerves behind the stomach called the celiac plexus, which is why losing someone you love feels like a chronic punch in the gut. I've learned that suicide is the tenth leading cause of death in the United States and the fourth leading cause for women my age. I've learned that, for women, the most likely method is pills.

But Feeney never was and never will be a statistic in my eyes.

I will never know what her last moments were really like, but this is how I like to imagine them.

She pulls her car into the parking spot at the beach, moved by the water at sunset, mesmerized at the way peach and rose can lay on top of blue and aquamarine without running into a muddy color that is no color at all. She watches the waves approach and recede, approach and recede, until she is almost hypnotized by their rhythmic comings and goings.

She feels peace. More peace than she's known in months, years, maybe a lifetime. She never wants it to end. If she thinks about us or her daughters or husband at all, it's in a dream-like trance where everything is in harmony, where there's no end or beginning, or rather all of it happens simultaneously and constantly so that hello and goodbye are just different ways of saying the same thing.

She reaches into her purse. Her hands close around a magic trick, one that can make this moment of peace stretch into eternity, one that can turn her into the sunlight on the waves, the peach on top of the blue.

All she has to do is ask one more thing of her body. One more stretch of discomfort and then nothing but wave after wave of blessed peace.

She unscrews the cap. She pulls out the stop on the water bottle. She is so close, she is almost there. She can taste it.

Acknowledgments

Writing a novel is a labor of sweat and love, and this one had some world-class doulas. Starting with Deborah Caust, therapist extraordinaire, who sat across from me years ago when I was a full-time copywriter with small kids, looked me dead in the eyes, and asked, "But what do you do for *you*?" When I couldn't come up with a good answer, she asked, "Okay, well, what did you do before you worked and had kids?" That's when I remembered that I loved to write. And, even though I was writing every day for work, once upon a time I wrote for joy. I'm pretty sure I wrote the beginning of this book the very next week. Next, is bestselling author and incredible writing teacher Laura Munson. Her wisdom on her Haven retreats gave me the confidence and motivation to turn an idea and thirty early pages into a full-blown book. And her friendship has been a heart-shaped rock of a gift. Finally, my Aunt Janet, who was one of the first people to read an early draft and who has been a wise woman in my head and heart my entire life, especially after I lost my mom to suicide.

To my early readers—Cathy Anderson, Janet Harding, Jane Bryan Jones, Brooke Cosgrove, Tommie Mattox, Sheila Bosworth, Kristen Gara, Amy Bessette, Michele Sloat, Jill Nieporte, Linda Willey, Katrina Reynolds, Jess Zucker, Missy Schneller, Katie Irvine, Amy Howard—you helped me shape this story more than I can say. To my "personal book club" (every writer should be so lucky to have friends who ask to book-club their book) Michelle Techel, Michelle Lewis, Jeannie Sucre, and Sarah Ting—thank you for being so incredibly thorough, insightful, and amazing in all ways. I hope you're able to see your wisdom reflected here. And to all my other friends who read drafts—you can't understand what a gift that is. Thank you for your friendship and for believing in me.

To the Northern California Writer's Retreat and its founder Heather Lazare, for creating an oasis of support, feedback, connection, and fun. Through it, I met best-selling author and amazing human Stephanie Danler, my brilliant copy editor Sarah Cypher, the world's best writing partners Caro Burke and Carinn Jade, and fellow author Martha Conway who has helped me navigate this journey. I'm so thankful for you all. Sorry about being allergic to trees.

To the various coffee shops and wine bars that fed, caffeinated, and wined me while I wrote—notably Café de la Press and Jane in San Francisco, and Kaffe Haus and Foreigner in San Mateo—thank you for the epic fuel.

To my family—Tim, Miller, and Lincoln Elliott—who waved me off supportively when I went on "business trips" that consisted of me locking myself in hotel rooms for days when I needed to focus and who make me laugh, smile, and beam with pride.

A giant thank you to She Writes Press—the reason this book is finding its way into the world—notably Brooke Warner and Samantha Strom.

And finally, I thank you, the reader, for spending time with my words. I hope they helped.

If you or someone you know is struggling or in crisis, help is available. Call or text 988 or chat 988lifeline.org to reach the 988 Suicide & Crisis Lifeline.

Permissions

Celebrate Me Home
Lyrics by Kenny Loggins
Music by Kenny Loggins and Bob James
Copyright © 1977 MILK MONEY MUSIC
All Rights Administered by UNIVERSAL MUSIC CORP.
All Rights Reserved Used by Permission
Reprinted by Permission of Hal Leonard LLC

Footloose
Theme from the Paramount Motion Picture FOOTLOOSE
Words by Dean Pitchford
Music by Kenny Loggins
Copyright © 1984 Sony Melody LLC, Sony Harmony LLC and Milk Money Music
All Rights on behalf of Sony Melody LLC and Sony Harmony LLC Administered by Sony Music Publishing
(US) LLC, 424 Church Street, Suite 1200, Nashville, TN 37219
All Rights on behalf of Milk Money Music Administered by Clear-Box Rights International Copyright Secured All Rights Reserved
Reprinted by Permission of Hal Leonard LLC

Hallelujah
Words and Music by Leonard Cohen
Copyright © 1985 Sony Music Publishing (US) LLC
All Rights Administered by Sony Music Publishing (US) LLC, 424 Church Street, Suite 1200, Nashville, TN 37219
International Copyright Secured All Rights Reserved
Reprinted by Permission of Hal Leonard LLC

Thorough efforts have been made to secure all permissions. Any omissions or corrections will be made in future editions.

About the Author

photo credit: Jeannie Sucre

JJ Elliott writes constantly, thanks to her longtime job as a freelance copywriter. In that role, she has penned everything from national television ads to urinal stickers.

She grew up in Northern California and received a degree in English from UCLA. She now lives in the San Francisco Bay Area with her husband, two teenage kids, and two bulldogs. She loves to read, play tennis, drink wine, and eat cheese. *There Are No Rules For This* is her first novel.

SELECTED TITLES FROM SHE WRITES PRESS

She Writes Press is an independent publishing company founded to serve women writers everywhere. Visit us at www.shewritespress.com.

Beginning with Cannonballs by Jill McCroskey Coupe
$16.95, 978-1-63152-848-4
In segregated Knoxville, Tennessee, Hanna (black) and Gail (white) share a crib as infants and remain close friends into their teenage years—but as they grow older, careers, marriage, and a tragic death further strain their already complicated friendship.

The Sound of Wings by Suzanne Simonetti. $16.95, 978-1-64742-044-4
What if a stranger held the secret to your past that would change your life forever? In this masterfully crafted tale of love, friendship, betrayal, and the risks we take in the pursuit of justice, three very different women's lives come together in unexpected—and life-changing—ways.

All the Right Mistakes by Laura Jamison. $16.95, 978-1-63152-709-8
When the most successful of five women who have been friends since college publishes an advice book detailing the key life "mistakes" of the others—opting out, ramping off, giving half effort, and forgetting your fertility—they spend their fortieth year considering their lives against the backdrop of their outspoken friend's cruel words.

Boop and Eve's Road Trip by Mary Helen Sheriff. $16.95, 978-1-63152-763-0
When her best friend goes MIA, Eve gathers together the broken threads of her life and takes a road trip with her plucky grandma Boop in search of her—a journey through the South that shows both women they must face past mistakes if they want to find hope for the future.

Brunch and Other Obligations by Suzanne Nugent
$16.95, 978-1-63152-854-5
The only thing reclusive bookworm Nora, high-powered attorney Christina, and supermom-in-training Leanne ever had in common was their best friend, Molly. When Molly dies, she leaves mysterious gifts and cryptic notes for each of her grieving best friends, along with one final request: that these three mismatched frenemies have brunch together every month for a year.